The Foreign Correspondent's Wife

The Foreign Correspondent's Wife

A Novel

JENNA HELWIG

CROOKED LANE
NEW YORK

Published in the United States by Crooked Lane Books, an imprint of The Quick Brown Fox & Company LLC.

Crooked Lane Books and its logo are trademarks of The Quick Brown Fox & Company LLC.

Library of Congress Catalog-in-Publication data available upon request.

ISBN (hardcover): 979-8-89242-705-0
ISBN (paperback): 979-8-89242-706-7
ISBN (ebook): 979-8-89242-707-4

Cover design by Lauren Harms

Printed in the United States.

www.crookedlanebooks.com

Crooked Lane Books
34 West 27th St., 10th Floor
New York, NY 10001

First Edition: October 2026

The authorized representative in the EU for product safety and compliance is eucomply OÜPärnu mnt 139b-14, 11317 Tallinn, Estonia, hello@eucompliancepartner.com, +33757690241

10 9 8 7 6 5 4 3 2 1

To my parents,
who made everything possible

War doesn't end when the weapons are silent.

—Sabine Bode, German journalist

Paris is so very beautiful that it satisfies something in you that is always hungry in America.

—Ernest Hemingway

Historical Note

On June 14, 1940, Nazi forces took control of Paris. The rest of France was divided into the Occupied Zone, run by the Germans, and the Free Zone, ostensibly run by the French-led Vichy government but with the close supervision of the Nazis. By the end of 1942, all of France was officially under German control.

In August 1944, Paris was liberated by Free French forces, closely followed by the Americans. The time after the Liberation was a period of hunger, political chaos, and recrimination. Thousands of Parisians were arrested and accused of collaborating with the Nazis. Over one hundred were executed.

By 1949, life was mostly back to normal, and a new force swept into the City of Light—the Americans. Thousands of American diplomats, businessmen, writers, artists, and journalists descended on Paris, ambitious and eager for adventure. Sometimes their secretaries joined them, and occasionally their wives.

Chapter One

Paris, 1949

Kat felt a wave of preemptive satisfaction when she saw the words *coq au vin* on the sheet of paper. She hadn't even gathered the ingredients yet, much less chopped an onion or lit the stove, and she could already taste the dish. The chicken would be fall-off-the-bone tender, rich, and savory thanks to the red wine it was cooked in. Chunks of lardons, or French bacon as Charlie called it, would add a salty chew to every other bite. Diminutive round pearl onions would be the subtle pops of sweetness that balanced out the savory ingredients.

Somehow the fact that it wasn't even 8:00 on a Monday morning did nothing to dampen her anticipation. Coq au vin. This is why she was in culinary school. In Paris.

Kat fished her notebook and a pen out of her bag and placed them on the worktable she shared with Toby. She hung her purse, hat, and coat on a hook at the back of the kitchen classroom. Often by 7:45 Toby would already be at their station, ingredients gathered and prep begun. But not today. And Kat enjoyed going to the pantry herself.

She tied on one of the two white aprons that the culinary school had given each student at the beginning of term. The words L'École de la Grande Cuisine were stitched in blue thread across the breast. The apron's dimensions were clearly designed for men. Kat had to wrap the strings around her waist twice before tying them in the back. But luckily she wasn't much shorter than the average Frenchman, so at least the garment wasn't comically long. In fact, on some of her American male classmates, the apron barely hit their knees.

Kat slipped her wedding ring off her finger and slid it into her skirt pocket. Then she pulled her dark hair into a tight bun—Chef Durand was appalled at her full, shoulder-length hair and threatened to make her wear a hairnet if she didn't keep it *sous control* at all times—and grabbed the recipe. She turned left from the kitchen classroom and headed to the pantry at the end of the hall. This was the room where all the culinary students who attended L'École gathered their ingredients at the beginning of each class.

Kat hadn't been sure what to expect when she visited L'École for the first time in August. A friend had told her that another culinary school that catered to Americans in Paris was woefully undersupplied in terms of both equipment and ingredients. "It's like the war never ended there. Students are still sharing knives and halving the amount of meat called for in a recipe," she had said.

Even if some of the culinary schools were limping along, Kat had quickly discovered that Paris itself was bubbling with energy. After four long years of war and then four more years of suffering through shortages, there was finally enough food to eat and coal to heat apartments, for most people at least. Theater, music, fashion, and literature were back in full force. At times, it seemed like Parisians were so desperate to make up for lost time that their eating, drinking, and dancing felt more fierce than fun.

L'École de la Grande Cuisine seemed to have risen above most postwar deprivations. There was a spacious, comfortable theater on the ground floor where visiting chefs offered demos for the students several afternoons a week. A set of wide stairs with polished wooden banisters led to well-equipped kitchen classrooms in the basement. The knives were sharp, with plenty to go around, and the pantry never lacked the ingredients that the day's recipes called for—Uncle Sam's dollars at work.

As she walked down the dim hallway, recipe in hand, Kat's eyes were drawn to the thin, metal staircase at the far end of the hall. Unlike the stairs that descended from the ground floor, these steps were stark and utilitarian, narrow and steep with an oppressively low ceiling. At the top of the stairs was a door that led directly outside, a fact Kat knew because on their first day of class, two months ago, the students had been directed to climb the stairs and actually go outside, a drill in case of emergency. It had been Kat's least favorite part about that day. She had never liked enclosed spaces.

Now Kat heard the shuffle of feet and the door at the top of the staircase creak open and bang shut. Perhaps it was the building's concierge, Madame Poitrine, or the school's housekeeper throwing something away.

When she opened the door to the pantry, the interior was still and dim. Weak sunlight streamed in from the high, dirty windows that ran along one wall. Kat could just make out the shelves of dry ingredients to her right and a row of refrigerators to her left. She grabbed a basket for her ingredients and moved toward the string hanging in the middle of the room that turned on the light.

Just as the string was near her hand, Kat slipped. She skidded and caught herself on the heavy metal table in front of the refrigerators. She carefully edged back toward the center of the room and pulled on the light.

The table blocked her view of the floor in front of the appliances, but looking down she saw a stream of red liquid slowly spreading its way across the room. Her immediate thought was that one of the refrigerators had been left open, and the juices from a defrosting protein had spilled out. But another part of her brain recognized that the thick, sticky substance on the floor was something else entirely.

Kat took a deep breath and walked around the counter. Splayed on the ground in front of the refrigerator was a man, his chest and belly stained red. A bloody chef's knife lay at his side. The man's face was covered by a striped kitchen towel. But Kat knew exactly who it was.

Chapter Two

In New York during the war, Kat often thought about women her age in France or England, or even Japan or Germany, where death became an uninvited yet regular guest at the table, and often horrific death at that. There seemed no end to the variations on the ways humans could die. Shot, of course. Drowned in the underground tunnels of London during the Blitz. Crushed when their home was destroyed by a bomb. And then near the end of the war, when she learned about the breadth of Nazi evil, she thought about the millions starved, tortured, and gassed in the concentration camps.

Here now was another way a person could die. Their body stabbed so many times the torso barely looked human. But of course it was human, and after a moment of utter disorientation, Kat knew that it was Toby Magnusson, her cooking partner and one of the few fellows who had been immediately friendly to her when the course at L'École started in September. Toby's face was covered, but she recognized his large frame, gray flannel trousers, and perfectly polished black shoes.

Kat turned away and caught her breath. She sank down to a crouch, not trusting herself to remain upright. She needed to call the police, but before that she needed to get out of the pantry, and before that she needed to move. She didn't know if any of those things were possible at that moment. Her eyes drifted downward, and she noticed her shoes were stained with blood. That realization sent a wave of energy through her body. She stood up, hurried out of the room, and went upstairs to alert the school and call the police.

Then Kat returned to the pantry, standing in front of the door to make sure no one entered. Her thoughts had slowed to a trickle and then to a mantra: *Toby is dead. Stay out. Toby is dead. Stay out. Toby is dead. Stay out.*

Monsieur Petit, the school's prim owner, approached the door, looking both ashen and agitated. "Perhaps it was an accident?"

The idea was so ludicrous that Kat didn't say a word. Her relationship with Petit had never recovered from their earliest meeting. When she had registered at L'École, he had insisted she take a recreational course offered in the afternoons to housewives. Joining one of the *vrai*—real—cooking courses for former American servicemen, whose training was mostly paid for by the GI Bill, was simply out of the question. Setting aside the financials, Petit was certain that no mere woman could keep up with men in the kitchen.

But Kat had been undeterred. It didn't hurt that she could speak to Petit in fluent French. Each time he said, "*Ce n'est pas possible*"—and he said it many, many times—she responded with "*Oui, c'est possible,*" until he finally sighed and agreed she could try. Despite, or maybe because of, his capitulation, Petit had been frosty to her ever since.

"Perhaps it was an accident," he repeated sharply.

Kat shook her head. *Toby is dead. Stay out.*

"Please step aside, Madame. I need to see."

"Toby is dead. Stay out."

Petit's chest puffed with annoyance. "Madame, step aside now."

Kat moved to one side of the door and leaned her head back against the wall.

As Petit opened the door to the pantry, she heard him mutter, "Perhaps it was an accident." His own mantra. He disappeared inside the pantry, and within five seconds she heard retching and vomit hitting the floor. She closed her eyes.

Petit stumbled out of the room. His shoes tracked blood, just like hers. She looked down and saw a dance of red footprints in front of the pantry door. Had some been there before and she just hadn't noticed?

"How can this be?" Petit demanded, like she might have an answer for him. "Who did it? What will I do? It will be a scandal! But perhaps it was an accident!" He looked at her, a flicker of defiance in his eyes.

Kat frowned but said nothing.

Footsteps echoed down the staircase from the lobby, and three men emerged in the hallway, two in suits and one in a police uniform.

The oldest man spoke first. "*Monsieur, mademoiselle.*" He nodded to Petit and Kat. "I am Detective Maurice Galland. This is Detective Faucher and Officer Martin. The body is inside this room?"

Kat nodded.

"Please wait here." He opened the door, and Kat caught a whiff of vomit. The three police officers walked into the pantry and closed the door behind them.

She looked squarely at Petit. "I don't think it was an accident." Speaking had taken effort, but she knew the police would want to talk to her soon. She needed to pull herself together. She closed her eyes and breathed in and out deeply.

The uniformed officer, Martin, stepped outside the pantry. He was very young, barely twenty, probably. "Is there a telephone I could use? I need to call in more men." He looked from Petit to Kat, clearly not sure which one he should be addressing.

"Of course." Petit sighed and began to lead the officer down the hallway. Before they got to the stairs, the detectives emerged from the pantry, closing the door behind them.

"You are Claude Petit, the owner of the building?" It was the detective called Galland.

Petit turned back. "*Oui*, I own the building and the culinary school that operates here."

"Do you have a key to this room? Can you lock the door?"

"I will get a key."

"*Merci*. But first, it is imperative that no one currently in the building leaves and that no one enters. Classes will, of course, be canceled today and probably the next two days, as well."

Petit opened his mouth to protest, but the detective cut him off. "*Monsieur*, a man was murdered here. I am sure you want us to conduct the most thorough investigation possible, *non*?"

Petit nodded, clearly reluctant. "Is there any possibility this was an accident? Perhaps if we said it was unclear . . . ?"

The younger detective, Kat couldn't remember his name, raised an eyebrow. "Parisians have heard enough propaganda to last a lifetime I think, *n'est-ce pas*?"

Petit colored a deep red.

Galland placed a hand on his colleague's shoulder. "Is there a room here that we can work from?" he asked Petit. "We will need to speak with everyone in the building, starting with you, *mademoiselle.* But first, remove your shoes, *s'il vous plait.*"

Chapter Three

The younger detective arranged three high stools around one of the workstations in the kitchen classroom. Kat pulled herself up on one. It took effort, and she was suddenly freezing. Her stockinged feet felt like blocks of ice. She wrapped her arms around herself.

"Faucher, please find a coat or a blanket for the *mademoiselle*." That's right; his name was Faucher.

He brought over Kat's coat and placed it on her shoulders.

"*Merci*." The warmth helped, and she forced herself to look up at the detectives.

"Now *mademoiselle*, your name please."

Why did he keep calling her *mademoiselle*? "Kasia Kelly." The name seemed to perplex both men, and for a moment neither said anything.

"You are not French?" Galland asked.

"My father is French, from Paris. I was born in New York and am an American."

"And Kasia?"

"My mother's family is Polish. I go by Kat."

"You speak perfect French." Galland said this almost to himself, as if to explain why he hadn't realized she was an *etrangère*, a foreigner. He looked up at her. "And why are you here?"

Kat studied the detective, finally alert enough to take in details. He was a large man but carried his bulk well. Perhaps about fifty years old, with a thick mane of silver hair that she suspected was the envy of his friends and colleagues. Why *was* she here? There were so many possible answers to that question that she didn't say anything at all.

Galland seemed to understand her confusion. "Forgive me. I should be more precise. Let us start with why you're in this building at this early hour."

Kat took a deep breath. She would be as thorough as possible for the detectives. "I am enrolled in a three-month long professional cooking course here. Classes start at 8:15, but I like to be here by 7:30 or 7:45 to prepare my ingredients and station."

"The front door is always unlocked when you arrive?"

"Yes. They told us that the building opened to students at seven. But most people seem to arrive closer to eight."

"So you came in the front door, and then what?"

Kat explained how she went to the kitchen classroom first to look at the day's recipes and then walked to the pantry to collect the ingredients she needed. She described slipping on the blood, the knife, and the body. "It was Toby." The image of his bloody torso came back to her, and she shuddered.

"Do you know the victim's full name?" It was Faucher, pen in hand and notebook on the worktable.

"Yes. Toby, Tobias, Magnusson. He's an American, from Chicago. We were in class together. We cooked together every day."

"I see." Galland picked up the questioning. "The face was covered. How do you know it was him? Did you touch the body, cover the face?"

"I didn't touch him. I just know. I recognized his clothes and . . . and . . ." Kat struggled to put it into words. "And his body, his shape." She saw Faucher's left eyebrow twitch slightly and knew she needed to elaborate. "I saw him every weekday for nearly two months. We were cooking partners. And friends."

"Friends?"

"Yes, we were friends," Kat said. "I was the only woman in the class." She thought back to the class introductions on her first day at L'École. It had been her and seven American men, all former GIs. The surprise that there was a woman enrolled in their course was palpable. "At first, most of the men were . . ." *Assholes* was the most precise word, but instead she went with, "Unpleasant. Except Toby. He was friendly from the first day." She didn't expect them to sympathize with this. But having an early ally had meant a lot.

She saw Galland appraising her, his eyes subtly stopping at her chest. "Did you and Magnusson socialize outside of class, Mademoiselle Kelly?"

She could see where this was going. "Yes, some. And it's Madame Kelly." She felt fully awake now. Why hadn't she corrected this *mademoiselle* business sooner? "In fact, just last week my husband and I went to dinner with Toby and his girlfriend."

"Ah, *madame*. Our apologies," Galland said graciously. "No ring." He nodded toward her left hand.

"We're not allowed to wear jewelry in the kitchen."

"I see."

Galland shifted on the stool and pulled a cigarette and matches from his pocket.

"We're not allowed to smoke in the kitchen, either," Kat said.

"I'm sure they'll make an exception. Faucher."

The younger detective looked up from his notebook. He stood up and returned with a small plate that he slid in front of Galland. Faucher didn't look at Kat.

The senior detective placed the cigarette in his mouth, struck a match, touched it to the cigarette, and inhaled. He waved the match to extinguish the flame.

"Now, *mademoiselle*." Kat opened her mouth to protest. "*Desolé. Madame.* I am going to ask this very forward question because this is a murder investigation, and we need to know what we're dealing with. Were you and Monsieur Magnusson romantically involved?"

"*Non*. As I said, I'm married, and Toby has a girlfriend. We were friends. That is all. *D'accord*?" She understood why the detective was asking, but she wanted to nip this line of questioning in the bud.

Galland gave a small smile and raised his hands as if in surrender. "*D'accord, d'accord*." He took another puff of his cigarette.

Suddenly Kat wanted nothing more than to exit this room. "When can I have my shoes back?"

"Soon. Just a few more questions. Speaking of your shoes, I'm sure you know they left bloody footprints at the crime scene, as did Monsieur Petit. When you walked in the room to gather your ingredients, did you see any other footprints?"

She shook her head. "It was dark. I felt the wetness under my feet, turned on the light, and saw Toby's body. It was such a shock that I didn't notice much else. Other than the knife. I think I would have noticed footprints outside of the door in the hallway before I walked in, but I can't be sure."

Galland nodded. "What did you touch?"

Kat traced her movements in her mind. "The knob on the outside of the door, the cord for the light, perhaps the metal table in front of the refrigerators. Then the knob on the inside of the door."

"Thank you."

"But I don't see how that will help."

"*Pardon*?"

"I don't know how often those surfaces are wiped down, but my fingerprints will be other places in the pantry, from yesterday and last week, and so will those of every other student at L'École."

"*Merci*, Madame. You can trust that the Paris police understand the nature of fingerprints," Galland said, with a trace of condescension in his voice.

She shifted in her seat. Her stockinged feet kept sliding off the footrest on the stool. When would they let her go?

"We're almost finished. Just a few more questions," Galland said again. "Faucher?" Galland stood up, subtly stretched his back, and lit a second cigarette.

Detective Faucher looked up. Kat estimated that he was in his early thirties, not much older than her, with a dark, well-trimmed mustache. "Madame Kelly, you said that Monsieur Magnusson had a girlfriend. Do you know her name and where she lives?"

"Her name is Marie-Hélène Arnaud. I don't know where she lives."

"How long have they been involved?"

Kat thought back to their conversation at that strange dinner the previous week. "Just a few months." She stared at Faucher. *Please, please let me leave.* Galland was now standing in a corner of the kitchen classroom, smoking and watching their conversation.

"Thank you for your patience, *madame.* Is there anything else you'd like to share that could help us?" Faucher asked.

In her old life, when she had been the one asking the questions, that was how she had always ended an interview, too.

"I heard the door close at the top of the back stairs. The metal stairs. As I went into the pantry. That was unusual."

She didn't tell them about Eugene.

Faucher nodded. "If you are in touch with any of your other classmates, please let them know we would like to speak with them. And where can we reach you if we have more questions? We likely will."

"Of course. Anything I can do to help." *As long as that means I can get out of this room right now.* "You can leave a message at my husband's office at the *New York Tribune*'s bureau. His secretary will get it to me."

Galland's and Faucher's eyes met briefly. Galland spoke from the corner of the room, almost to himself at first. "Kelly. Kelly." He looked at Kat. "Your husband is Charles Kelly, the foreign correspondent?"

"Yes." Kat was still getting used to the fact that seemingly everyone in Paris knew her husband's name.

Galland walked back toward Kat and stubbed out his cigarette. “Faucher, go fetch Madame Kelly’s shoes immediately. Can’t you see that she’s freezing?” He offered Kat his arm as she slid off the high stool. “We greatly appreciate your assistance in this tragedy. I am sorry for the loss of your friend. We will find who did this; you have my word.”

Chapter Four

When Kat left the building, she walked into a cluster of students milling around the entrance, their curiosity palpable. She took a few deep breaths of the crisp early November air, grateful to be outside.

"Kat!" It was Vaughn Harris, standing with Eugene Sizemore, both classmates, both dismissive of Kat from the first day, before she had proven that she could more than keep up with the boys. Since then, their other classmates had warmed to her. Not these two. "What's going on? Why won't he let us in?" He gestured to young Officer Martin standing in front of the door.

She looked up at Vaughn as she spoke. He was well over six feet tall and as skinny as a *haricot vert*. "We can't go back today or tomorrow, at least. Classes are canceled; demos too. But you should tell him that you're a student. They want to talk to you, to everyone."

"Who? Why?" It was Eugene. Kat studied his face for any indication of guilt or deception but saw only his typical hauteur underneath his slicked-back white-blond hair.

At that moment, an ambulance pulled around the corner and double parked in front of the school. Two men in coveralls pulled out a stretcher. As they carried it toward the front door of the school, Kat thought about bringing Toby's body up that flight of stairs. He had been a tall, solidly built man. She was suddenly afraid she would throw up.

"Kat?" Vaughn prompted her.

Officer Martin stepped aside to let the men with the stretcher inside. At the same moment, a young man with a camera around his neck jogged up to the entrance. Were there already press here? Kat saw him shake hands with the officer and enter the building. No, that photographer must work for the police.

She turned back to Vaughn and Eugene, swallowed hard and steadied herself. "Toby is dead. Someone killed him."

"What the fuck?" It was Vaughn. He looked at Kat. "Excuse my language."

It was an appropriate question, and she took no offense. She nodded toward the building. "I already spoke to the detectives. They want to talk to everyone in our class."

Vaughn shook his head. "I can't believe it. Murdered?" He looked to Kat for confirmation, and she nodded.

Eugene said nothing, just stared at Officer Martin.

Vaughn started walking toward the entrance. "You coming?" he said to Eugene.

"I don't have time for this bullshit. If they want to talk, they can come to me." He turned and walked away.

Kat watched Eugene go. From the first day of their course, he and Toby had shared an almost instant antipathy. With his immaculately styled hair and impeccably tailored suit, Eugene had made an odd culinary school student, at least to Kat's eyes.

Upon seeing Kat in the mix of students, he had immediately approached Chef Durand and, without bothering to keep his voice low, insisted that he had signed up for a serious course, not one for housewives.

"Rest assured, Monsieur Sizemore, this course will be *très serieux,*" Chef had said placidly, instantly winning Kat's affections.

As they ascended the main stairs after class that first day, Toby had caught up to her. "Don't worry about Sizemore. His unpleasantness is only skin deep. Spend a little time with him and you'll discover that he's actually just a pathetic, empty shell of a man." She had laughed gratefully, and they ended up getting lunch along with a third classmate, the slight, mild-mannered Roy Kasden from St. Louis.

And then there was the notebook business. But it was ridiculous to think that it could have led to murder. Wasn't it?

Toby's notebook. It was leather-bound and handsome, and Toby took notes in it throughout class and demos. Whenever he had an idea for the restaurant he was planning to open in Chicago, he jotted it down. Sometimes he even sketched an image of how the food would look on the plate. Kat could barely draw a stick figure and so was impressed by his drawings.

Toby had shared some of his menu items with Kat, and she had been astonished. The ideas were unlike anything she had ever seen or tasted before. He was starting with traditional French dishes like vichyssoise, boeuf Bourguignon, and duck confit, but reimagining them.

Kat couldn't predict whether Toby's restaurant would be a success, of course. Would steak and potatoes–loving Americans embrace such novelty on their plates? In a large, cosmopolitan city like Chicago he had a chance, especially since so many former soldiers had tasted French food during the war. Whether or not his restaurant flourished, Kat was certain that Toby was graced with a touch of culinary genius.

Last week, Toby couldn't find his notebook. He was sure he hadn't left it at home. Kat helped him search every corner and cabinet of the kitchen classroom, but it had vanished.

"Kat, you don't understand. I have to find it." She could see the tension on his face. He must have weeks or even months of ideas in there that he didn't want to lose.

Toby spent the remainder of class curt and anxious, and afterward he was the first person up the stairs and out the door. When Eugene and Vaughn exited the building, Toby blocked their way. He was a tall man, about six feet tall, Kat estimated, with broad shoulders. In another life he would have been a Viking warrior. Kat had watched the scene from a few feet away.

Toby positioned himself just a few inches from Eugene's face. "Give it back."

"I don't know what you're talking about, asshole. Let me by."

"I know a no-talent hack and thief when I see one. Give it back, now."

The two men were nose to nose. Eugene was a few inches shorter than Toby and several inches less broad. But presumably he had the lanky Vaughn on his side if things turned violent. Eugene gave a forced laugh that came out like a bark. "Is that the best you can do? I can say a lot worse about you."

Toby had taken a step back, and Kat saw immediately that he was going to punch Eugene. Vaughn had seen it too and forcibly stepped in between the two. "Fellas! Fellas! Let's cool it. There's a lady present. Eugene, let's take a walk."

Toby's body was still tensed, his right fist clenched. "Toby! Cool it, buddy. If you don't, I'm going to call Madame Poitrine, and no one wants that." Toby let out an involuntary snort. Vaughn's joke about the small but fierce concierge had broken the tension. Toby stepped back, and Kat breathed a sigh of relief.

Now, as Kat walked toward the Boulevard des Italiens, she wondered if that fight had escalated without her knowing it. Eugene was a weasel and a big talker. But she had to admit that, if anything, she could imagine Toby killing him, not the other way around. No, she didn't regret not telling the police about their conflict. She didn't want them to be distracted from tracking down the real murderer.

All Kat wanted at the moment was to find Charlie. But she knew she needed to make another stop first. She had been truthful when she told the detectives that she didn't know where Marie-Hélène Arnaud lived. But she did know where she worked. And she needed to tell the woman that her boyfriend was dead.

Chapter Five

As she walked, Kat thought back to the evening that she, Charlie, Toby, and Marie-Hélène had spent together the week before. It had been gusty out, dry leaves swirling through the streets and onto the sidewalks. Kat held her hat on her head to keep it from flying into the Seine as she and Charlie made their way to Chez Daniel, a decidedly more upscale restaurant than they usually ate at. She had decided to wear her best new outfit—a soft, dark green skirt and jacket with a shawl collar that she had bought after they arrived in Paris in August.

Toby had invited them to dinner just that day, and it would be the first time the two couples had socialized. Kat had met Marie-Hélène once before, at lunch with Toby and Roy after class. The French woman had been barely cordial, not at all interested in Kat, or Roy for that matter. She spoke mostly to Toby and seemed to resent his friends' presence. Marie-Hélène clearly wanted her American boyfriend all to herself.

Kat knew Charlie would be game for dinner at Chez Daniel. He was always game—it was one of the things she loved about him. Plus, neither of them could turn down what promised to be an excellent meal. Kat also suspected that Charlie wanted to meet this Toby Magnusson that Kat had spoken so much about. Charlie wasn't the jealous type, exactly, but he would want to take his own measure of the man.

The meal was one of those that made Americans want to uproot their lives and decamp to Paris. The couples started with a bottle of champagne and Breton oysters on the half-shell. Kat ordered escargots in herb butter for her appetizer and truffled duck suprême for her *plat principal.* She tasted Charlie's lamb Navarin and regretted not ordering Marie-Hélène's pommes Dauphinoise.

Although Marie-Hélène was reserved, overall the conversation was smooth, if not exactly scintillating. They covered the usual ground. Kat explained how she and Charlie had met: "I was a reporter at the *New York Tribune* during the war, technically a copy boy, but also a writer. Charlie was a reporter there but had been in the service. Then he came back." *And within a couple of months, I lost my job and basically my whole career. But that's a whole other story*—none of which she said, of course.

"And I thought, hot damn! These copy boys got a lot better looking while I was away." Kat smiled and subtly rolled her eyes at Charlie. It was a practiced line, but a crowd-pleaser. Kat lightly grazed his thigh under the table with her hand, and he interlaced his fingers through hers. He looked especially handsome tonight in a double-breasted charcoal suit. For all his dark good looks, it was Charlie's eyes that still made her swoon—a warm brown at first glance but shot through with specks of gold when you looked more closely.

Toby described growing up in Chicago, working in his family's grocery store. His father had put him and his brother to work as soon as they were old enough to hold a broom.

Charlie talked about being the *Tribune*'s Paris correspondent, reporting on whatever governing coalition had just collapsed, labor strikes, the struggle between the communists and the socialists in the Assemblée, occasional human interest stories, even sometimes crime.

Now Marie-Hélène was intrigued. She leaned forward. "And do Parisians open up to you? Tell you their secrets?"

"Sometimes," Charlie said. "Have any you want to share?"

The truth was that a lot of people told Charlie their secrets. Kat's husband had an innate ability to talk to people from all walks of life. He charmed the secretaries of important men into sharing their bosses' schedules, became buddies with the bartenders who passed along the gossip they overheard, spoke to men in uniform like he was one of them—because he had been—and used his Harvard education to adopt the bearing of the powerful statesmen, businessmen, and politicians he interviewed. He was a chameleon, and that made him an excellent investigative journalist.

And now his charms were working on Marie-Hélène, who was finally opening up. She told them about working at her uncle's publishing company and the quirky writers whose egos she had to massage on a daily basis. She ate every bite put in front of her with obvious pleasure, and she looked especially beautiful in a silky violet dress that was cinched at the waist and ended in a billowing skirt.

After they finished their second bottle of wine and conquered the cheese course, Toby asked the waiter for the check. "This is my treat, and I won't take no for an answer." He removed a thick bundle of francs from his wallet and counted out several bills.

The wind had died down, and the evening had turned crisp, with the faintest scent of wood smoke in the air. Toby suggested a nightcap, and the couples walked to Café du Vent, one of Kat and Charlie's favorite spots, around the corner from their apartment on Rue du Bac.

The owner, Jules, greeted them with a broad smile, kisses for Kat and Charlie, and handshakes for the newcomers. Kat reveled in the warmth that came with being a regular. They ordered cognacs all around.

Jules's wife, Claudine, came to the table to greet Kat and Charlie. She dropped off three desserts they hadn't ordered—a small dish of mousse au chocolat, a plate with a petite slice of apple cake, and a dish of crème caramel, classic bistro desserts. "Just try these. My brother-in-law is a chef. He and his wife have come to live in Paris and are working here with us now." She smiled and returned to the bar.

Marie-Hélène scraped a small bit of chocolate mousse onto her spoon. "I don't think it's possible to eat anything more, but I will try in the name of *politesse*." She took a bite and purred with pleasure. "*Mais*, it's real chocolate! Good chocolate!"

Kat followed suit and almost purred herself. It was the first dark, rich chocolate she had eaten in Paris since they had arrived in August. And not only that, she detected the barest hint of coffee in the dessert, which was unusual. The coffee was more of a suggestion than a flavor, just there to make the chocolate taste chocolaty-er.

"Marie-Hélène," Kat asked. "When did rationing end?"

"April, *finalement*. Good coffee and chocolate are the last foods that are hard to find. But somehow this new chef has found them." The mousse was truly extraordinary.

Toby took another sip of cognac. "Charlie, buddy, how have we come this far tonight without telling our war stories?"

It was true. Kat had discovered that no social gathering ended in France without an exchange of *where-were-you's* and *this-is-what-I-did's*. This was especially true when there was a Parisian in the mix, since the war had literally been on their doorstep. She had noticed that some French people were eager to share their personal experiences. But others preferred to talk only in generalities or not at all.

Kat looked at her husband. It was impossible to avoid talking about the war. He gave Toby his standard answer.

"I was a low-ranking Army officer here in Europe, mostly in Germany. We saw a lot of action, but I was lucky."

"And he wrote for the *Stars and Stripes* throughout it all." Kat always hopped in at this point to keep the story moving. "What about you, Toby?"

Marie-Hélène stood up and excused herself and walked toward the spiral staircase in the middle of the café that led to the *toilettes* downstairs.

Toby looked slightly abashed. "She's heard my stories a million times." He watched her walk down the stairs before continuing. "I came up through Italy and southern France until we got to Paris. On our way, we marched through village after village. All the Italians were over the moon for us. And some French, too, of course. But not everyone. The people that hitched their wagon to Pétain were screwed, pardon my French."

Charlie nodded. "I've taken a couple of trips south to report on how the region is getting back on its feet post-Vichy, but no one seems eager to talk about it, except for the butcher who wants to denounce the baker as a collaborator. Then it turns out that the baker is sleeping with the butcher's wife."

Claudine arrived at their table with a friendly-looking man in an apron and chef's hat. She introduced him as their new chef, Jules's brother Jacques. They all stood and shook the chef's hand.

"These desserts were the best we've had in Paris, and we eat at a lot of restaurants," Charlie said. Claudine beamed.

"*C'est mon plaisir.* I'm so grateful to be here in Paris, at my brother's restaurant."

"Did you own a restaurant where you lived before?" Kat asked.

"Yes, but after the war, well, you know . . ." He shrugged. "It is better here in Paris. People are back to normal and don't dwell on the past." Charlie inclined his head at Toby, as if to say, *see?*

"We're certainly glad you're here," Kat said. "Charlie and I live in the neighborhood. Claudine, you won't be able to get rid of us."

Jacques continued, "We have also updated the café menu, just a bit. It was very good before." He nodded to Claudine with respect. "But we can make it special."

Kat saw that Claudine was not offended but excited at the prospect. It was a quartier full of cafés, and Claudine had confided that business had been slow over the past several months, longer actually. If Café du Vent became known as a restaurant with superior food, it would only help. Jacques gave a slight bow, said good night, and headed back downstairs.

Charlie ordered another round of cognacs from Claudine. Just then, Marie-Hélène returned to the table. She didn't look at Kat or Charlie. "Toby, it's time to go."

"We just ordered another round. Come, sit down." He patted the seat next to him.

Marie-Hélène shook her head.

"Are you okay?" Kat asked. "Can I help you with anything?" She wondered if Marie-Hélène had unexpectedly gotten her period.

She ignored Kat and said to Toby. "This was a mistake, and I'm leaving now. If you want to stay, stay." Marie-Hélène picked up her coat and walked outside without stopping to put it on.

Charlie looked at Kat quizzically. She shook her head, as baffled as he was. Toby seemed frozen, unsure what to do.

"Go," Charlie said to Toby. "Don't worry about us; I've got this."

Toby stood, clearly embarrassed. "She doesn't like to talk about the war much. See you tomorrow, Kat. Good to meet you, Charlie." Then he hurried out of the café.

Chapter Six

Kat stood in the hallway on the second floor of a stately, if slightly shabby, office building just a ten-minute walk from school. She took a deep breath and knocked on the heavy wooden door in front of her. A nameplate on the side read Guillaume Publishing.

Why was she here again? Kat easily could have left this wrenching job to the police. She barely knew this woman. There had been just that one night that had ended so awkwardly. Kat had felt sure that the two couples would never socialize again.

But still, she felt a responsibility to tell Marie-Hélène that Toby was dead. Better to hear it from, well, not a friend in this case, but at least an acquaintance? One that you didn't really like very much? Maybe she shouldn't have come at all.

"*Entrez!*" It was Marie-Hélène's voice. Too late to escape now.

Kat opened the door and was immediately accosted by a small, enthusiastic white dog. He balanced on his hind legs in his eagerness to reach Kat's hands. She bent forward to scratch him behind the ears.

Marie-Hélène was sitting behind a neatly organized desk in the middle of the room. There was a small sitting area to one side and open doors to the left and the right. One door appeared to lead to an office—Kat saw a desk piled high with stacks of papers—and the other to a small kitchen. Large windows behind Marie-Hélène's desk overlooked the tree-lined street below. Bookshelves filled nearly every wall. Aside from Marie-Hélène and the dog, the office appeared to be empty.

Toby's girlfriend stood up. "Kat. *Bonjour.*" She didn't come from behind her desk to offer Kat kisses near both cheeks, the customary French greeting, especially between two women who had socialized together. She didn't even offer her hand to shake.

Despite the woman's chilliness, Kat was struck again by her delicate beauty. Marie-Hélène was petite and fine-boned. Her warm, chestnut hair was cropped close to her head, a style that Kat saw more and more in Paris. Her chocolate-brown eyes seemed to take up half of her heart-shaped face. From sitting next to her at Café du Vent the week before, Kat knew that she had a fine scar along her left jawline. But it was only noticeable up close.

"I'm sorry to come unannounced, but I need to talk to you. Can we sit down?" She gestured to the seating area.

Marie-Hélène didn't budge. She shook her head, a look of disgust on her face. "I can't believe you would stoop to being Toby's messenger. Tell him I am not changing my mind. There is no discussion."

Kat noticed the dog sniffing intently at her shoes. Her stomach flip-flopped, and she gently pushed the creature away. "I don't understand. I'm not here with a message from Toby."

"He didn't send you here to talk with me, woman to woman, to convince me not to break up with him?" Her voice dripped with disdain when she said *woman to woman.*

Kat shook her head.

"Good. Because that's not happening. It is over between Toby Magnusson and me." She sat down and began shuffling papers around her desk.

It is over, Kat thought, *but not in the way you think.* "Toby is dead."

Marie-Hélène stopped moving, one of her hands in mid-air, holding a piece of paper. She put it down and looked at Kat. "It was an accident? At school?"

Kat shook her head. "He was murdered."

A flash of what looked like panic ran through Marie-Hélène's eyes, and after a moment of stunned silence she began to breathe quickly, almost gasping for air. She took one long, sharp breath after another. Kat had never seen anyone hyperventilate, but that must be what was happening. Kat hurried toward her and took the woman's hands. "Marie-Hélène, look at me. Look at me! Now, breathe with me."

Marie-Hélène locked eyes with her, and Kat was reminded of a frightened animal. She could see Marie-Hélène's pulse beating wildly in her pale neck. Kat slowed down her breathing and willed Marie-Hélène to do the same.

Once she was calmer, Marie-Hélène slipped her hands from Kat's, stood up, and moved in front of one of the windows looking out to the street below. "We broke up."

Remembering how their evening had ended the week before, Kat wasn't entirely surprised. "When?"

"Yesterday."

Kat couldn't help herself. "Why?"

Marie-Hélène turned to her. "He broke my trust, and it was unforgivable."

This time Kat held her tongue, even though she was desperate to know more. She joined Marie-Hélène at the window, looking out over the treetops. Most of the leaves had already fallen, but some still clung to branches, fiery oranges, pale yellows, and deep reds. Kat looked at the passers-by on the sidewalk across the street, besuited men, women pushing baby carriages. Everyone was going along their way because they didn't have a friend who died that day.

Marie-Hélène rested her forehead and hands on the window. She closed her eyes. The women stood together in silence.

Kat decided she might just stay and look out the window all day. It was like she was watching individual members of an ant colony, unceasingly going about their business. She watched without judgment, following people with her eyes—a couple, arm in arm, a woman wearing a green suit, a young man struggling with a heavy box—until they strode out of her line of vision. It was soothing and distracting.

Then her eye snagged on someone, a man who looked like he was in a French military uniform. Just after the Liberation, there would have been men in uniform—American, French, British—all over the city, but it was less common these days. And this man wasn't moving but standing stock still on the sidewalk. In fact, it seemed like he was staring right up at them.

"Do you see that man?" Kat pointed, and Marie-Hélène followed her gaze. Kat felt her stiffen and then sway slightly. She saw what looked like alarm pass over Marie-Hélène's face. "Are you okay?" She held onto the woman's arm to support her.

"Bijou." The little dog trotted over. Marie-Hélène scooped the animal into her arms and hid her face in its fur.

Kat turned her eyes back to the man, but he had disappeared. She scanned the sidewalk, but there was no trace of him.

Marie-Hélène sat back in her chair, the small dog on her lap, her face more composed. "Kat, thank you for coming, but please, I need to be alone now."

"I don't think I should leave you."

"It is fine. My uncle, who I work for . . . I told you the other night, yes? He will be back soon and will help me get home." When Kat still didn't move, she continued, "Please. I need to be alone!" Her voice rose, almost in desperation. Or was it fear?

"Marie-Hélène, who could have wanted Toby dead?" Kat knew it was a terribly insensitive question, but she couldn't leave without asking.

The French woman's eyes welled up with tears. She didn't answer for a long time. Finally, she shook her head briskly. "I don't know. And it doesn't matter."

"It doesn't matter?"

"He's dead. Knowing who did it won't bring him back." She set Bijou on the floor, stood up, and walked to the door. She opened it, gesturing for Kat to leave.

Kat didn't know what to do. She didn't feel right leaving Marie-Hélène alone, but she also didn't feel like she could stay when Marie-Hélène so clearly wanted her gone.

"I will leave on one condition. Give me your home address, and I will come check on you tomorrow."

Marie-Hélène walked to the desk and swiftly wrote an address on a slip of paper. She handed it to Kat. "Please go."

As Kat walked toward the stairs, she heard the door lock behind her.

Chapter Seven

If she kept walking, maybe she could leave every trace of blood on her shoes behind her on the sidewalks of Paris. She walked down Boulevard des Italiens, past the ornate Palais Garnier, and down rue de la Paix, not giving any of the expensive jewelers on the street a second glance, not that she ever did.

She turned off onto a small, much less glamorous side street before Place Vendôme, the expansive, elegant square that was home to the Paris Ritz and France's Ministry of Justice. One could argue that the Place was the epicenter of wealth and power in Paris, and the *New York Tribune* bureau sat in its orbit. Charlie spent a not insignificant amount of time at the bar at the Ritz, meeting sources and conducting background interviews.

Kat opened the door, climbed the stairs, and was immediately enveloped into the comforting cacophony of a newsroom. She let the ringing telephones, clacking typewriters, occasional holler across the room, and the familiar smell of ink envelop her. For a second she forgot the terrible reason she was there. *I miss this*, she thought.

The paper's Paris operation wasn't large. There was Charlie; his editor, Tom Granderson; and a researcher named Peter Ericson, who sometimes wrote smaller stories. A few other Europe-based correspondents kept desks there as well. And there was a copy editor, a copy boy, and a couple other people whose roles Kat was unsure of.

"Kat, my darling!" It was Florence, the formidable American woman who kept the paper's Paris bureau running smoothly. She sat at a desk near the front door, greeted visitors, answered the telephone, made sure "her boys" never ran out of paper and typewriter ribbon, and supervised the cleaning crew, among many other things. Kat was certain the woman must work twelve or more hours a day, at least six days a week, maybe seven. Charlie had said that Granderson had offered to hire Florence an assistant, but the woman had replied that she would quit if he did. Florence had been widowed fifteen years earlier, and both her sons had died in the war.

"Florence." It was all Kat could muster. Discovering Toby's bloody body, being questioned by the police, and the emotional toll of sharing the news with Marie-Hélène had finally caught up with her. Kat wasn't sure how much longer her legs would hold out. Maybe she would just sit down on the ground here next to Florence.

The older woman hurried around her desk and put her arm around Kat's shoulders. "Kat, honey, you look like you're about to melt." Florence led her to the conference room. Kat saw Charlie at the far end of the bureau, talking with Ericson, the young researcher. "Kelly!" Florence hollered. *She should have been a general*, Kat thought hazily. Her voice would have carried over any battlefield.

Charlie looked over, saw Florence with her arm around Kat, and strode over, worry etched on his handsome face. Kat wanted to reassure him. She was fine, really. She just needed to sit down. But the words wouldn't come out.

Florence sat her in a chair in the conference room. "I'll be back with coffee."

"Kat, what's going on?"

Florence returned immediately with a mug of black coffee and a bottle of whiskey. She handed both to Charlie and left the room.

He added a splash of whiskey to the coffee and slid the mug to Kat. She inhaled and then took a sip. It was warm and calming and helped her focus. She looked up at Charlie, who was staring at her with both concern and impatience on his face.

"Toby is dead. He was murdered, and I found his body."

"Jesus Christ." He sat down and took Kat in his arms. This was what she had needed all day. Just this. She started to cry. She couldn't help herself. She cried and cried, and then she stopped and told Charlie everything that had happened, from finding Toby's body in the pantry to the detectives questioning her without her shoes to Eugene's strange reaction to telling Marie-Hélène that her lover was dead. Charlie added another splash of whiskey to her mug, checked that the door was closed, and took a swig himself directly from the bottle.

"Do the police have any idea who did it?"

Kat shrugged. "I don't know."

"But do you think it was random?"

Kat was confused. "I don't know! How would I know?"

"I'm sorry. It's just . . . what if you had been the first person in that pantry today?"

Kat exhaled. She hadn't thought of that.

There was a knock at the door. "Come in," Kat said. She already felt better, the atoms in her body realigning into their usual configuration. This was exactly what she had needed. Coffee, whiskey, and Charlie.

It was Florence. "Kat, my dear, the police just called. A Detective Laurent Faucher. He asked if I could get a message to you requesting you to come to the prefecture. I didn't tell him you were here. Shall I call back and tell him I wasn't able to locate you?"

Kat shook her head. "Please call back and tell him that I'm on my way. I'd like to help them if I can."

Florence looked pointedly at Charlie and closed the door.

"Let me get my hat. I'm coming with you."

Kat stood up. "Thank you, but no. I can handle it." She tilted her head up and kissed him softly on the lips, savoring the faint scent of his shaving cream. "Besides, you'll need to report the story."

Charlie held her to him, her cheek pressed against his broad shoulder. "Not if my wife found the body. I'll tell Tom to put Ericson on it. And don't worry, I'll keep him away from you."

"Charlie." She looked up at him. "I asked Marie-Hélène if she had any idea who would want to kill Toby."

"And?"

"She said she didn't."

"But?"

"But I didn't believe her."

Chapter Eight

Kat spent two hours in a small office at the prefecture answering more questions. It had taken some effort, but she had convinced Charlie that she would be fine on her own.

Working from a list, Faucher asked about each student in the class; the instructor, Chef Durand; Monsieur Petit, the school's owner; and even Madame Poitrine, the concierge. This time, Kat told the detectives about Eugene and the nearly instant loathing he and Toby seemed to experience for each other. Faucher asked if Toby had been in Paris before. Kat remembered their conversation at Café du Vent the week before and replied that he had been in Paris soon after the Liberation in August 1944, but that she didn't know for how long.

The detectives had been courteous when she arrived, thanking her for coming to answer more questions. Galland had been especially chivalrous, pulling out her chair, delivering her coffee, and ensuring that his cigarette smoke didn't travel in Kat's direction. This time, when she felt more herself, she was able to observe the two men more closely. They were almost physical opposites. Silver-haired Galland was thick-set. It was hard to imagine he had ever been hungry during the war. Faucher was lean and compact. He was focused and intense, while Galland was expansive and gregarious. Galland was clearly in charge and didn't want anyone to forget it. Faucher was younger, and obviously Galland's junior, but he seemed to have a quiet confidence. She didn't think he would be a lackey for long.

After Kat shared her very limited observations on Monsieur Petit—his desire to avoid scandal, primarily—Faucher sat back. Galland stubbed out his cigarette and leaned forward.

"Tell us more about Marie-Hélène Arnaud, Toby's girlfriend. We spoke with her briefly, and she said you went to see her this morning . . . despite telling us you didn't know where she lived," he added in a mildly disapproving tone.

Kat didn't apologize. "Yes. I wanted to tell her about Toby's death myself. I thought it might be easier for her than hearing about it from the police."

"And how did she seem to you?"

"She told me they broke up."

"Did she say why?"

"She said she couldn't trust him."

Galland pulled another cigarette from his pocket, glanced at Kat, and set it down on the table, unlit.

"Do you suppose there might have been another woman?"

Kat thought about it. "I have no way of knowing. Toby and I were friends. We spent time together in school and then often had lunch or a coffee after. But we didn't share personal details like that."

"I'm not asking you to be certain, just to give me your instinct."

"My instinct is that he wasn't seeing anyone else."

Galland nodded, thought for a moment, and then lit the cigarette. "I'm curious, did Monsieur Magnusson ever try to be more than friends with you?"

"Never." Kat was firm.

"Even before he knew you were married? Because it wouldn't be so shocking, would it? You are a very beautiful woman."

Kat didn't bother to say thank you. She could barely remember what had happened in their interview that morning, but she was pretty sure she had been clear that there had never been anything romantic between her and Toby. "He always knew I was married." She changed the subject. "Do you think the killing could have been random?"

Galland held up a finger and smiled, barely. "One moment, please. You mentioned that you and your husband socialized with Monsieur Magnusson and Mademoiselle Arnaud. How did that go?"

"Fine. Well, it ended abruptly. Marie-Hélène suddenly wanted to leave. But before that it was fine."

"How did your husband and Monsieur Magnusson get along?"

Kat stared at him, frustrated and annoyed. Why were they wasting time with these pointless questions? She took a deep breath to calm herself, and responded, "Beautifully." She raised an eyebrow, as if to say, *proceed further at your own risk*, and then repeated her earlier question. "Do you think the killing could have been random?"

Galland accepted defeat, at least for the moment, and briefly considered her question. "*C'est possible*, but unlikely. The killer would have had to wander into that building, find themselves downstairs and in the pantry at just the right time when not many people were around."

"Could it have been a robbery?"

"A poor one, if so. Magnusson's wallet was in his pocket."

"And the victim's wounds suggest the crime was personal." It was Faucher. Galland gave him a sharp glance.

Kat was intrigued. "How so?"

"It is still too early to tell." Galland stood up. "Thank you for your valuable insight, Madame. It is good to have someone 'on the inside,' as they say."

Chapter Nine

Behind the Club Margaux bar, Philippe shimmied a cork out of a bottle of Côtes de Nuit and brought three glasses over to the table where Kat and Charlie were sitting. He gave them each a generous pour.

"Do you want something stronger, Kat?" he asked. "I would probably be at the bottom of a bottle of whiskey in your shoes."

Kat winced slightly at the mention of shoes but shook her head. "If you had asked me this morning, I would have said yes. But I want to stay clear-headed. I'm meeting Chef Durand and my class early tomorrow morning." Monsieur Petit had gotten the message to her at Charlie's office. Since the building would be closed to students, Chef would show them around Les Halles, the sprawling covered market in the heart of the city. Petit also asked her to come to the school on Wednesday to meet Toby's brother, who was traveling in from Chicago. They would need a translator.

Tomorrow night at about this time, people would start trickling into Club Margaux for the evening's poetry performance.

Philippe would get a modest, devoted crowd. But nothing like Friday or Saturday nights when American jazz acts played sets until the early hours of the morning. Then the room would be packed with people on a high of drink and music and who knew what else.

While Philippe liked the music and, especially, the money it brought in, it was no secret that his heart was in the literary and theatrical events the club hosted on weekdays. Walk back to his cramped office and you'd see shelves lined with books and a desk full of writing, both his and other people's. The poetry readings and short theatrical events brought in a loyal crowd of local intellectuals and a few tourists looking for the likes of Jean-Paul Sartre, who actually did drop in occasionally.

The club was named after Kat's late aunt, her father's sister Margaux, Philippe's mother. Kat thought of herself and her cousin as mirror images. Kat had an American mother and French father and had grown up in New York. Philippe had an American father and French mother and had grown up in Paris. His father had been a Negro musician who came to Paris to perform. He had met Margaux, stayed, had a son, and opened the club. Philippe's parents died in a car accident before the war. Philippe had dreamt of becoming a writer and one of the intellectuals who frequented his club now. But he had felt the pull of obligation in keeping the club, his father's dream, open. Adding the literary events was an indulgence he allowed himself.

Club Margaux was closed on Mondays, but Philippe lived upstairs, and there was always something to do—like open a bottle of wine and read a book at the bar. That's where Kat had found her cousin tonight.

"*Patron*, I'm ordering more champagne." It was Vivienne, a petite woman in her forties. A striking streak of silver ran through her short, dark hair, and Kat couldn't remember ever seeing her without a cigarette in her hand or mouth.

"Fine, fine," Philippe waved her away.

"You should be nice to her," Charlie said, loud enough for Vivienne to hear. "She runs this joint." It was true. Aside from booking the acts, Philippe left most hiring and firing, stocking the bar, and general operations to Vivienne.

"I know. I don't know why she bothers telling me things like that. Of course she should order more champagne!" Philippe said, exasperation in his voice.

Charlie grinned. "She just wants to remind you of everything she does around here."

Philippe crossed his arms and thought for a moment. "Vivienne!"

The woman came back to their table.

"Thank you for all of your hard work and managing everything so well."

"I'm glad somebody finally noticed." She winked at Charlie and went back behind the bar. She liked Charlie. Everyone did.

"Do you think someone in your class killed him?" Philippe asked. Murder was like a gravitational force, impossible to resist talking about.

"He and Eugene hated each other, and Toby accused Eugene of stealing from him. But would that actually lead to murder? And if he did do it, how would Eugene ever expect to get away with it?"

"Maybe he's on a flight back to the U.S. as we speak," Charlie said.

"And what about his girlfriend? Didn't you go out to dinner with them last week? I remember because you skipped the literary salon I hosted here that night," Philippe said pointedly.

Kat patted Philippe's hand. "Don't worry. We'll be at the next one for sure." Charlie looked sideways at Kat, and she stifled a grin. Charlie loved the jazz at Philippe's club but had to be dragged to the literary happenings. They could be a little too artsy for his taste, but he was generally a good sport about it.

"When I saw Marie-Hélène today she seemed so surprised that Toby was dead. If she faked that reaction, she's the next Anouk Aimée. And, again, why kill him at school? It would be too easy to be spotted and caught."

Kat had been running various scenarios through her head since leaving the police station that afternoon. That conversation hadn't engendered any confidence in the detectives' instincts. She looked at Charlie. "They asked me if you and Toby got along."

"Me? I barely knew the guy."

"I know. But it seems like one of their theories is that Toby was involved with another woman and it got messy."

"Another woman, meaning you?" Charlie sat back and folded his arms across his chest.

"I told them it was ridiculous and that they're wasting their time. I guess there's no reason they would take my word for it."

"I mean, the situation isn't so far-fetched," said Philippe. Kat and Charlie stared at him, and he quickly continued. "Not with you two, of course! But maybe he was seeing another woman, and she was married. And maybe her husband killed him."

Kat frowned. Had Toby been cheating on Marie-Hélène? She remembered the woman's words. *He broke my trust, and it was unforgivable.*

"What else did the police ask you?"

Kat thought for a moment. "They wanted to know if Toby had been in Paris before."

"And had he?"

"Yes," Charlie answered. "He told us he was a GI in Paris right after the Liberation."

"Interesting." Philippe sat back.

"Is it?" Kat asked.

"Potentially. You weren't here," he said to Kat. "And you," now to Charlie, "were only here for a week or so. You don't know what it was like in those days. We all knew that even though French troops marched into Paris first, it was only because the Americans allowed them to. Without the Americans, we never would have been liberated." He finished his wine, refilled Charlie's, topped off Kat's, and then poured the remainder of the bottle into his glass. "Girls kissed them on the streets, people gave them the bottles of champagne they'd hidden from the Germans in their cellars, children cheered for them. The American soldiers were gods."

"And then?" Charlie prompted. Kat noticed a familiar look in his eyes.

Philippe shrugged. "It didn't last. Some GIs became too accustomed to the attention. When a French woman asked for a cigarette, they expected much more than a kiss in exchange. There were rumors that teenage girls were being taken advantage of, and there was talk of other crimes."

"What kind of crimes?"

"Robbery. Thieves wearing American military uniforms robbed banks and stole cars. Were they actually Americans, or had they just stolen the uniforms? It's hard to say. I heard that Americans were running some of the biggest black-market rings in the city, dealing in coffee, gasoline, tires, cigarettes, ammunition, and whiskey. I don't know if it's true, but there was gossip that some soldiers worked with French drug dealers, supplying morphine." He took a sip of wine. "There was even talk of murder."

Kat could practically feel the energy crackling off of her husband. She knew this wasn't just an interesting bit of history to him, but potentially a lead.

"So," Philippe continued. "If Toby was in Paris during that period, it's possible there was unfinished business."

Kat was intrigued too, but not for the same reason as Charlie. After discovering Toby's body, she felt entitled to know what happened to him. "I wonder if the police are thinking along those same lines."

"I will ask Marcel." Marcel was Philippe's latest paramour.

Kat looked at him, not understanding at first. Then it clicked. Even though the club was empty, she lowered her voice out of habit. "Your new beau is a *flic*?" The relationship between club owners and police officers in Paris was traditionally quite adversarial, to say the least.

Philippe looked pleased with himself. "He came with other officers to arrest two men who were wanted for fraud. And then he showed up again the next night and the next." He stood up and walked behind the bar in search of another bottle of wine.

"When do we meet this fellow?" Kat asked.

"He's on duty tonight but will be here tomorrow for a new one-act play we're premiering."

"In that case, we'll be here too."

"Weren't you coming anyway?"

"*Mais, bien sur.* Obviously." Kat could practically feel Charlie's sigh of resignation. She grinned and kissed him on the cheek.

Chapter Ten

Kat had been to Les Halles, the enormous and lively covered market in the center of Paris, just once since she and Charlie had arrived in Paris in August. They had stayed out all night with two other American couples, dancing, drinking, and watching the Folies. They capped the evening, or rather started the morning, in the traditional way by devouring bowls of onion soup and small glasses of white wine at 5 AM at Les Halles. The cafés there served real food all night and into the morning for the people who worked at the market overnight, unloading and selling the meat, produce, and fish that came in from all over France for Paris's restaurants, markets, and housewives.

The iconic French writer Emile Zola had called Les Halles "the belly of Paris," and it was a world unto itself, gritty and literally splashed with blood. And yet, there was something alluring, romantic about it, at least for people who were just passing through looking for a spectacle. For the hundreds of French people who worked here, it was a job like any other.

Only three other students had gotten the message to meet Chef Durand at Les Halles that Tuesday morning: the beanpole

Vaughn Harris, typically inseparable from Eugene; mild-mannered Roy Kasden, who usually joined Kat and Toby when they had lunch or a coffee after class; and Peter Perilla, Kat's fellow Brooklyn Dodgers fan. They had celebrated when the Dodgers made it to the World Series in October and then commiserated when their team lost to the dreaded Yankees.

Kat wondered if Eugene hadn't gotten word about the field trip or had just decided not to show up.

"Kat, um, you doing okay?" It was Roy, easily Kat's favorite classmate after Toby. What he lacked in confidence, he made up for in kindness.

Peter chimed in, "Yeah! The detectives said a female student found Toby's body, and that had to have been you." Kat could see that he was hoping for details. Murder seemed to bring out the chattiness in people.

"I'm doing okay, thanks." Actually, she was exhausted. She was already on her second coffee and yearning for her third. It didn't help that most coffees these days were still at least partially ersatz.

Kat's sleep the night before had been fitful, like those nights as a child when she had a fever and recurring images played through her brain, warping and twisting as she drifted in and out of sleep. The image last night had been Toby's face, covered by a towel. Every time she ascended from sleep to something like wakefulness, she thought of that towel. Why was his face covered with a towel? And that was just one of many questions about Toby's death that ricocheted through her mind.

"I still can't believe it. Toby was such a good guy," Roy said.

From the corner of her eye, Kat saw Vaughn shake his head. She stopped and faced him. Chef walked ahead, into the maze of stalls, unaware that his students were no longer following him.

"You disagree?" she asked Vaughn.

"I'm not going to talk shit about a dead man. Let's just say he had it coming."

"So, I guess you are going to talk shit," Kat responded.

"What do you mean by that, Vaughn?" Roy asked. "He was the first fellow that was nice to me in this group. Unlike that snob Eugene." *And unlike Vaughn himself,* Kat thought. He followed Eugene's lead in everything. They had set themselves apart from the rest of the class from the very beginning.

The four of them were clustered around each other in the middle of the passageway. People gave them annoyed looks as they were forced to maneuver around the group, often with arms full of provisions. It was that hour when housewives shopped Les Halles, picking up whatever was leftover for a *bon prix.*

"Where is Eugene?" Kat asked Vaughn. "Did he ever go back to talk to the detectives yesterday like he said he would?" Kat tried to imagine him stabbing Toby, blood spattering his clothes. She suspected that the fastidious Eugene would have preferred a cleaner form of murder.

"Chefs!" Chef Durand had finally noticed that his students weren't following him. They hurried to catch up. Kat was determined to finish this conversation with Vaughn later.

Chef Durand led the students past stalls with flowers, fruit, and vegetables on offer, past stall after stall stained with animal blood. Most of the meat vendors were closing up for the day. Their group stopped periodically for Chef to introduce them to a vendor he knew. A fishmonger from Bretagne offered them samples of oysters. Kat couldn't remember having an oyster this early in the day before, and it wasn't her first choice of breakfast, but she accepted. When at Les Halles . . .

As they stood in front of a cheesemonger, Kat noticed an adjacent, pocket-sized café and wondered if she could get a quick coffee. No matter what it was made from, it should have at least some caffeine, enough to keep her on her feet anyway. As she scanned the space to see how busy it was, she noticed two men seated at a small table involved in a quiet yet heated discussion, espressos untouched in front of them. Kat was sure that one of the men was the new chef at Café du Vent, Jacques Roche, Jules's brother who had recently come to Paris. Jacques, whose chocolate mousse and apple cake had impressed them all, Toby too, just a few days ago.

Kat barely listened as the cheesemonger explained the differences between washed rind and bloomy rind cheeses. Jacques and his companion were standing now, both gesticulating angrily. Jacques shoved a stack of francs across the table and picked up a paper bag from the floor. Then, before she—or Jacques—realized what was happening, the other man landed a punch to Jacques's cheek and stormed out of the café. People gasped, and everyone in the vicinity stopped to stare at Jacques, who grimaced and pressed a napkin to his face. Without making eye contact with anyone, Jacques dropped a few coins on the table and quickly wound his way through the tables and toward one of the market exits, paper bag in hand.

While she had no way of knowing for sure, Kat's guess was that it was coffee in that brown paper bag, good coffee, bought under—or, in this case, over—the table. According to Marie-Hélène, it was one of the last remaining ingredients that was hard to source in Paris, and Kat was sure she had tasted it in the chocolate mousse at Café du Vent. But based on the appearance of that transaction, this might be the last time Jacques secured such good coffee unless he had another source.

"Attention, chefs!" Chef Durand raised his voice slightly to reclaim his students' focus. Then he continued to explain how to assemble a balanced selection for the cheese course.

"*D'accord*, now we will leave the stalls to see a very special store just outside the market." Chef began leading them down a long passageway.

Kat hurried to catch up with him. Roy, Peter, and Vaughn moved slowly behind them, distracted by slabs of beef and pork hanging from the ceiling.

"*Ca va, ma chère?*" Chef asked quietly. Kat was surprised but touched by the endearment.

"*Oui, merci*, Chef. I have a question."

"Proceed, *bien sur*."

"What can you tell me about the black market for food during the Occupation?"

She could see this wasn't the question Chef had been expecting. He inhaled deeply and slowed his walking pace a touch. "In those years that the Nazis ran Paris, 1940 to 1944, the most important thing to remember is that Parisians were close to starvation, and that many people died from lack of food. As you can see here at Les Halles, France produces wondrous fruit, vegetables, meat, dairy, and seafood, plenty to feed the city and the country. But when the Nazis invaded France and occupied Paris, they sent most of the food France produced back to Germany to feed their own people."

They were outside now, crossing a busy pedestrian street. Chef held his arm in front of her to stop Kat from walking in front of a speeding bicycle.

"Parisians had ration cards for meat, butter, and bread. But there was never enough food. One could wait in line for several hours at the bakery only to discover that they'd sold their last loaf before you reached the front of the line. What were you to feed your children or your parents? And there was no guarantee you'd get anything the following day either."

Chef shrugged and continued. "People were desperate. Some raised rabbits in their bathtubs to have a source of meat for their families. The story goes that once a German horse died in the streets, and housewives carved it up with knives for meat. Fortunate people had families with farms outside the city, and they could occasionally get vegetables or eggs."

The Paris Kat had known both before and after the war was practically overflowing with good things to eat. She struggled to imagine the city being so hungry.

"*Alors*, the *marché noir*. The butcher might keep extra cuts of meat in the back for people with the francs to pay a premium. A farmer in Normandy might come to Paris with a suitcase full of blocks of butter he had managed to hide from the authorities. He could get a good price for it, better than he would get from the Germans, and people could have butter on the table. Of course, the black market was illegal, but, *madame*, I would implore you not to judge the participants, especially the buyers, harshly. It was often a choice between life and death."

"I understand." She had known that the war had been a hungry time but wasn't aware to what extent. She put herself in the shoes of a mother without any food to feed her child. She too might do anything. "The black market was mostly on a small scale?"

"I cannot say for sure, but I think not. War is a time of chaos, and there is always someone to step in at a time like that to take advantage."

They had stopped outside a shop called E. Dehillerin. Kat saw gleaming pots and pans and various tins for baking displayed in the window. Peter and Roy caught up with them. Vaughn had disappeared. What had he meant that Toby had it coming?

A tall, stately man approached, shook Chef's hand, and introduced himself to the students as the owner of the shop, a kitchen supply store beloved by chefs and home cooks alike. He invited the students to explore on their own. He and Chef continued to chat.

As she, Peter, and Roy entered Dehillerin, Kat was still thinking about what it must have been like to live in Paris during those desperate years. But almost immediately she was distracted by the spectacle in front of her. She had never seen so many pots, pans, bowls, hand mixers, whisks, strainers, and spoons in one place. Kat walked down the aisles, letting her hand brush lightly against the items on the shelves. The number of whisks alone was astonishing, from the tiny, barely bigger than her index finger, to the gargantuan, large enough to make mayonnaise for a giant.

She walked by a mammoth mortar and pestle and wondered how anyone would get it home, much less up the stairs of their apartment building. She admired the shiny copper mixing bowls and sighed a little in longing. She paused before the gleaming cast-iron pans. She lifted a 10-inch skillet and felt its heft.

And then she made her way to the knives. They were so beautiful. Her eyes wandered past the chef's knives, their imposing silver blades catching the light, the paring knives, bread knives, carving knives, and even the curved *tourné* knives, whose job it was to cut vegetables into small football shapes, something Kat could never quite get the hang of, no matter how many times Chef demonstrated the technique. Toby had mastered the *tourné* cut almost immediately but vowed never to use it at his restaurant. "Too old-fashioned," he'd said.

Suddenly she shivered, remembering the crimson-stained chef's knife next to Toby's body, the vicious slashes on his torso, and all the blood. So much blood.

She closed her eyes and forced her mind back to the clean knives in front of her. Before starting at L'École de la Grande Cuisine, she hadn't understood the power a good, sharp knife could bring to cooking. She shook her head, thinking of the dull knives she had worked with back in Brooklyn.

She had always adored eating; she was half French after all. But about the same time she had met Charlie four years ago, it was like a new dimension opened in her brain, a new understanding. Food became her hobby, almost her obsession. She religiously read all the weekly cooking columns in the city's newspapers, checked out cookbooks from the library, and dragged Charlie to Yorktown for bratwurst, Chinatown for dumplings, and Arthur Avenue for pasta fagioli. She planned elaborate dinner parties for their friends. Charlie joked that the real reason she married him was so she could sit in the kitchen with his Italian mother and scribble down her recipes.

At first, part of her rebelled against this new culinary enthusiasm. She was a modern woman, after all! The last thing she wanted for herself was domestic drudgery.

But she kept coming back to it. And this was all happening as her journalism career was falling apart. Food and cooking gave her something to hold onto, to dig into.

What she loved best about it was that, for the first time in her life, it wasn't just all in her head. Being a student and then a reporter and writer were cerebral occupations. Once she started at L'École, she was able to put the feeling into words: Cooking literally uses all of one's senses. Taste was obvious. Sight, too, as she would observe how much a sauce had reduced or if a pie crust was brown enough. Smell to determine when a gateau aux figues baking in the oven needed to be checked. Touch, pressing a piece of meat to determine its level of doneness. It was how much she used her sense of hearing that continually surprised her. How the burble of hot oil changed when its temperature rose too high or sank too low. The tap, tap, crack of a spoon on glossy toasted sugar when breaking into a perfect crème brulée. Cooking brought her out of her mind and into her body.

School had also been physically challenging in a way that Kat relished: filling and carrying giant stockpots of water, mastering precise chopping styles—often so small you could barely see the individual pieces of food once you had cut them—and scrubbing every surface and pan after cooking with a devotional fervor. Kitchen cleanliness seemed to be Chef's religion.

L'École had been her fresh start. But now, instead of being a place of happiness and discovery, it was a place where she had found death. Would she ever be able to walk into the pantry again? And Toby wouldn't be there to make her laugh and rescue her when she was in the weeds.

She knew that it was human nature to adjust and persevere, even in the wake of violence. The people in this city had proven that. For four long years, the Germans had occupied Paris. Thousands of people had been deported and killed. Many businesses closed and families were separated. Homes had been destroyed. And yet, just five years later, aside from a few rubble-strewn lots, Paris felt almost like it had when she visited with her family before the war. There was life in the streets, laughter in the bars, and excitement in the late-night quartiers. Kat didn't know what emotional scars were under the city's exuberant surface, but she was sure they existed. It was impossible to escape that kind of trauma unscathed.

Chapter Eleven

An hour later, Kat opened the door to Café du Vent and saw that it was bustling. Most of the tables were full, and some of the ones that weren't still had dirty plates on them waiting to be bused.

"Kat!" Claudine seemed surprised to see her in the middle of the day. She looked frazzled, her usually impeccable French twist lopsided and her apron dirty.

"It looks like business is good," Kat said as they exchanged kisses.

"Oh yes, ever since Jacques and Annette arrived. I'm even considering hiring a server." She led Kat to a table. "Do you know what you'd like?"

"I haven't stopped thinking about that chocolate mousse since last week. But I suppose I should start with some real food first. A croque madame please." The day before, after she had found Toby's body, Kat's appetite had deserted her. But it was back again today, like a loyal friend.

"*Bien sur.* How are things at school?"

Kat suddenly remembered that Claudine had met Toby the week before, but Kat didn't have the energy to tell the whole story. Instead she said, as lightly as she could, "I love it, but it isn't always easy—the mayonnaise took me a while to master."

Claudine looked at her closely, as if she suspected Kat wasn't telling her the whole story. But she said only, "I remember when Jules took his course there so many years ago. Ooh la la, mayonnaise was difficult even for him."

"I didn't realize that Jules went to L'École."

"Oh yes. He had planned to be a chef but later realized he preferred managing the café. Speaking of chefs, let me get your order to Jacques." She hurried away from the table. Kat had forgotten all about Jacques and the altercation she had seen at Les Halles that morning. Now she imagined him cooking downstairs with a purple shiner under one of his eyes. What had the fight been about?

Kat pulled her notebook out of her bag and flipped through looking for the first blank page. The notebook was a hodgepodge of recipes, notes from cooking demos, shopping lists, observations of Paris street scenes, and the beginnings of essays that she never quite finished. Opening her notebook whenever she had a moment had become a habit.

A few minutes later Claudine appeared with Kat's lunch.

"How is Mélisse?" Kat asked.

"You are so kind to ask. She's doing well at her new school. It is the best decision we ever made." Claudine seemed to catch the eye of another patron. "*Bon appetit!*"

A croque madame had been Kat's favorite café lunch since coming to the city with Charlie in August. As a child, when she had visited with her parents, she preferred the croque monsieur, a toasted ham and cheese sandwich covered with a rich béchamel sauce and broiled until golden. The madame was the same sandwich but with a sunny side up egg on top. As a child, the egg didn't make sense to her. But now, as she cut into the thick slices of bread and the egg yolk spilled down the sides, she understood the appeal. She quickly ate the rest of the yolk and the parts of the sandwich it had touched. One thing she didn't like was cold, congealing yolk.

Once the yolk was taken care of, Kat continued to stare at the blank page in her notebook. She had carried a notebook everywhere with her since starting the journalism program at Brooklyn College, when she had decided that she was going to be a *serious* journalist.

There were serious women journalists of course—look at Martha Gellhorn, who had reported from Spain and even smuggled herself into Normandy on D-Day. And, not only that, she had married Ernest Hemingway while doing it. "Well, that was your big mistake," Charlie had told Kat once. "You should have married someone more famous!"

Kat had laughed, but they both knew he was wrong. Gellhorn had been a foreign correspondent before marrying Hemingway. Kat was certain that if she had married first, somehow Gellhorn wouldn't have made it into war zones. She would have been a foreign correspondent's wife, just like Kat.

During the war Kat had worked as a copy boy at the *Tribune*—even the copy girls were called copy boys, and even the grown men in the job were called boys. Her primary task was to move copy from desk to desk—God forbid the writers or editors had to stand up and walk across the newsroom—fetch coffee, and run other errands. In normal times, all of the copy boys would have been young men. But during the war, three women, including Kat, had been hired. Kat had been jubilant.

Being a copy boy was hands down the best way to start a career in journalism, *real* journalism: hard-hitting stories, exposés, investigative pieces. Her father had congratulated her on the job but cautioned that when the war ended, so might her position. Kat felt that she could be the exception. The editors would get to know her, value her, and understand what she could contribute. She would work harder than anyone before her had ever worked.

And she did, and they did notice her and come to value her and even assign her pieces that ran with her byline. Her first assignment was to profile a boy in Queens who had collected 847 pounds of scrap metal for the war effort. After that, her editor, Mr. Shields, gave her two or three stories a week. Kat never quite escaped the human interest category of news, but she figured, if she just kept showing up and working hard, that would change.

After the war ended in Europe in May 1945, a few men began to trickle back to the *Tribune*'s office. The other two female copy boys left to get married, but Kat kept her head down and lodged a fervent prayer to the gods of journalism that she would be an exception, that Mr. Shields and his higher-ups would recognize that she wasn't just a copy boy but a real newspaper woman.

One of those returning men appeared in the *Tribune*'s office on a sunny morning in June. He exchanged hearty handshakes and friendly greetings with the old-timers who stood up to welcome him. Then he disappeared into Mr. Shields's office. Kat noticed how the energy in the room changed when the man arrived. It was like the sun shone a little more brightly through the windows and laughter came a little more easily.

Even the clackety-clack of the typewriters sounded more jaunty. Later, Kat would call that transformation the Charlie Kelly Effect.

While Charlie was in with Mr. Shields, a writer in his late forties named Perkins stood up and began putting the contents of his desk into a stray box. In this newsroom, the best desks were in the middle, and this was one of them. He walked the box over to an empty desk next to the bench where Kat and the other copy boys sat, and she silently groaned. Perkins was notorious for his body odor, fully deserving the nickname the copy boys had bestowed on him, PU Perkins.

"Mr. Perkins? Why are you switching desks?"

"Charlie Kelly's back."

"So?" Perkins had seniority, for sure.

"He spent three years in who knows what hellholes while I sat on my duff here. Not to mention he's what they would call a rising star, and I most certainly am not." There was no bitterness in his voice.

Kat instantly made up her mind to dislike this Charlie Kelly with his easy confidence and almost certain sense of entitlement. He'd probably gone to a fancy college, fancier than her alma mater Brooklyn College anyway, and had the world on a platter and took it for granted. She hadn't said one word to the man and had barely gotten a look at him—although she couldn't help but notice how his dark, wavy hair curled at the ends, the slightly crooked smile that lit up his whole face, and his broad shoulders that were skinny but would surely fill out now that he was eating civilian food again. Anyway, the point was that she wasn't going to be taken in by his charm like everyone else seemed to be. And she vowed to stop thinking about his shoulders. She would treat him with frosty professionalism if she had to interact with him at all.

When Charlie emerged from Shields's office, he strode straight to the desk Perkins had vacated. He tested a few keys on the typewriter, removed his jacket, and slung it on the back of the seat. He looked around the room for Perkins and gave him a friendly smile and a nod. Perkins raised his hand in acknowledgment. As he was turning back to his typewriter, Charlie's eyes caught Kat's. She wanted to look away, but her body wouldn't obey her brain, and she felt a shiver of electricity run through her. They stared at each other for a long moment before someone called Charlie's name.

Kat would never suggest that it was love at first sight—she didn't believe in that—but it was true there was some essential understanding that passed between them the first time their eyes met. Looking back, she thought that they had recognized something in each other, a kindred spirit.

Within a few days, Kat realized she was almost completely wrong about Charlie, at least mostly—he had, in fact, gone to a fancy college.

By September, Kat and Charlie were inseparable, spending as many days and nights together as possible.

By October, Kat was out at the *Tribune*—too many men needed jobs now—but quickly landed a staff job at *Delight*, a woman's magazine that offered beauty tips, strategies for landing the fellow of your dreams, and career advice along the lines of how to anticipate your boss's every need. Kat hated it.

By May 1946, Kat and Charlie were married. She was both happier than she had ever been and miserable, thanks to her job.

Kat didn't blame Charlie for the implosion of her newspaper career. It wasn't his fault that the profession, and the whole world really, thought a woman couldn't hack anything serious. He believed in her and respected her ambition.

But she also didn't consider it a fair trade, like some of her friends did. "Even if you lost your job, it was all worth it, wasn't it? Let's face it, Charlie is a catch," one of her high school pals had said. Or like, cosmically, she had been at the newspaper just to meet her husband, and once she had there was no reason for her to have the job anymore. Kat wanted both. Charlie had both. Why shouldn't she?

Now she was moving on, leaving journalism behind and learning more about food at L'École. What she would do with her new knowledge she wasn't entirely sure. But she was collecting recipes with an eye toward teaching cooking classes to other American wives in Paris with their husbands. Now, sitting in Café du Vent, was her time to edit what she had and fill in any gaps.

Without even thinking about it, she wrote the words "Toby Magnusson" at the top of the first empty page and started writing. She jotted down what she remembered from the scene where she had stumbled onto Toby's body. Then she wrote, "MH scared? If so, of who? What did Vaughn mean, Toby had it coming?" Kat was itching with questions. Somehow seeing them on paper helped her organize her thoughts.

"Madame Kelly." It was a smooth voice with a Texas twang.

Kat looked up to see Jeanette Ketchum with her hand on the back of the table's other chair. "May I?"

"Yes, please!" They exchanged kisses, and Kat admired Jeanette's slim, olive-green trousers and matching jacket. "You look smashing today, as usual."

"Oh stop, you're going to make a girl blush. So, how is the *Trib*'s man in Paris? And, more importantly, how is his wife? I heard about what happened yesterday."

The community of American journalists in Paris was small, and Kat wasn't surprised that Jeanette had heard about Toby's murder and Kat's discovery of his body.

Jeanette wrote a biweekly column about life in Paris for *The American*, a New York–based weekly that covered news and culture and included some fiction and humor as well. Jeanette's columns ranged in subject from the power struggles in the French government to the latest Sartre play, to the drama of a big murder trial, to observations on the superiority of race relations in France as compared to the United States. She had come to Paris the week after it was liberated in August 1944 and was a fixture on the avenues and in the cafés in her trademark suits and hats.

Kat never asked about Jeanette's love life, but she was fairly certain there were no men involved. Jeanette was confident, a little brash, and undoubtedly successful in a milieu where women rarely permeated. She understood the city in a way that neither Kat nor Charlie did yet, and she seemed to be fearless. She had the career that Kat had dreamed of, but Jeanette was so uniquely herself that Kat never thought to be jealous. It would be like a runner being jealous of a prize-winning racehorse. The natural thing to do was to admire its power.

Claudine stopped by the table. Jeanette ordered an espresso. Kat asked for a noisette, an espresso with a dollop of foamy milk on top, and two chocolate mousses. "Trust me," she said to Jeanette.

"So? How are you?"

"I was a mess yesterday. It surprised me. I've always thought of myself as level-headed."

Jeanette frowned. "I've covered a lot of violence over the years, including murder, and if it doesn't affect you there's something wrong with you."

"Perhaps."

"And he was your friend."

"Charlie and I had dinner with him and his girlfriend last week."

Jeanette opened her hands as if to say, *you see?*

Claudine dropped off their coffees and two dishes of chocolate mousse. Kat hoped it would be as good as she remembered, and she wasn't disappointed. She tasted the hint of good coffee behind the chocolate. Even just the whisper of it was so much deeper and richer than most of the coffee she encountered in Paris. She closed her eyes to fully savor the bite and let out a small moan.

When she opened them, she saw Jeanette watching her. "That Charlie Kelly has all the luck. Where do I find someone who eats chocolate mousse like that?"

Kat grinned. "Paris probably isn't a bad place to start." She took another bite of the mousse and thought of a question for her friend who knew the city and its players so well. "Jeanette, are you familiar with a Detective Galland? I think his first name is Maurice."

"He's the one investigating your friend's murder?"

Kat nodded.

Jeanette let out a big breath. "I know him." She leaned toward Kat, serious. "The most important thing to remember about Galland is that he's a survivor. He's been around forever—through various changes of the political guard, through the Occupation, and then after. Sure, he solves some murders; I think he's probably actually a good investigator. But what he's really good at is reading the political tea leaves. Let's just say that I don't think getting to the truth is his top priority."

"What is?"

"Self-preservation. Sometimes that means arresting the bad guy; sometimes it means arresting someone else altogether. And sometimes it means arresting no one at all."

"And what about his sidekick, Detective Faucher?"

Jeanette shook her head. "I only know that he's young and ambitious."

"Thanks, Jeanette. I've got to run." Kat put a handful of coins on the table and bent down to exchange kisses with Jeanette. She smelled like sandalwood. Kat started out toward the door.

"Kat!" Jeanette called after her, and she returned to the table.

"There's someone I want you to meet Friday night."

The U.S. embassy was hosting a party for American journalists on Friday. "Sure, who's that?"

"Ethan Prentice. He's an editor at the *International Star Herald*. He's looking for someone to write a regular recipe column. You should meet him."

Kat felt a little hum run through her. A recipe column. Now that was intriguing. "Of course. I would love to meet him."

"Do you have something prepared, in case he wants a sample quickly?"

Kat's mind skipped through the hodgepodge of her notebook. She didn't have anything presentable now but would pull something together. "Yes, yes. *Merci, mon amie*!" She kissed Jeanette on the cheek once more and hurried toward the door.

"Kat!" Jeanette called again.

Kat turned back.

"Don't get mixed up with Galland."

Kat nodded her thanks but didn't say anything. She knew she couldn't promise that.

Chapter Twelve

Kat stood in front of a modest apartment building on a busy street in Montparnasse. She couldn't be sure if Marie-Hélène had given Kat her real address or just a random one in order to be rid of her. Now the trick would be getting into the building to find out. She didn't think this was a concierge building but one where she'd need a key for the front door. Kat resolved to just wait until someone came out.

After about ten minutes, a middle-aged woman with an impossibly small dog on a leash in one hand and a wheeled shopping trolley in the other awkwardly pushed open the door. Kat hurried to help her. The woman thanked Kat and didn't give a backward glance as Kat slipped into the building behind her. This was clearly a building where there were a lot of comings and goings, not one where neighbors were overly vigilant.

She climbed two flights of stairs to the apartment number written on the piece of paper and knocked. She heard steps inside, and the door opened to reveal a stocky, dark-haired man with a weather-beaten face. "*Oui?*"

"*Desolée*," Kat said in French. "I must have the wrong apartment. I'm looking for Marie-Hélène Arnaud. Is she a neighbor of yours?" If Marie-Hélène had given her the wrong address on purpose, Kat resolved to go straight back to Guillaume and ask her uncle where she lived.

The man studied Kat for a moment, opened the door wider, and inclined his head, as if inviting her in.

Kat was confused. She realized this man looked familiar, and her confusion only grew. She didn't move.

"*Elle est dans la chambre*." She was in the bedroom, he said.

Suddenly Kat registered that this man was wearing casual French-style military fatigues, and she knew where she had seen him before—yesterday looking up at her and Marie-Hélène inside the Guillaume office building. She took a step back.

"*Allez-y*," he said, gesturing for her to enter. "I'm going out." He grabbed a jacket from a hook next to the door and stepped outside the apartment, keeping the door ajar.

Kat traded places with him, and he started down the hall to the stairs. "Who are you?" she asked.

He stopped but didn't look back. "Her husband." He continued walking, and she heard his footsteps on the stairs and the building's heavy front door open and close.

Her husband! Last night Philippe had speculated that Toby had been seeing a married woman whose husband might have found out, become enraged, and killed him. It never occurred to her that Marie-Hélène might be the married one.

Kat closed and locked the door, although the man—Marie-Hélène's husband!—probably had a key. The front door opened into a small hallway with doors along either side. Kat peeked into the kitchen and the living room but didn't see Marie-Hélène. One door at the end of the hall was closed. Kat knocked quietly, and when there was no response, she opened the door.

The room was dim. Only thin slivers of light escaped the heavily curtained windows. But Kat could see Marie-Hélène lying on the bed, on top of the covers. She was wearing the same gray dress as the day before when Kat had gone to her office to tell her that Toby was dead. Marie-Hélène was lying on the far side of the bed, facing Kat, with her eyes open. She didn't say anything, and she didn't look at Kat. The little white dog, Bijou, was curled up next to her.

Kat sat on the bed. She saw a tear slip down Marie-Hélène's cheek. Kat couldn't know how long she had been there like that, but she thought it must have been a very long time.

Without consciously making the decision to do so, Kat laid down on the bed facing Marie-Hélène. It felt good to lay down. She had been doing well today, but suddenly it all caught up to her. Was it only yesterday that Toby had died?

Marie-Hélène finally looked at her. The tears began spilling from her eyes more quickly, and she made no effort to wipe them away.

Kat squeezed her own eyes closed tightly. She had no business crying in front of this woman. But she couldn't help it. "I'm sorry," she whispered.

"For what?" Marie-Hélène's voice was barely audible.

"I don't have the right to be this sad, not like you."

"There's so much sadness. Too much for one person." She moved a hand to the middle of the bed, and Kat reached for it. They held hands for a moment before Marie-Hélène retrieved hers and shifted onto her back.

They lay there in silence for a few minutes before Marie-Hélène asked, "Did you meet Nico?" Her voice was stronger.

"He said he's your husband."

"Yes."

"Did Toby know?"

"There was nothing to know. I haven't seen Nico in years. He is only my husband on a piece of paper." Kat wondered if Nico felt the same way.

Marie-Hélène seemed to read her mind. "I have asked him for a divorce many times, but he always refuses. That is why I couldn't marry Toby."

Kat propped herself up on her elbow. "Did he ask you to marry him?"

"He wanted me to marry him and move to Chicago where he would open his restaurant. I would work the front of the house. He said my accent would bring in more customers than his cooking." She smiled slightly. "But I couldn't marry him because I was already married."

"What did you tell Toby when he talked about marriage?"

"I laughed and told him that we had just met."

"Would you have married him if you could have?"

"If it meant I could leave this place I would have married anyone."

"But you broke up."

Marie-Hélène shifted and sat up, her back to Kat. "I need coffee. Or what passes for coffee these days." She stood up and walked out of the room.

Kat followed her into the kitchen and sat at a small round table as Marie-Hélène prepared a cafetière. "Sugar?"

"*Oui, merci.*"

Marie-Hélène brought two cups and spoons and a sugar bowl to the table. She poured them both coffee and sat down at the table.

"How long have you been married?" Kat asked.

"Six years. I left Paris when the Germans came but returned in the fall of 1942. That's when I met Nico, and we got married. It was a bad time, and he made me feel safe."

"But then he left?"

Marie-Hélène nodded. "Left to fight with the Free French; he is a soldier. And then after the war he was in the proper French army. He came back occasionally, but I realized soon that I had made a mistake. It is one of the things I am best at, making mistakes." She took another sip of coffee.

"And, this time, when did he come back?"

"Yesterday. At least that's when I saw him for the first time. You saw him too."

Kat nodded at the confirmation; it had been him on the street in front of Marie-Hélène's office. So he had been in Paris, and even in the neighborhood, the morning that Toby was murdered.

Once again, Marie-Hélène seemed to read her mind. "He didn't know about Toby."

"How can you be sure?"

Marie-Hélène shrugged. "I would have known if he was following me, watching me. He wasn't trying to hide from me. You saw how obvious he made it yesterday."

Kat pressed the subject. "Had he known, would he have been jealous or violent?"

Marie-Hélène shrugged again. Kat wanted to shake her. Her boyfriend had been murdered! Didn't she care who had done it? She decided to push more.

"When I was with you yesterday, at your office, you looked scared."

"I was in shock. And I was surprised to see Nico outside." Usually, Kat could reliably judge when someone was telling her the truth, but not Marie-Hélène.

"He's staying with you?"

"For now."

"Did you tell the police about him?"

Marie-Hélène shook her head. "*Non*, why get him in trouble? I am sure he wouldn't kill Toby."

Kat wasn't as certain. Should she tell the police? The presence of Toby's girlfriend's husband in Paris would certainly be interesting to them.

"Promise me, Kat, you won't tell the police about Nico."

Kat didn't respond.

"I know he didn't do it. Please, Kat, don't drag him—and me—further into this. If the police know about him, they won't leave me alone. Please, I need you to promise me."

It was against her better judgment, but Kat couldn't refuse. "*D'accord*. I promise. But, if it wasn't Nico, who could it have been? Marie-Hélène, you knew Toby and his life better than anyone." At least Kat assumed that was true.

Marie-Hélène stood up and collected the empty cups from the table. "How could I possibly know? Maybe it was a robbery, or maybe it was that ass at L'École. Toby couldn't stand him."

"Eugene?"

Marie-Hélène nodded as she washed the cups.

"What did Toby tell you about Eugene?"

"Just that he was a shit."

Kat couldn't really argue. There was something off about Eugene besides just run-of-the-mill jerkiness. She had dismissed him as a suspect, but maybe she needed to consider him more seriously.

Kat stood up to leave, stopping to scratch Bijou behind the ears. At the door, she said, "Toby's brother will be here tomorrow from Chicago. Would you like to meet for lunch?"

Marie-Hélène looked surprised. After a moment's pause she replied, "*Oui*. I'd like that very much."

Kat nodded, and after they arranged a location near Marie-Hélène's office, she asked, "Will you be okay now?"

"Yes. I am going to take a bath and finally get out of these clothes." She held Kat to her for a moment as they exchanged kisses. "I didn't want to go out to dinner with you and your husband last week. Toby talked about you so much that I thought there must be something going on with you. But I saw at dinner that wasn't the case. You and your Charlie only have eyes for each other."

"It was the same with you and Toby," Kat assured her.

Marie-Hélène nodded sadly and gave Kat a quick kiss on the cheek. "*Merci*."

Chapter Thirteen

At five o'clock, Kat walked to the post office near their apartment on Rue du Bac to use the pay phone. Like most Parisian apartments, they didn't have their own telephone.

"Hello, Florence."

"Kat, honey, how are you doing today? I was so worried about you yesterday."

"Better, thank you. What's the plan tonight?"

"Charlie is meeting someone at LPB and says that, if you're up for it, you could come around 6:30. Do you want me to get him a message?"

"No, that's okay. I'll be there. Thank you!"

If Kat and Charlie couldn't use Florence as a telephonic go-between, they'd never know where the other one was. Thankfully, the indispensable *Tribune* secretary was happy to transmit their nearly daily messages.

Ninety minutes later, Kat walked down the long corridor to Le Petit Bar at the Ritz Hotel on Place Vendôme. When he was off the clock, Charlie drank at the nearby Hôtel de Crillon with all the other American journalists. Since he was at the Ritz, he was likely wrapping up a more professional meeting.

Le Petit Bar was certainly more discreet than the Crillon, where every other writer in town would know who Charlie Kelly drank with. And with only about thirty seats, it felt cozier, clubbier, and more intimate than the ornate main bar closer to the hotel entrance.

Kat had changed into a soft gray jersey dress that gathered at the waist. There were a couple of other women at the bar, and she noticed that both were wearing the full-skirted style that was so popular. Kat admired the look but didn't want to wear it on a daily basis. Too much material to manage. She preferred sportier clothes that she could move in, even when the occasion required some polish, like drinks at LPB.

Kat saw Charlie sitting at a table with a man in an American military uniform. Her husband was leaning in and listening closely to whatever the man was saying. She had assumed his meeting would be over by the time she arrived, and she was about to leave and walk around the block. But at that moment Charlie saw her and waved her over. As she approached, both men stood up.

"Smithson, this is my wife, Kat. Kat, this is Brigadier General Martin Smithson. He's based in Paris helping to coordinate implementation of the Marshall Plan."

"Pleased to meet you, Kat." They shook hands, and Kat sat next to Charlie. The bartender came over, and Kat ordered a Tom Collins. She wanted to compare it with the Crillon's version, which was justly famous. Charlie ordered a second whiskey, but Smithson declined. "I have to go meet my wife and a few friends for dinner."

"How long have you been in Paris?" Kat asked.

"This tour, just over a year. But I've been back and forth since '44, and this time I was able to bring my family." Martin Smithson looked to be in his early to mid-forties, clearly a career military man with close-cropped hair and impeccable posture.

"Two girls, right?" Charlie asked.

Smithson pulled his wallet from his back pocket and extracted a small photo of two young children in pajamas in front of a Christmas tree. "Linda and Nancy," he said, pointing. "They're nine and eleven now."

"They were just babies during the war!" Kat said.

Smithson nodded. "Patty had her hands full."

"And now you're in Paris helping with the Marshall Plan. Are the French as grateful as they should be?" Kat asked this last question with a smile on her face. Despite the fact that the United States was giving France over two billion dollars—an astronomical sum—to rebuild its industry and economy, gratitude wasn't an especially strong quality among the French, especially when it came to Americans. And then her mind flashed back to what Philippe had said about Americans in Paris after the Liberation. Maybe gratitude was overrated.

Smithson laughed. "Some of them are. The finance men in the French government are. They know they would be up a creek without a paddle if it weren't for this investment." He tipped back his glass to swallow the last of what looked like a gin and tonic. "Actually, I think they all know it, but one faction likes to pretend it isn't true."

"How come?" Kat asked, although she thought she knew.

"Pride. They hate the Brits because, well, they've hated them for centuries and because they held out against the Nazis when the French couldn't. And they want to pretend they're as powerful and important on the world stage as anyone else."

"And how do they feel about the Soviets?"

"That's the million-dollar question. The communists in the government are always trying to drive a wedge between the U.S. and France. You know, you ask as many questions as your husband here." Smithson said it good-naturedly.

"We never run out of conversation; we can both ask each other endless questions," Charlie said with a grin.

Smithson stood. "Then you're lucky." He looked at Kat and said to Charlie, "But you probably know that."

"Thanks, buddy," Charlie said. "I'll see you soon." They shook hands.

"It was a pleasure to meet you, Kat."

"Likewise. Enjoy your dinner."

Kat and Charlie sat down. "Do you want another drink?" he asked.

She took another sip and shook her head. It was good but not quite up to Crillon standards. "So, what's the scoop?"

Charlie drummed a finger on the table and smiled. "I'm not sure yet, but I think it could be something big." Kat could feel the energy emanating from his body. He got an almost electric charge when he was excited about a story. "I couldn't stop thinking about what Philippe said about Americans committing crimes in Paris after the Liberation."

"That isn't something the public has heard much, if anything, about."

"Exactly," Charlie said. "Smithson and I are meeting again tomorrow, and he's going to bring me something."

"Why would he do that? Surely it would reflect badly on the military."

Charlie thought for a moment. "I've known Smithson since the war, when he was an official, on-the-record source when I wrote for the *Stars and Stripes.* We got along from the beginning. And it became clear pretty fast that he actually believes in honor and integrity and those other supposed Army values. Not just covering your ass and covering things up like the rest of them." There was a touch of bitterness in his voice, and Kat couldn't blame him. But part of her wondered if there was something personal in his pursuit of this story, which, if it unfolded the way she thought it could, would leave the Army scrambling. She raised her eyebrow slightly, and that's all it took.

"I know what you're thinking," Charlie said. "But no investigative journalist worth a drop of newsprint would ignore a story like this. And if I dig and it turns out the Army comes out smelling like roses, I'll publish that too." He swallowed the final sip of his drink. "Ready?"

She nodded, and he helped her on with her coat.

They walked past the imposing obelisk at Place de la Concorde across the river to one of their favorite spots, the famous Brasserie Lipp. Over the choucroute garni for him and the duck confit for her, Kat told Charlie about her excursion to Les Halles, seeing Jeanette at Café du Vent, and visiting Marie-Hélène and briefly meeting Nico.

"She doesn't think Nico killed Toby, even though she hasn't seen him in years and he has every reason to be jealous. But it's more than that. It's like she isn't even interested in who might have killed him."

The duck confit was salty and rich. Kat reached over for a bite of Charlie's tender, porky choucroute. The French were truly culinary wizards if they could make cabbage taste that good.

Kat continued, "And I can't stop thinking about what Jeanette said about Detective Galland not always caring about getting to the truth. And Vaughn saying that Toby had it coming. It's all tangled up in my head." She felt like she needed to organize everything she knew about what had happened in the last thirty-six hours and everything she knew about Toby. She realized that if the police didn't know about Nico, she might be the only one with the whole picture. Of course, they might have other evidence by now, fingerprints, footprints, an autopsy report. How could she find out about that? Then she remembered Marcel, Philippe's police officer boyfriend, would be at Club Margaux tonight.

Charlie frowned. "When do classes start again?"

"Thursday."

"Blind faith is against my religion, so I'm not going to say you should trust the police to do their job. But, Kat, I know you. And I know you're going to get yourself mixed up in this."

"I *am* mixed up in this. I found Toby's body, and I'm meeting his brother tomorrow. There's no getting out of this even if I wanted to."

"But the point is, you don't *want* to get out of this."

Kat didn't deny it. He knew her as well as she knew him. And at this moment, she thought he knew her better than she knew herself. Her plan had been to channel her energies into culinary school. But ever since she had found Toby dead, Kat's brain had been inching toward investigating his murder. She just hadn't known it. But Charlie did.

She didn't say anything, and he continued, "All I'm saying is, be careful. Someone was murdered. The stakes will be high for whoever did it."

"I know." She wanted whoever killed her friend to be arrested, of course. But she was honest with herself. Charlie had a new story to sink his teeth into. Now she did too.

Chapter Fourteen

Kat told Monsieur Petit she would be at school at nine o'clock that morning. It was 9:13 when she dashed up the steps and hurriedly opened the big front door.

They had stayed too late at Club Margaux the night before. The play was well-received by the small but enthusiastic audience; miracle of miracles, even Charlie enjoyed it. Then Philippe had brought over a bottle of wine to their table and introduced them to his new friend Marcel Arsenault.

Since they were teenagers, Kat had understood that Philippe was attracted to men. Early on in their relationship, she had told Charlie about her Black cousin who dated men, lived in Paris, and was like the sibling she never had. She held her breath as she waited for his reaction. Despite their connection, if he had shown an ounce of disapproval, that would have been the end of the Kat and Charlie Show.

To her relief, after only the briefest moment of surprise, Charlie hadn't batted an eye. Despite growing up in a traditional Catholic family, he was one of the most liberal-minded men she knew. He genuinely liked and was interested in people, no matter who they were, a quality that served him well as a journalist. And he didn't have much patience for societal conventions. Charlie's quick acceptance made her fall even harder and faster for him.

Marcel looked to be in his late thirties, with smooth, olive skin and a well-trimmed mustache. Kat immediately liked his relaxed, friendly manner. She hadn't expected that from a cop. And while he was subtle, of course, he was clearly besotted with her cousin. He could barely take his eyes off of Philippe.

"Are you in uniform or a detective?" Charlie asked.

"A detective. I mostly investigate financial crimes, like fraud and bribery."

He couldn't shed any light on Toby's case but promised to discreetly ask around.

"Do you know Detective Maurice Galland?" Kat asked him.

"*Bien sur*. But just by reputation. He's a legend in the force."

"How so?"

"He has gotten into scrapes with the higher-ups before, but he always slips out of any trouble. He'll be there longer than all of us, as long as there are French in France."

Despite the late night at the club, Kat would have been on time to meet Toby's brother that morning, but everything had gone wrong. Just as she was walking out the door, Charlie had pointed out a hole in the side seam of her dress. She had hurriedly pulled on another that, she admitted to herself, probably needed to be washed. She still would have been on time if the metro hadn't been delayed.

Now, she said good morning to the concierge, Madame Poitrine, and quickly walked to Monsieur Petit's office. The door was closed. She paused for a moment and listened for voices. If they were in the middle of a conversation, she might give them a moment.

Kat heard nothing, so she knocked.

"*Entrez*!"

Petit and a second man stood. Kat saw relief wash over both of their faces.

"Mrs. Kelly, I'm Harold Magnusson. Thank you for coming." It was easy to tell that this man with his hand outstretched was Toby's brother. Although Harold was stockier, he was just as powerfully built. His hair was light brown while Toby's had been sandy blond, but their cleft chins were nearly identical. Kat judged that Harold was the elder, probably by about four or five years.

They shook hands. "I'm so sorry for your loss, Mr. Magnusson. Toby will be missed."

"That he will."

Petit looked pointedly at his watch and raised an eyebrow. Kat apologized for being late in both French and English.

Petit walked around his desk and over to the office door. "Madame Kelly, I will leave Monsieur Magnusson in your capable hands." He bowed to Harold and left the room.

"Mr. Magnusson, how can I help?

"Please call me Harold. For starters, I barely speak a lick of French, despite being stationed here for several months. That was the longest fifteen minutes of my life. Petit and I just sat here staring at each other. Every time he said something all I could muster up was a different pitch of 'mercy bocoupe.'"

Kat smiled. "I am more than happy to be your translator."

"Swell. Can I enlist your services at ten o'clock with a detective called Galland?"

"Of course." Kat tried not to betray her excitement. She was eager to hear what the police would tell Toby's brother. She looked at her watch. "And, in that case, we should get going. It's about twenty minutes away. Do you mind walking?"

"Not at all." Harold collected his hat and coat, and they made their way out of Petit's office.

"Also, Toby wrote that he had a girlfriend, a French woman."

"Yes, Marie-Hélène. I thought you might want to meet her, so I arranged for us to have lunch today. If not, I can call her office and cancel."

"No, don't cancel. I'd like to talk with someone who knew Toby well. I just can't believe he's gone." He held the door for her as they exited the building, his shoulders slightly slumped.

Kat felt a pang. She was an only child but knew intimately that losing a sibling was devastating. Harold seemed to be keeping his emotions in check, but it couldn't be easy.

"How are your parents?"

"They're crushed, of course. Both of their sons survive a war, and then one gets killed going to chef school."

"It does feel like a cruel twist of fate," Kat agreed.

"I know they feel better with me being here to see what's what and to bring him home."

"How long are you planning to stay?"

"I'm not sure yet. Do you know if they have any suspects?"

Kat shook her head. She weighed telling Harold that Galland didn't have a sterling reputation but held her tongue.

"Do you have a family back home?" Kat asked.

Harold stopped walking. Just as Martin Smithson had the night before, he pulled a photo out of the breast pocket of his jacket. He handed it to Kat. It was an image of Harold, a pretty woman, and two young, smiling children. "James is four years old, and Maggie is two. I miss them already." He returned the photo to his jacket. Did Charlie want to be able to pull a photo from his pocket to show people his smiling family?

Having children was a fraught topic that she and Charlie went back and forth on, usually one deciding that the time was right, but the other disagreeing. They'd set the topic aside for a month or two, and then the discussion would start again, this time switching sides. Kat secretly believed that they were both grateful that the other person reliably took the opposite side of the discussion. Someday they would agree, and then their whole world would change.

"Are they in Chicago?" she asked.

"Just outside." Harold told her about his family's small chain of grocery stores. There had just been one location in the city when he and Toby were growing up, but since Harold had taken over the business after the war, he had opened up two more in the suburb where he and his family lived. "I've got my eye on Wheeling and Northbrook for two more stores. Everyone wants to leave the city these days."

Kat was fairly certain she would never want to leave the city, but she didn't say that. "You said that you were in Paris during the war. Is this your first time back?"

Harold shook his head. "I brought my wife once." They were stopped at an intersection, waiting for the cars to pass. He looked up at the buildings on the opposite side of the street.

"But you don't really like it here," Kat guessed.

"You caught me." Harold grinned. "I didn't want to say. I know you're French."

"Only part French, but I do love Paris."

"Just like Toby."

"In class, he would tell me about his adventures the night before, at a bar or club or restaurant."

"I'm a family man, but my little brother loved the nightlife. I don't know if he would have ever settled down. Now, we'll never find out."

Chapter Fifteen

At the police station, Kat asked for Detective Galland, telling the officer at the front desk that Harold Magnusson, the brother of the murder victim Tobias Magnusson, was here.

It was the younger detective, Faucher, who came to fetch them. He stopped abruptly when he saw Kat.

"Madame Kelly, we weren't expecting you."

"I'm here to translate for Mr. Magnusson."

"I see. That is a fortunate coincidence, because we were going to call your husband's office and ask you to come in today."

"A fortunate coincidence indeed." Kat had a few questions for the detectives herself.

Kat was reminded of a newsroom as the detective led them through a maze of desks to a room with a large table. Kat and Harold sat down. A young officer asked if they would like a coffee, and both said yes. They grimaced when they tasted it. Surely good coffee would be available again soon.

Detective Galland strode into the room, immaculate in a well-tailored, charcoal gray suit that set off his extravagant mane of hair. Both Harold and Kat rose to shake his hand.

"Monsieur Magnusson, let me start by offering you my condolences." He spoke rough but understandable English.

"I appreciate that. It's appalling that a fellow who helped liberate and secure your city at the end of the war gets brutally murdered when he comes back a few years later. And while I do appreciate your condolences, what I would appreciate much more is you finding the bastard who did this, excuse my French."

This very direct speech was not what Kat had expected from the seemingly mild-mannered Harold. She looked at the detectives and saw immediately that they unfortunately did need a translation. While cringing internally, Kat repeated his statement word for word and saw the detectives' faces shift. Playing hardball out of the gate wasn't a tactic Kat would have recommended to Harold. This situation called for more finesse.

Harold continued, "I know that's what the American embassy would like as well. I've been told that the ambassador is paying special attention to this situation." He didn't raise his voice and spoke without overt emotion. But the threat was clear. If the detectives didn't solve this case quickly, it could turn into a political and bureaucratic headache.

Kat saw Faucher purse his lips just slightly as she translated. Galland maintained a placid façade. "I understand, *monsieur*. You can put your faith in this department to bring your brother's killer to justice. While it's too soon to rule anyone out, we already have several suspects."

Kat was intrigued. Who could they be talking about? Eugene? Did they find out about Nico? Then she remembered what Vaughn had said. *Toby had it coming*. Maybe it was someone else entirely.

"We will also have fingerprint analysis very soon. Have you been to your brother's apartment yet?" Galland asked.

"No. I was planning to go this afternoon."

"*Bon.* You will see that we have been there. We tried to maintain things just as they are. But we did find a significant amount of money, many thousands of francs in cash." He stopped as Kat translated, as if he wanted to watch Harold's reaction to this news. Kat also watched Harold's face, but he betrayed no surprise.

"And?"

"And can you shed any light on why or how he might have had that much money? Is your family particularly well-off?"

"I suppose you could say that. We run a successful chain of supermarkets in the Chicago area."

Faucher chimed in. "Why would your brother keep so much cash at home instead of in a bank? That seems unnecessarily risky, no?"

Harold's voice turned harder. "Perhaps Toby thought the real risk was the security at some of the banks in this town. At the end of the war, armed robberies seemed to happen every other day."

Kat saw Faucher subtly roll his eyes.

Galland responded. "That was an unusual time, to say the least. I assure you that our banks are now just as safe as those in Chicago. Perhaps safer. We have heard of Al Capone here too, Monsieur Magnusson."

Now Kat cringed on Galland's behalf. These men, always trying to one up each other.

After a moment of awkward silence, Harold asked, "Anything else, fellas?"

Galland pursed his lips. "Not at the moment."

Harold rose from his chair. "Then I'm going to be on my way. But I'll be back tomorrow. And every day until you have the man who killed my brother behind bars." He looked at Kat.

"I'll be out in a moment."

Harold nodded and left the room without shaking hands with Galland or Faucher, a major snub.

"*Charmant*," Faucher said under his breath.

Kat didn't say anything but privately agreed. There were strict, if unspoken, rules of politeness in France, and one was physically greeting and taking your leave of people, whether by shaking hands or exchanging kisses near the cheeks. She guessed that Harold thought bluster would get him farther than finesse. Maybe he was right. She wondered if the part about the American embassy being interested in the case was true. It seemed likely. Of course they would care if an American was killed here.

"Madame, we will let you join your friend momentarily. Just one or two more questions," Galland said.

"I just met Harold Magnusson this morning. He's not my friend." She couldn't help but distance herself from his bad behavior. "How is the investigation going? You mentioned that you have suspects."

Galland lit a cigarette and took a deep inhale. "I am going to let you in on a secret. We have reason to believe it was a woman who killed Monsieur Magnusson."

Kat was shocked. It had never occurred to her that a woman could be responsible for such a violent, bloody scene. But she quickly chastised herself for her lack of imagination.

Galland shrugged and leaned back in his chair. "It's too soon to say for sure, of course, but there is no question this was a *crime passionnel*."

"What do you mean?"

Now he leaned forward and looked directly at her. "As you yourself saw, this was not a clean killing. There was emotion behind this murder. I don't know what: perhaps rage, fear, or jealousy."

Kat didn't respond. She didn't want to call up the image of Toby's body in her mind. But she understood what Galland was saying.

"Who had such strong feelings against Monsieur Magnusson?"

She thought immediately of Eugene and Nico.

"I told you about our classmate Eugene Sizemore yesterday. Did you speak with him?"

Galland dismissed her question with a wave of his hand. "Yes, we questioned him. But he has an alibi."

She wasn't sure Galland should eliminate Eugene as a suspect so quickly, but she didn't pursue it. That left Nico. Of course, she had no way of knowing how Nico felt about Toby, but if he was still in love with Marie-Hélène, it seemed logical that he wanted his rival out of the picture.

Still, Kat couldn't quite betray Marie-Hélène's trust and name him. "You should ask Marie-Hélène Arnaud. She knew Toby better than anyone. And there may have been other men in her life." Hopefully that would set them on the right path.

Galland nodded. "*C'est possible.* Yes, Mademoiselle Arnaud is a very interesting woman. Tell us what you know about her."

"I'm not sure I know much more than you do. She works at her uncle's publishing house. She has lived in Paris for many years." What did they want to know? "Do you suspect her?"

"At this point, we suspect everyone who had a strong enough emotional tie to Mr. Magnusson to want to do him harm. Do you think Mademoiselle Arnaud would be jealous if she thought her boyfriend was seeing another woman on the side?"

"Wouldn't most people be?"

Galland gave a small smile. "True, true." He stamped out his cigarette, leaned back in his chair, and crossed his hands over his belly, like he was settling in to tell a story. "Hear me out. This is just a theory at the moment. Suppose Mademoiselle Arnaud suspected that her boyfriend was having a dalliance with someone else, perhaps someone he saw every day in culinary school—"

Kat visibly bristled.

"Calm down, Madame Kelly. I'm not saying it's true. But perhaps she *thought* it was true, and no matter how much Magnusson denied it, she didn't believe him. Perhaps she was so convinced that she couldn't take it anymore and went to confront him at the scene of what she considered the crime, the crime against her. Perhaps she didn't even plan to kill him."

"That's a lot of perhaps," Kat said with ice in her voice. She couldn't explain why, but she felt a loyalty toward Marie-Hélène. Galland's theory wasn't impossible, but Kat didn't want to believe it. "In fact, Marie-Hélène told me just yesterday that, yes, she had been a little wary of me. But when she, Toby, Charlie, and I had dinner together, she realized that there was nothing between us."

Galland shrugged his shoulders. "Perhaps. Or perhaps she was trying to divert suspicion." Kat didn't want to admit that it was possible.

"Do you have any actual evidence against her?"

Now it was Galland's turn to bristle. He stood, indicating that the conversation was over. He walked to the door of the interview room and turned back to look at her. "Rest assured, Madame Kelly, evidence will be rolling in shortly. We will see if it indeed points to Mademoiselle Arnaud, or elsewhere. You know an interesting thing about murders?"

"What?"

"Surprisingly often, the person who 'finds' the body is actually the killer."

Chapter Sixteen

Kat found Harold leaning against the side of the building.

"I was starting to wonder if they arrested you," Harold said.

"Let's go." Kat began walking. She needed to collect herself. Galland's parting words had left Kat speechless. She guessed that he was simply being provocative, needling her, but she wondered if perhaps her name was on their suspect list.

"Do you think I was too much in there?" Harold looked at Kat. In her incredulity at the suggestion that she might be a murderer, she had almost forgotten how Toby's brother had dealt with the detectives. He had acted like a typical American—loud, entitled—the type that French people love to hate.

"I'm not sure you made any friends." She didn't add that people like to help their friends.

"I don't care if they like me. I'm not here to have a tea party. I'm here to make sure those detectives do their jobs."

Kat was silent as they crossed a busy street back toward the quartier where Marie-Hélène worked.

"Maybe you're right. I'll tone it down when I go back tomorrow. Anyway, this blustery persona doesn't come easily to me." He winked and grinned.

Kat laughed. "You could have fooled me."

They walked in silence for a few moments before Kat spoke. "Did you keep in close touch with Toby while he was in Paris?"

"A few letters back and forth, but neither of us were big writers. He told me he had a girlfriend and that school was going well, but that's about it."

"He didn't mention any other friends?"

"Are you asking if he mentioned you?"

"No! No. I was just wondering if . . ."—she thought quickly—"there's anyone else in Paris who should know what happened." What she really wanted to know was if there was anyone else she should talk to, anyone else who might shed some light on why Toby Magnusson was murdered.

Harold shook his head. "Not that I know of."

Marie-Hélène cried off and on throughout their lunch with Harold. She told Toby's brother about how they met and how much Toby loved her little dog, Bijou. Harold talked about growing up in the family's grocery store business.

As they chatted, Kat's mind drifted. Kat wished she could pull out her notebook to jot things down but made do with organizing her thoughts in her head.

What brought the killer to that place and time, to that kitchen with Toby? Despite what the detectives had said about it being a crime of passion, she wanted to at least consider that the murder had been impersonal. Perhaps a vagrant or unstable person had followed Toby into the school and killed him. But what would have been the motive? Not robbery. While Toby did carry a lot of money on him, the detectives had said that his wallet hadn't been stolen.

More likely the killer had a connection with Toby. As much as she loathed Galland at the moment, she took his theory that it was a crime of passion seriously. Someone would need to have been angry enough with Toby to kill him in such a bloody, brutal way. It wasn't a cold murder. It was a hot one.

Plausible suspects: Eugene, Nico, and, Kat had to admit, Marie-Hélène. She studied Marie-Hélène as Harold told a story about the two brothers' escapades in Paris after the Liberation. Although the woman wasn't showy in her grief, it did seem genuine. But as much as Kat was growing to like Marie-Hélène, she still couldn't quite trust her. Kat was sure there was something she wasn't telling her.

Then Kat considered Galland's parting line. Was he truly thinking about her as a suspect? Looking at the situation dispassionately, she understood that it was at least something they should contemplate. They wouldn't be doing their jobs otherwise. But she had no motive, and they had no evidence that wasn't circumstantial. And accusing a foreign correspondent's wife on flimsy to nonexistent evidence seemed like a recipe for disaster, or at least extremely bad press.

As Harold paid the check, Marie-Hélène excused herself, saying she had to get back to her office. She kissed Harold on both cheeks. "Let's meet again before you leave Paris." She kissed Kat good-bye as well, and when her lips were near Kat's ear, she whispered. "Come see me soon."

Kat looked up at her, surprised, but Marie-Hélène had already turned to leave the restaurant.

"She's a peach," Harold said admiringly as they left the restaurant. "Do you think she killed my brother?"

Kat was startled by his directness. Here was someone else she couldn't quite get a handle on. "Don't beat around the bush there, Harold!" She almost laughed but could see he was serious. She paused a moment before answering. "I don't think so. In fact, I would be very surprised. But, as Detective Galland said, it's too early to rule anyone out."

Harold nodded, seemingly satisfied with her answer. "I would be surprised too. But love does crazy things to people, and Toby was always a romantic. Where are we walking to, by the way?"

Kat stopped on the sidewalk. "Good question. I'm going back across the river to an appointment in my quartier. You?"

"I'm going to Toby's apartment."

"Then we should probably split up here. If you need anything else from me, leave a message either at L'École or the *Tribune*."

"Will do. Thanks for being my translator today."

They shook hands, and then Kat turned to go.

"Kat."

She turned back. "Do you think they"—he lifted his chin toward the restaurant they had just come from—"were in it for the long haul, Toby and Marie-Hélène, or was it just a fling? I know my brother always had delusions of grandeur when it came to women."

"How do you mean?"

"He was one of those types that believed in the fairy tales. That you fall in love with a woman and, I don't know, become two halves of the same whole." His voice was slightly mocking, but then it turned serious. "That there should be no secrets."

In fact, there had been at least one big, husband-sized secret between Marie-Hélène and Toby.

Kat did her best Gallic shrug. "Everyone has some secrets they keep, *non*?"

Chapter Seventeen

Claudine looked nervous when Kat arrived at Café du Vent. The evening before, on their way to Club Margaux, Kat had popped in to ask if Jacques would share the recipe for his extraordinary chocolate mousse. It had come to her that it would be the perfect recipe to show Ethan Prentice, the newspaper editor who was looking for a cooking columnist. If the *Star Herald* didn't want it, she would try to sell it elsewhere. Plus, she really wanted the recipe for herself. Kat had pitched it as good publicity for the café, if indeed it was published, and Claudine had responded with a hesitant, but still affirmative, *oui*.

And now she looked nervous and exhausted. Kat wondered if she had changed her mind since yesterday. Or perhaps she was just busy.

"*Bonjour*, Claudine. *Ca va?*"

"*Oui, ca va, ma chère.* I heard that your friend, the one you were here with, died. I'm so sorry."

"It was a shock." To say the least. Kat didn't know if Claudine realized she was the one who had found the body, but she wasn't going to bring it up. Even polite people couldn't help asking questions when there was murder involved. It had been hard to tear herself away from thinking about Toby's murder that afternoon, but once she realized that the mousse was perfect for her first story, she couldn't delay. Plus, she wasn't quite sure what to do next in the investigation. She had a lot of questions but wasn't sure where to go for answers. Hopefully a break would help focus her mind.

"Do the police know who did it?"

"I don't think so." Kat changed the subject without elaborating. "What we discussed yesterday . . . is now a good time for me to talk with Jacques about the chocolate mousse recipe?"

Just then a second woman, about Claudine's age, slid behind the bar next to Claudine. She was slim and blonde, with a few gentle lines on her face. Her hair was pulled back into a chignon, and she carried an apron in her hand.

"*Bonjour.* I am Annette Roche, Claudine's sister-in-law."

"The chef's wife!" Kat shook hands with Annette.

Annette looked at Claudine, eyebrows raised. It seemed to Kat that they were in the middle of a silent conversation.

Claudine paused for a moment and then nodded to herself as though she had made a decision. "*Bon.* Kat, I told Annette that you were interested in writing a story about the chocolate mousse."

Kat didn't say, *if I can find someone who will publish it.* "Yes. It's one of the best versions I've ever tasted. And a story in the paper could draw even more customers to the café." She knew that would be hard for Claudine to refuse. "If your husband is too busy now, I can come back later."

Before Claudine could say anything, Annette jumped in. "I am the pastry chef here."

Kat was surprised. And then delighted. A female chef of any sort was practically unheard of!

Claudine looked pained, and Kat guessed her concern—that people wouldn't take their food seriously if they knew a woman was preparing it. But she disagreed.

"*Formidable*! Claudine, I think the novelty of the situation would only draw more customers, for curiosity's sake if nothing else. And then once they tried the desserts, they would only be impressed. The proof is in the pudding or, in this case, the mousse and tarts and creme brulées."

"You think so?"

Kat nodded. "Especially American tourists, once the story is published." She also thought the fact that there was a woman cooking at Café du Vent gave her story an irresistible hook. She could barely believe her good fortune.

Kat looked at Annette. "And you don't mind sharing the recipe?"

"*Pas du tout.*"

Claudine gave a small smile. "*D'accord*, go ahead." Kat knew that she was a businesswoman at heart and wouldn't pass up the chance to bring in more customers.

Annette made two espressos. Kat inhaled their rich aroma with pleasure as she followed Annette downstairs to the kitchen. Yes, they definitely had the good coffee here.

Downstairs, she found herself in a modestly sized but well-organized and gleaming space that reminded her of L'École. Pushed against one wall was a wooden table with large containers of flour and sugar on top. Rolling pins, whisks, and tamis—large sieves—hung on the wall. All manner of ramekins, cake pans, tart pans, and madeleine tins were stacked on the shelf under the table.

"Do you make desserts every day?"

"Every day but Sunday, when we are closed. I make apple cake, mousse au chocolat, crème caramel, a lemon tart, and profiteroles with ice cream and chocolate sauce. Everything is made ahead, not to order. It is only the four of us working here, along with Raoul who washes the dishes and helps clean."

Kat was already taking notes. Annette brought a dozen eggs, sugar, vanilla, and butter to her workstation.

"First we melt the chocolate and the butter."

Annette turned on the heat under a large pot that held a couple of inches of water. Once the water was simmering, she fitted a second pot on top. Kat knew that this was a double boiler and that the steam from the water in the lower pot would heat the ingredients on the upper level more gently than if they had been directly over the heat themselves. This made a double boiler ideal for chocolate, which was prone to breaking if it was heated too aggressively.

Annette added discs of milk and dark chocolate to the pan, along with a big block of butter. She told Kat that they were making sixteen servings and what the measurements of chocolate and butter were for that number. "But I don't need to measure at this point. I can tell how much the butter weighs by just holding it in my hand."

She stirred the mixture with a large wooden spoon. The butter was now mostly melted, and the chocolate discs were beginning to get soft around the edges. Soon, Annette switched to a whisk.

"Where did you learn this recipe and all the others?" Kat asked.

As Annette whisked, she explained that she had grown up in Moulins, a city about 300 kilometers south of Paris, where her father owned a much-loved neighborhood patisserie. She was an only child, and despite her mother's disapproval—girls weren't pastry chefs—she spent as much time as she could with her father in the back of the shop, learning how to make the beautiful tarts and cakes for the display case to entice passing customers. By the time she was sixteen, she had left school and was helping her father make the shop's confections every day.

Once the mixture was completely melted and smooth, Annette lifted the top pot off the stove and carried it back to the pastry workstation, placing it on a towel. She glanced at Kat. "Everything I do with this mousse is traditional; you will find the recipe in LaRousse." Kat knew she was referring to *LaRousse Gastronomique*, the encyclopedia-style bible of French cooking. "Except for this." She poured the two shots of espresso and a large glug of vanilla into the chocolate and butter mixture and whisked until smooth. She pushed the pot off to the side.

"Did your father add espresso to the mousse?"

"*Non*. That is something I thought of." There was a hint of pride in her voice.

"Now we start with the eggs." She quickly cracked a dozen eggs, separating the yolks and whites into separate bowls. She whisked the yolks with sugar until they were uniform and then got a new whisk—the third of this recipe Kat noted—and started to whip the whites. "You must start with fresh eggs; they'll whip better. And you must use a perfectly clean whisk for the whites. If there's any fat on the whisk or in the bowl, they won't whip properly."

Kat thought of making mayonnaise at school and the amount of elbow grease that went into that. She knew that process would feel like a cakewalk compared to whipping a dozen egg whites to firm peaks. She watched as the whites turned foamy, then creamy, then smooth and thick. She always felt like this transformation from clear and runny to snow white and billowy was a small miracle. Annette handled the whipping with ease, never taking a break. The clacking of the whisk against the metal bowl was fast and even.

"*Bon*," said Annette. She scraped the chocolate, butter, and espresso mixture into the egg yolks and whisked them together. "Since the chocolate mixture had a few minutes to cool, it does not cook the eggs."

"When did you first make the mousse this way? Here in Paris?"

Large dollop by dollop, Annette gently folded the egg whites into the chocolate mixture until it was perfectly smooth and uniform. "*Mais, non*. Jacques and I owned a café in Moulins. Like here, he cooked and I made the desserts. Our restaurant was very popular." Again Kat saw pride on her face. "One afternoon, it was after my oldest was born, I was so tired. I was drinking espresso and eating a cup of mousse, alternating bites with sips, and something clicked in my brain. I didn't want the mousse to taste like coffee. But there is something about the coffee that intensifies the flavor of the chocolate."

Annette grabbed a small teaspoon, ran it into the mousse, and handed it to Kat. The mousse was less dense now than it would be after chilling, but it was deeply, sublimely chocolaty, and Kat couldn't help but sigh with contentment. Annette nodded her agreement and transferred the mousse into a large pastry bag fitted with a metal tip.

"Can you please get the ramekins? Over by the sink."

Kat saw the tray of clean dishes and carried them over to Annette.

As Annette was expertly piping the mousse into the ramekins, Kat asked, "What did you do for coffee and chocolate during the war?"

"Things were not so bad in Moulins as they were here. We could get ingredients, at least at the beginning. We were not political." She began smoothing the tops with a small offset spatula.

"Not political?"

"We had two children, and we needed to make a living. We just went about our business as usual, made food, served desserts, and helped people forget about the war."

She stood back to survey her work. "Now they chill for at least four hours." She carried the tray to the large refrigerator across the kitchen. "*Voilà, c'est tout.*"

As Annette cleaned up, Kat continued to ask questions. "Why did you leave Moulins?"

Annette's voice turned hard as she scrubbed down her workstation. "After the war, everything went to shit. People had a short memory. So we went south to Nice. But then Jules wrote to Jacques and said that he and Claudine needed help. So here we are."

"What do you mean that people had a short memory?"

"They forgot how we all lived on a knife's edge. The dividing line between the Free Zone and the Occupied Zone ran through Moulins. We had the worst of both worlds—Vichy and the Nazis. Every man, woman, and family had to figure out how to make it to the next day and the day after that. It may not have been noble, but it was reality."

Kat nodded. Annette was right. It didn't sound noble, not in these days when fighting with the Resistance was practically a requirement for public office and a shining badge of social status—even if many of those claiming to be on the right side had only joined up in the final weeks or even days of the Occupation, when anyone could see that France would be liberated. But, for millions of ordinary French, going along to get along was their survival mechanism.

She hoped that if she were in the shoes of Annette or anyone else when the Germans marched into town that she would have been one of the people resisting, no matter the consequences. But you never really knew until you were in the situation what kind of stuff you were made of. And, if you had children, perhaps protecting them should be your highest aim, whether you were buying food on the black market or serving Germans in your café.

Kat asked about Annette's children and learned that she had two boys, ages twelve and fifteen.

"Mélisse is twelve years old too, isn't she?" This was Jules and Claudine's daughter.

Annette nodded. "Although she goes to a special school, not the same as my boy. It's very expensive. You know about that, yes?"

Kat did. Mélisse was born with a condition that made walking difficult and painful. She used crutches, although Claudine had once confided that the condition was degenerative, so even crutches wouldn't be enough someday.

"Does it bother you that everyone thinks that your husband makes the desserts here?"

Annette sighed. "I appreciate the daily routine and work of it, watching the chocolate melt into the butter, slicing apples for the cake just so. And I know that people enjoy my desserts. I am proud of that. And maybe that should be enough. What do you think?"

Kat knew her answer to this question. "I think the desire for a certain amount of recognition and validation is human, not just male."

For the first time that morning, Annette truly smiled. "We understand each other. And maybe this article you are writing will change things for me."

Kat heard someone coming down the stairs and looked up as Jacques came into the kitchen. Kat had forgotten all about the altercation she had witnessed at Les Halles the day before, but his mottled purple left eye reminded her.

"*Bonjour. Excusez-moi.*" He gestured toward his eye. "My wife loses her temper sometimes." He grinned as he reached over to kiss Annette, who shook her head in mock exasperation. "I hear that you're interested in the best pastry chef in Paris."

Kat noted his support for his wife. He didn't seem to mind that she would finally be getting some of the credit she deserved. As much as she admired his attitude, she couldn't resist asking a potentially provocative question.

"I'm curious, are there any ingredients that are still hard to get?" she asked in her best innocent voice.

Jacques's grin vanished. He turned away from Kat and busied himself putting on a chef's jacket and apron. "Rationing ended last spring. But high-quality coffee and chocolate are still scarce and expensive." Kat had an inkling that she knew where he found them.

"Many neighborhood cafés like this one don't care about the quality of the food they serve," Annette said. "But Jules and

Claudine agree that if the food and drink are exceptional, the rest will follow."

Jaques added. "It seems to be working. Even only a couple of weeks after we arrived, the café is much busier."

"I, certainly, am glad you came to the neighborhood," Kat said. "For the chocolate mousse alone." *And for this juicy story.* Kat suddenly realized that she hadn't thought about Toby's murder once in the past hour, and she felt both relieved and guilty.

Chapter Eighteen

Throughout class at L'École the next morning, Kat had trouble concentrating on the recipes. Today was all about choux, that incredibly versatile dough made on the stovetop from milk, eggs, sugar, and flour. You could add cheese and turn it into savory gougères or pipe it into profiteroles to split, stuff with ice cream, and drizzle with chocolate sauce, a dessert that Annette made at Café du Vent, Kat remembered. As she stirred the mixture over the heat, the pan scorched, filling the room with a burnt smell. Kat was grateful that Chef had allowed her to cook alone instead of joining another group. At least no one else would have to bear the brunt of her mistakes.

Kat had purposefully arrived early this morning so she would be forced to confront the pantry on her own. Her heart thumped in her chest as she opened the door and turned on the light. But of course, everything was normal, the floor immaculate.

As she had returned to the kitchen classroom with her ingredients in a basket and opened her notebook to make notes on the recipes, her mind drifted back to Toby's notebook, his sloppy handwriting but clear, detailed sketches. How had it just disappeared into thin air?

Then an image of the concierge Madame Poitrine flashed in her mind. Kat almost groaned. Why hadn't she or Toby thought of this before? If the notebook had simply been lost or misplaced, and someone had found it, Madame Poitrine might have kept it for safekeeping, just waiting for the owner to claim it.

Kat was ready to immediately dash up the stairs and knock on the concierge's door, but at that moment Chef Durand entered the classroom, and Kat knew she would have to wait.

Now, as she piped the choux into puffs, she couldn't stop her mind from running through the facts of the case, no matter how much she tried to focus. And her gaze continually wandered to Eugene. As he and Vaughn smirked at some private joke, he caught Kat looking at him and his smirk turned to a glare.

After class, Kat hurried up the stairs, eager to talk to Madame Poitrine. But Monsieur Petit intercepted her.

"Madame Kelly. There is someone here who wishes to speak with you. You may use my office." He didn't wait for a response, just turned and headed in the opposite direction.

Kat tried to tamp down her impatience, but she was also intrigued. Surely if it had been the police or Harold, Petit would have said so.

When Kat entered the room, a light-haired man with a bow tie stood up from his seat in one of the two chairs on the near side of Petit's desk. He extended his hand. "Mrs. Kelly. My name is Bob Braeburn, from the United States embassy. How do you do?"

She shook his hand. "How can I help you?"

Braeburn gestured for Kat to sit down.

"Any time an American is killed overseas it becomes a matter of great concern for us, as you can imagine. I heard that you were close to Mr. Magnusson. This must have been quite a shock."

Braeburn was trim and good-looking in a generic sort of way. He didn't look like a spy. It was common knowledge in journalism circles that many people who "worked at the embassy" were actually part of the intelligence community. Although perhaps the people who didn't look like spies made the best spies.

"It was."

"Naturally, we are in touch with the police to make sure that American citizens involved in horrible crimes like this are given all due consideration. And, in this case, that means Magnusson and, well, you."

"I am involved as a witness."

Braeburn didn't respond directly but asked, "How long have you been in Paris?"

Kat explained her background and that she had been in the city since August on account of her husband's job at the *Tribune*. As she said these last words she saw a flare of surprise in his eyes, but he quickly recovered his placid expression.

"Ah, Kelly. I should have made the connection. You're married to Charlie Kelly, one of the USA's finest."

"The one and only."

As so many people did in this city when they learned who her husband was, she could tell he was looking at her with new eyes. But she couldn't discern if it was with respect, wariness, or was it possibly dislike? Few people disliked Charlie Kelly. Maybe this Braeburn would make a good spy after all. He was inscrutable.

Braeburn paused and nodded, his eyes squinting over her head, seemingly distracted by his own thoughts. After a long moment he pulled his attention back to Kat. "Mrs. Kelly, I'm sure you've covered some of this same ground with the police, so forgive me. But can you tell me anything more about Mr. Magnusson and the day of his murder?"

Kat told Braeburn about meeting Toby back in September and working together in the kitchen almost daily. Then she explained how the morning had unfolded just three days ago.

He listened without interrupting and then seemed to come to a decision. "Thank you for that detailed account. As you know, the police are investigating Mr. Magnusson's murder, and we, of course, have full confidence in them . . . officially."

"And unofficially?"

"This is off the record." He looked at her squarely, and she nodded. "You may be aware that the French and the Americans have a complicated relationship these days. The United States is investing billions of dollars in France's recovery, and, well, there's a fine line between gratitude and resentment in some quarters. The fact that an American was killed in Paris complicates things further."

"You're saying that there is extra pressure on the police to solve the case quickly?"

"Exactly. And they're in a tough spot. We've expressed our desire that Mr. Magnusson's killer be found without delay and that they do everything by the book. Detective Galland is one of their most experienced investigators, but let's just say that he has a tendency to ignore the rules from time to time. How have your dealings with him been?"

Kat sighed. "Odd and uncomfortable. On the surface he's respectful, but underneath, condescending and almost threatening. He made a strange comment to me when I saw him yesterday."

"What was that?"

"He said that surprisingly often the person who finds the body actually committed the murder.

Braeburn nodded his head, as if she confirmed something. "That's exactly what I was concerned about."

"Do you think I need to be worried?"

"I think Galland was just trying to show you who's boss. Not very subtle. But the sooner this is over, the better. Thankfully, it seems like the police have zeroed in on a suspect."

"Who?"

"Mr. Magnusson's girlfriend." Kat's heart sank, and he must have seen it on her face. "You know her?"

"I do, and, well, I have a hard time believing she did it."

Braeburn looked at her appraisingly for a moment. "May I offer you a word of advice?"

"Of course."

"Stay out of it." His tone was friendly, but she detected a slight edge underneath it. "If the police are looking elsewhere, count your blessings and let them do their job."

Kat didn't say anything, and Braeburn stood to leave. "It was a pleasure to meet you, Mrs. Kelly. Say hello to Charlie for me."

Chapter Nineteen

After Braeburn left, Kat sat in Petit's office on her own, thinking. Kat knew that any evidence against her could only be circumstantial—ugly gossip about her relationship with Toby, his blood on her body. As Braeburn said, with that comment Galland was probably just trying to put her in her place. She wasn't going to worry about it. But she also wasn't going to stay out of it. She brushed past Braeburn's last comment, "Say hello to Charlie." She'd come back to that later.

Now, once again, she contemplated Marie-Hélène. Kat felt equal parts suspicious, perhaps because she had hidden Nico's existence for so long, and protective of Toby's girlfriend. The woman seemed both calculating and fragile, steely and vulnerable. Kat couldn't get a handle on her, but she wasn't ready to accept her as a murderer. That left the question, if Marie-Hélène didn't kill Toby, who did?

Kat left Petit's office and walked down the hall to the concierge's apartment. She knocked on the door's frosted glass window. A figure approached and opened the door a couple of inches, just enough for Kat to see part of the older woman's thin face. "*Oui*?"

"Madame Poitrine, I'm Kat Kelly, a student here. We've met a couple of times. May I come in?"

The concierge opened the door wider. Kat found herself in a short hallway lined with hooks. The space was full of cleaning implements, an umbrella, two pairs of shoes, and a couple of coats and jackets. It was crowded but well organized.

Madame Poitrine gestured to a chair. "I was just making tea. Would you like a cup?"

"*Oui, merci.*"

Madame Poitrine disappeared into a nook behind a screen, a tiny kitchen, Kat surmised. She returned with two cups of tea, filled just half full, and then disappeared again. Kat suspected that the concierge had heated only enough water for one cup but divided it into two to share with her guest. Electricity was still unpredictable; you could never be sure when one of the periodic rolling blackouts would happen.

Kat knew from Philippe that, in addition to food shortages during and after the war, fuel was a precious commodity. During the Occupation, French coal had been requisitioned for the Germans, and particularly in Paris, families had suffered from extreme cold in the winters. After the war, strikes by miners in the north of France took another toll on the supply of coal. The supply chain seemed to be stabilizing, but even four years after the war, a few hours without power was still a normal fact of life.

Kat sipped her tea. It was strong and good and calmed her down.

The concierge returned with a small ramekin of what looked like a creamy cheese and a few thin slices of fresh baguette. "It's fromage fort, my mother's recipe."

Kat spread some of the cheese onto a slice of baguette and took a bite. It was deep and savory. "*Merci, madame. C'est delicieux.*" Kat was curious about the recipe but knew she needed to focus. "How are you, Madame? It must be quite a shock to know that someone was killed here."

"People are killed everywhere, Madame Kelly. Were you here during the war?" Kat shook her head. "Well, people died for the stupidest reasons. They died because they didn't have enough food or enough heat or because they fought with their neighbor over whose turn it was to use the toilet down the hall. Or they died for good reasons. Because they were hiding a Jew in the basement or because they passed messages to the Resistance. I don't know why Mr. Magnusson died, but I hope it was for a good reason."

"I don't know either, but I would like to find out."

The concierge grinned. "I know you're an American, but that doesn't mean you're a *détective privé*." American detective novels were all the rage in France.

Kat smiled. "It's just in my nature to ask questions, I'm afraid, and Toby was my friend."

Madame Poitrine swallowed the last of her tea. "How can I help you?"

"Have you or the housekeeper found a notebook?"

The concierge looked surprised. "In fact, yes. *Un moment.*" She walked across the room and came back with a tobacco-colored, leather-bound notebook.

It was Toby's, and if the concierge had it, did that mean that Eugene hadn't stolen it? Toby had been so certain. Perhaps he had just lost it. Madame Poitrine handed her the book.

"Where did you find it?"

"Ida, the housekeeper, found it in one of the *poubelles* downstairs. She was sure that it was a mistake that it was in the trash. It is not full and a very nice notebook. So she brought it to me."

"When was this?"

"Friday. In all the disruption with the police here this week I forgot about it. Is it yours?"

Kat quickly flipped through the notebook. She didn't want to study it in front of the concierge. "No, it was Toby Magnusson's. He lost it last week. Madame Poitrine, may I take this? I am seeing Mr. Magnusson's brother later and will give it to him." Kat hoped Madame Poitrine wouldn't insist on turning it over to the police.

The woman appraised Kat closely. "*Allez-y*," she said finally. "Take it. The police are useless."

That would be another thread to tug, but later. Kat thanked Madame Poitrine for the tea and the snack and left the building, notebook tucked under her arm.

As soon as she got outside, she leaned against the building and started paging through the notebook. It was clear almost immediately that several pages were torn out. Kat realized it was missing some of the detailed drawings of plated food that Toby had shown her before. She guessed there were about ten pages missing.

As the heavy door opened beside her, Kat quickly tucked the notebook into her bag. Vaughn Harris stepped outside.

"What are you still doing here?" she asked.

"Our Kat, always so curious. If you must know, I was talking to Chef about doing a stage at a local restaurant. I'd like to stay in Paris for a while after the course ends."

Kat simply could not imagine this tall American who barely spoke any French landing work in a highly regimented French kitchen. But right now, that wasn't her problem.

"Vaughn, where does Eugene live? I need to talk to him."

"About what?"

"It's private. But he can either talk to me or to the police."

Vaughn considered for a moment. "He stays at the Plaza Athénée."

It was one of the most expensive hotels in Paris, and to live there for months on end would cost a fortune. Kat's surprise must have been evident.

"C'mon, Kat, he's loaded. It's like Monopoly money to him."

Again, Kat wondered what Eugene was doing in culinary school. He certainly didn't have to work for a living, and chefs rarely came from the wealthy set.

"Thanks," she said and walked past Vaughn toward the metro. Then she stopped and turned back toward her classmate.

"What did you mean that Toby had it coming?"

"Huh?"

"When we were at Les Halles a couple of days ago, you said that Toby had it coming."

"Ask Eugene."

Chapter Twenty

The first word that came to mind when Kat approached the Hôtel Plaza Athénée on Avenue Montaigne not far from the Champs Élysées was *splendid*. The red awnings on its many windows added a touch of vibrancy to the gloomy day. There was a boutique by the wildly popular fashion designer Christian Dior across the street, and beautifully dressed women and men streamed in and out of the hotel. Kat prided herself on not being intimidated by wealth, but this was another level. She wished she had worn something other than her navy shirtwaist today, but L'École's aprons were not foolproof, and she'd already ruined one dress in the past two months. *Tant pis*, oh well.

Kat approached the reception desk and asked the clerk to please call up to Eugene Sizemore's room and request that he come down to the lobby to meet her. Perhaps they could sit in the restaurant and Kat could buy an exorbitantly priced coffee or even a drink. She could use one at this point. The clerk asked her name and made the call.

Kat watched as he spoke with someone on the other end of the line. "*Oui, monsieur. Bien sur.*" The clerk hung up the phone. "Madame, he asks that you go to his apartment."

Kat was taken aback. "*Vraiment?*"

The clerk's face revealed nothing—no surprise, judgment, or disapproval. "*Oui, madame.*"

Kat thought for only a moment and then asked for directions.

The elevator opened onto a hallway lit by opulent gold sconces. There was a door at either end, and Kat knocked on the one to the left.

There was no response. Kat waited a moment and then knocked again. After the call from the lobby, Eugene had to be expecting her. Finally the door opened.

"Mrs. Kelly, to what do I owe this pleasure?" He looked anything but happy to see her. Annoyed or bored were more like it.

"I need to talk to you. Can you please come downstairs and we can get a coffee?" Or a shot of whiskey, or an entire bottle of gin.

"Afraid to be seen going into a man's hotel room? Don't worry, there are no witnesses here." He smirked. "But I suppose the whole hotel saw you get into the elevator alone."

Kat didn't care what people thought of her, but she also didn't want to be in a hotel room with a man who might be a murderer to ask him about said murder. She hesitated.

"Either come in or leave. I'm not going to stand here all day, and I'm not coming downstairs. I'm in the middle of something."

Kat walked into a grand sitting room and immediately caught a delicious aroma. It was savory—chicken and wine and thyme, she thought.

"Are you cooking?"

"Is that such a surprise? We are in culinary school." He strode through a luxurious sitting room, and she followed him into a small but well-appointed kitchen. He pulled a pot out of the oven and removed the lid to check the contents.

"Coq au vin?"

"Yes."

Kat would have been less surprised if he outright confessed to killing Toby.

Eugene replaced the lid and put the pot back in the oven. "If you recall, we didn't actually get to prepare the recipe the day your friend died." He said the word *friend* with the slightest of sneers.

Even though he hadn't invited her to, she took off her coat and hat and sat down on one of the stools flanking the counter. "Why are you at L'École?"

"Why are you at L'École?" he asked right back.

"I'm thinking of teaching cooking classes to other Americans," she answered. She wasn't about to mention the potential recipe column Jeanette had told her about. It was still too much of a long shot.

He looked at her for a moment, and she thought he was weighing whether to tell her the truth or give a typically careless reply. "My father made a fortune and a half in the retail business in San Francisco. I'm supposed to join him, but I convinced him to finance a year in Paris first. My parents don't know that I'm in culinary school."

"I still don't understand."

"What's to understand? I want to open a restaurant, to be the chef. That's why everyone, except for you I guess, is in the course. Do you mean, why does a rich guy want to open a restaurant?"

"I guess I do."

"Then you should have just asked that."

"Why does a rich guy want to open a restaurant—and be the chef?" She could understand a rich man wanting to open a restaurant. It could be a prestige-filled sideline, a place to entertain wealthy friends. But cooking in a restaurant was a brutal, taxing business.

"I'm not saying I'll be the day-to-day chef. But I want to know as much as the chef. I want him to know that I could do his job." Bingo. This sounded more like the Eugene Kat knew and didn't love. Leveraging his knowledge to lord it over an employee. Still, she gave him a soupçon of credit for taking culinary school seriously.

"So the plan is to open a restaurant in San Francisco."

"That's right. Dessert's on the house if you come."

"Gee, thanks."

"What are you doing here, Kat?"

"May I borrow a napkin?"

He opened a drawer and handed her a pressed linen napkin. She used it to pull Toby's notebook out of her purse. She watched some of the color drain out of Eugene's face.

"What's that?" he asked. She could tell he was aiming for nonchalance, but he wasn't convincing.

"As you know, since you saw it every day for nearly two months, this is Toby's notebook. I'm holding it with a napkin because I'm betting that the police will be able to lift your fingerprints off of it." Kat actually had no idea if that would be possible. The housekeeper's, Madame Poitrine's, her own fingerprints, and Toby's of course were already on it. Would the detectives be able to isolate someone else's? Maybe, maybe not. But Eugene didn't know that.

She continued. "I don't know if anyone in our class told the *flics* about the fight you and Toby had about the notebook. Before, it didn't matter because there was no way to prove that you took it. You thought the notebook was long gone. But the housekeeper rescued it from the trash."

Eugene's face was hard. "But you're bringing it here and not to the police. Why?"

"You admit you stole it?"

"I didn't steal it. But maybe I helped it find its way to the trash."

"There are pages missing."

For the first time Eugene looked embarrassed. He didn't say anything.

"If you don't tell me the truth, Detective Galland will have this within the hour."

He turned away from her to look out the window. "I cut out some pages."

"What was that?" She had heard him but took pleasure in seeing him squirm.

Now he looked directly at her. "I cut out some pages."

"The plates and menus?"

He nodded, almost imperceptibly.

"Why?"

He looked at her like she was an idiot. "Because they were good, obviously."

"Do you still have them?"

He shook his head. "I burned them after Toby died."

Kat thought back to that morning and how Eugene had left so quickly without talking to the police. "You burned them in case the police made a connection and searched your apartment?"

He nodded again.

"Were you inside the school when Toby died?"

"Are you asking if I killed him?"

Kat shrugged. "I guess I am."

"You think I'm going to confess that I killed Toby?" Eugene laughed, derision in his voice. "Tell me, why do you think Toby hated me?"

Because you're an asshole, Kat thought. But, truthfully, she had never thought about it. The two men seemed to take an instant dislike to each other from the first day of class. It seemed chemical, intrinsic. "It looked like the feeling was mutual and without bothering to get to know each other."

Eugene shook his head, like he was disappointed in her. "He never told you."

Kat was losing her patience. "Told me what?"

"We were in the same unit in forty-four. Vaughn too."

Kat was stunned.

"We were in Paris together, just after the Liberation. Toby was a shit then too, but I didn't put up with it."

"What does that mean?"

"It means he was no choir boy. Magnusson always liked to skirt the rules, play the big man. Let's just say he left Paris with more money than he came with. Pretty unusual during a war, don't you think?" Kat heard Philippe's voice in her head, explaining that some American servicemen committed crimes after the Liberation. Could Toby have been mixed up in that?

Eugene continued. "And then in school he treated me like a hack. So, no I'm not sad he's dead. But I didn't kill him. Besides, I have an airtight alibi." His lips curved into a slight smile. "She'll be down at the bar around eight o'clock tonight. The most beautiful whore in Paris. She may not look it, but don't worry, she's eighteen. Barely." He said all of this without a drop of embarrassment and the last word with a leer.

That was enough for Kat. She put the notebook back in her purse, gathered her things, and started for the door.

"I'd think the police would want to talk to you, or maybe your husband, about Toby's murder."

She whirled around. "Excuse me?"

"Look, Kelly, everyone knows what you two were up to. And while there's no accounting for your taste, I can't say I blame him." He raked his eyes up and down her body and began walking toward her.

Kat felt a jolt of adrenaline race through her. She clutched her purse more tightly, ready to swing it in Eugene's face if necessary. It wasn't especially heavy, but it was the only defense she had on such short notice.

He stopped a few feet from Kat. "Although, on closer inspection, you're a little geriatric for me."

Kat had never hit anyone in her life, but the impulse was so strong she suddenly understood how fights broke out. She forced herself to turn back to the door and walk out. Once she was over the threshold she turned to face Eugene. "You're wrong about it all, except for one thing."

"Oh yeah?"

"Toby did think you were a hack, a pretentious, pedestrian, uninspired hack. He was right, and everyone—I mean everyone—knows it."

Chapter Twenty-One

Kat's instinct was to get as far away from Eugene as possible, but she forced herself to stop outside the hotel and make a plan. First things first, she needed a drink.

She walked a few blocks and then ducked into a nearby hotel bar. It wasn't as upscale as the Plaza Athenée, but she knew they would make good cocktails. She quickly discarded the notion of ordering a glass of white wine and asked for a dirty martini instead. She needed serious reinforcement.

Kat couldn't care less that Eugene had called her old, and unfortunately, like most women, she was used to men looking at her body like she was their property. But it was the first time ever that she had feared for her physical safety. Although the moment had passed quickly, the fear and anger still coursed through her body.

As she took the first bracing sip of the cocktail, she forced herself to focus on the rest of their encounter. Eugene had said that everyone knew what she and Toby were up to, implying that they were having an affair. Is that truly what her classmates believed? Kat was sure that Roy didn't. He was with Kat and

Toby during most of their lunches, and it would be obvious to him that they were no more than friends.

But if that's what, say, Vaughn thought, or even what he pretended to think, and he told the police that, it would only buttress Galland's theory that Marie-Hélène killed Toby out of jealousy.

There were two olives on a cocktail skewer resting in her drink. She pulled one off with her teeth and began turning the pages in Toby's notebook one by one. She saw his notes from class and demos and the recipes he had copied down. These were the pages she was familiar with, glancing over during class. She saw where the ten or so pages had been that Eugene had ripped out and then burned.

She kept turning pages and saw a list with three columns: dates, cities, and numbers. The dates began in August and stretched into this month. Kat paused on the list but couldn't figure out what it meant.

Next were a series of portraits made in pencil. She had seen Toby's renderings of food, but never these. She saw drawings of Marie-Hélène, Chef Durand, herself, and a self-portrait. There were a few other people she had never seen before. The drawings were simple, just pencil, but the likenesses of the people she knew were stunning.

Kat took the final sip of martini and ate the last olive. Why hadn't Toby told her that he and Eugene had served together? And what did Eugene mean that Toby wasn't a choir boy, that he liked to skirt the rules and play the big man? That he left Paris with more money than he came with. She had to find out, and this time she wasn't going to take no for an answer.

Twenty minutes later, Kat walked up the staircase to the second floor of Marie-Hélène's office building. She stopped in front of the door marked Guillaume Publishing and gave two firm taps to the door before trying the knob. It was locked. Kat checked her watch. It wasn't yet 5 PM. Maybe Marie-Hélène hadn't come back to work after Toby's death.

Kat heard movement behind the door and the lock being turned. As the door opened, Kat saw a middle-aged man in well-kept but rumpled clothes and glasses.

Kat introduced herself. "I'm looking for Marie-Hélène. Your niece?"

The man nodded and invited her in. "*Oui*, I'm Etienne Arnaud. It's very nice to meet you." They shook hands, and he gestured to her to have a seat on the sofa. "May I offer you a coffee or some water?"

"No thank you. I'm just here for a moment. Is Marie-Hélène here today?"

He shook his head. "My niece mentioned you. She said that you had been kind to her following the death of her boyfriend."

"I wish I could do more. This must be a terrible time for her."

"Yes, but unfortunately she is used to terrible times."

Kat paused to see if he would say more, but he didn't. "Has Marie-Hélène left for the day?"

"No." He ran his hands through his thinning hair and looked around the room at Marie-Hélène's desk. "Actually, she quit."

"Quit?"

"Yes. She came to visit her aunt and me yesterday and said she was leaving town. She apologized for giving no notice. She said she couldn't stand to be in Paris any longer."

Leaving. Was she running because she knew the police suspected her? Surely they wouldn't just let her leave. "Where is she going?"

"She wasn't sure yet. Not back home I don't think."

Kat looked over at Marie-Hélène's desk, stacked with papers and mail. Was she leaving to escape the police or something or someone else? Or did she just want a change after the shock of Toby's death?

"I am sad to lose her, and I wish she wasn't making such a hasty decision. But if leaving Paris is what's best for her, then . . ." He trailed off and shrugged his shoulders. Then, he straightened up. "You are an American, yes? I wouldn't know except Marie-Hélène mentioned it."

"*Oui.*"

"Are you looking for a job? I need someone who speaks French and English. It isn't easy to find someone bilingual."

Kat smiled. "Thank you, but I'm enrolled in a course at L'École de la Grande Cuisine through December."

"Ah. If you change your mind, please let me know."

She stood up. "I will. *Merci*, Monsieur Arnaud."

Chapter Twenty-Two

Kat was fairly certain Marie-Hélène was drunk, or at least on the far side of tipsy. When she saw Kat at the door of her apartment, she was exuberant with her kisses. Bijou was excited too, wagging his tail and balancing on his hind legs to get Kat's attention. She crouched down to stroke his head behind the ears.

When Kat followed Marie-Hélène into the living room, she saw two open suitcases on the floor, one almost full, and clothes strewn on nearly every available surface. Clearly Monsieur Arnaud was correct; his niece was packing up to leave.

Marie-Hélène had disappeared into the kitchen, and Kat heard the pop of champagne opening. Marie-Hélène returned with the bottle and two glasses. "Drink with me, Kat, to my last nights in Paris."

Kat clinked glasses and obliged. "When are you leaving?"

Marie-Hélène looked around. "Probably day after tomorrow. I was hoping to leave right away, but it is hard to pack up a life so quickly. And I need to take care of things like bank accounts."

"What will happen to your apartment?"

"Nico will live here and pay rent for now. When the lease is up, he can do as he pleases." She finished her glass of champagne and poured another. They were standing awkwardly in the middle of the room.

"May I sit?"

"*Desolée, bien sur.*" Marie-Hélène scooted a few coats on the sofa to a corner, and Kat sat. Marie-Hélène did not. She flitted around the room, folding clothes, tucking things into the suitcases, reconsidering others and removing them.

"Where will you go?"

"I still need to decide! What do you think? Should I go to Montréal or Los Angeles? I have narrowed it down to those two places." There was excitement in her voice. She sounded like a child choosing between two flavors of ice cream.

Kat was surprised. "You're leaving France? I thought you were just moving out of Paris." Bijou jumped onto Kat's lap, and she narrowly saved her champagne from spilling.

"Staying in France would not help." Marie-Hélène turned so her back was to Kat. She began folding a pile of sweaters on the table. "I have been thinking about this, leaving, for a long time, you know. When I met Toby, I thought things would change, would get better for me. But now that he is gone, I need to escape."

The word put Kat on high alert. Who was Marie-Hélène running from? "Escape?"

Marie-Hélène waved her hand, dismissing the word. "Leave. I need to leave. This country is haunted, but no one will admit to seeing the ghosts." She turned to face Kat. "I feel like a crazy person. I want to say to everyone, look! Look!" She gesticulated broadly. "The ghosts are all around you! I know they see them, too, but they pretend they don't."

"From the war?"

"Yes, yes. Everyone has decided that what we did to each other doesn't matter. They pretend that it was the Germans, and yes, obviously it was. But they were the first match. The French spread the fire. Well, some of them did." She finished her champagne and set the glass down. "It doesn't matter now. I'm leaving. So where to, Kat? Los Angeles with the movie stars or Montréal with the . . . who is in Montréal?"

"The Québécois. And it's frigid in winter."

"Los Angeles it is. Then I don't need to pack these sweaters." She pushed a carefully folded stack across the table. A couple fell to the floor.

Kat set down her glass. She had taken only a few sips. The martini was still making its presence known, and she wanted to stay sharp. She needed to remember why she was here.

"What about the police?"

"What about them?"

"Will they let you leave?"

Marie-Hélène looked surprised. "Why wouldn't they let me leave?"

Kat hesitated. "Marie-Hélène, you're a suspect."

Marie-Hélène waved her hand dismissively and turned back to folding her clothes. "No. That cannot be. Why would I kill Toby? We were in love."

"The detectives seem to think there was some sort of love triangle and you were jealous."

Marie-Hélène gave a short laugh and shook her head. "*Quelle stupidité*. Love triangle with who?"

"Well, with me."

Marie-Hélène laughed again and said matter-of-factly, "If I thought you and Toby were lovers, I would have killed you, not him."

Kat was only somewhat reassured by this but had to admit it made a kind of sense.

"And why would I go to L'École to do it? I've never even stepped foot in there. Didn't they say that the killer took a back way out of the building? How would I know about that?"

More good points, but Kat didn't say anything.

Marie-Hélène abandoned her folding and came to sit next to Kat on the sofa. "Do you believe that I killed Toby?"

"No." Kat hesitated before continuing, "But I think you're hiding something."

It was like a shadow fell over Marie-Hélène's liquid brown eyes. She looked at Kat but said nothing for several long moments. Kat resisted filling the silence, hoping that Marie-Hélène would say something, anything that would help Kat understand what was going on.

Finally, Marie-Hélène spoke, "I did not kill Toby." She stood up and plucked one of the coats from the sofa and placed it in a pile of discarded clothes in the corner of the room.

Kat sighed. She believed Marie-Hélène, but she wasn't getting any closer to understanding who might have left Toby's body in a pool of blood on the floor. Kat stood up and walked over to stand next to Marie-Hélène.

"You must have some idea of who could have done this. Even if it's just a guess. Or even if it's just someone else Toby knew in the city."

"Help me close this suitcase."

Both women crouched down next to the now overflowing suitcase on the floor. Marie-Hélène folded one side over the other and tucked in the fabric that spilled out. She placed her weight on the suitcase and nodded to Kat to fasten it.

Miraculously, the suitcase locked easily. Both women stood up, and Kat continued, "Did Toby have any other friends here in Paris? Or any other connections, maybe from the war?"

"We didn't talk about our pasts. We were just starting to at the end. At the very end."

"How do you mean?"

When Marie-Hélène spoke, there was something like fondness in her voice. "The last weekend we were together, Toby told me something terrible and I told him something terrible. It was beautiful. I felt so at peace, like I finally found someone who accepted me for me." Her face grew hard. "But, then . . ."

"Then what?"

"Then he betrayed me."

"I don't understand. How did he betray you?"

Marie-Hélène quickly shook her head and then looked at Kat with a new sharpness. "Toby had his life in Paris, and I had mine. I don't know exactly what he did or who he saw."

"Marie-Hélène!" Kat couldn't hide the frustration in her voice.

The woman sighed audibly. "*Mon Dieu*, you don't give up. Fine. There was something, but I don't know what." She drank another swallow of champagne. "He always had money, so much money. I told myself that all Americans had so much money. And he had a gun."

A gun. It wasn't unheard of. Charlie had once written a story about how some discharged soldiers broke the rules by keeping their service weapons as souvenirs. The story was killed. The paper's owner didn't want to say anything negative about the brave boys home from the war.

"What did he say about the gun?"

"He didn't know that I found it." Kat pictured Marie-Hélène quietly going through her lover's things while he was bathing or out buying croissants for breakfast.

"It didn't bother you?"

Marie-Hélène shook her head. "*Non*, it made me feel safe." It was the same thing she had said about Nico. She went on. "The only person I know that Toby saw in Paris was a grocer at Les Halles."

Kat didn't understand. "Why would he go to a grocery store at Les Halles?"

"He was friends with someone there. Gaspard. I never met him, but Toby went at least once or twice a week."

"In the covered market itself or the general vicinity?"

Marie-Hélène shook her head dismissively. "That is all I know, and I need to finish packing."

Kat nodded. It was time to leave. "*Merci*."

At the door, she reached into her bag for one of Charlie's business cards and felt Toby's notebook. She briefly considered offering it to Marie-Hélène but decided she needed to hold onto it. Kat gave her the card. "Keep in touch." The women kissed good-bye. Despite their unusual relationship, Kat would miss her.

As she walked out into the dusk, Kat realized that Marie-Hélène had never said how Toby had betrayed her.

Chapter Twenty-Three

It was nearly seven o'clock by the time Kat got back to their drafty apartment on Rue du Bac. She had called Florence from a pay phone on her way. The *Tribune's* secretary said Charlie was headed home. Kat was glad. She needed to talk through the day with her husband.

Charlie was waiting to talk to her as well. He swept her into his arms as soon as she walked in the door. "Finally! Sit. Or do you want to go out?"

She thought about popping over to Café du Vent, but it was so busy lately that it would likely be faster to cook. "No, let's stay in."

"Good, yes."

She kicked off her shoes and sat at the kitchen table. As Charlie spoke, he opened a bottle of red wine and poured glasses for both of them. "I met up with Smithson again today, and he gave me something, something good."

"Tell me."

"In October 1944, so just weeks after the Liberation, a French doctor and his wife were murdered, shot, driving home after a party."

"Oh God, that's terrible."

"Yes, of course. But it gets worse. Rumor has it that it was American servicemen who pulled the trigger, and the case was never solved. In fact, it was buried. The French police couldn't find the killers, and the Army kept mum."

Yet more Americans behaving badly in Paris. A group that might have included Toby, if Eugene was to be believed. "So Philippe was right."

"It seems like it." Charlie put his hand around her wrist and stroked her arm with his thumb. "Kat, this is a huge story. Even if I can't find out who did it, if I can prove there was a cover-up, that the Army hid something this big from the French and the American public . . ." He didn't have to finish. Kat knew that this was the type of story he had gotten into journalism to tell. It was the type of story she had wanted to tell, too.

"You trust Smithson?"

"I do. He isn't claiming to know the whole story, just that this was the talk. But what I need is the original police report. You're buddies with those two detectives now, right? Do you think either of them would slip it to you?"

Kat snorted. "Highly unlikely. I told you about that crack Galland made yesterday about the person finding the body often being the killer. Why not ask Marcel? Or better yet, ask Philippe to ask him. I think the detective is smitten." She stood up to look in the fridge. Every day she felt lucky they had found an apartment with an icebox. Many Parisians still kept their milk and other perishables outside a window. She pulled out some lardons, eggs, butter, and a nub of hard cheese. There were a few mushrooms and some day-old bread on the counter. The makings of a very nice omelet.

Charlie nodded. "Good thinking."

As she started dinner—slicing mushrooms, whisking eggs, and grating cheese—she began walking Charlie through her day, starting with meeting the man from the embassy. "He confirmed that the police are seriously considering Marie-Hélène as a suspect. And while I know it's logical, I just don't see it."

She continued through her conversation with Vaughn and then talking with Eugene in his apartment at the Plaza Athénée. She left out the moment when she thought she might have to defend herself. She felt her body tense at the memory, but she didn't need to tell Charlie every detail; she was already pushing her luck by sharing that she had been alone with Eugene. She hurried to the punchline. "You won't believe it, but it turns out that he and Toby were in the same unit and stationed together in Paris."

"Hold up. What do you mean, you went up to his apartment? By yourself?"

Kat swore to herself. She had hoped to skate over that part of the story without him latching onto it. No such luck. She lit the stove, dropped a knob of butter into a pan, and prepared to brazen it out. "Yes, by myself. Who was going to go with me?"

Deep down she knew that what she had done was risky. But she wasn't about to admit that to her husband.

Charlie stood up and turned off the stove. He turned her body to face him. "And it was just the two of you there? Do I have that right?"

"Seriously? You're upset because I went up to a man's apartment? Because maybe people saw me?" She was trying to distract him, to turn the tables, but he didn't take the bait.

"C'mon, Kat. You know me better than that. I don't give a damn what people say or think. But I do give a damn about you being alone with someone who maybe, just maybe is a murderer. Did you ever think of that?" His voice had risen in volume as he spoke, and now he was on the verge of yelling.

"I can handle myself!"

Charlie shook his head with exasperation. "You don't know that! You can't know that! You put yourself at risk, and for what? To figure out who killed some guy you went to culinary school with? Jesus Christ!"

His eyes were blazing with anger, and Kat felt the anger building up inside her as well. The realization that her husband thought she needed to be protected, that he couldn't see that she knew what she was doing, that not so long ago she had been a professional journalist chasing down leads just like him, was maddening.

Now she was yelling, too. "You don't trust me! You run around Paris or New York or goddamn Nazi Germany, and you don't need anyone's permission." She was livid, her frustration at losing her job at the paper and her lack of professional prospects pouring out of her. "You're Charlie Kelly, and you can do anything, go anywhere, talk to anyone no matter who. But I have to just be the good little wife, the supportive wife who cheers you on and learns to cook!" She slammed the wooden spoon in her hand down on the counter.

His face softened a degree, but his voice was still hard. "It's not about me not trusting you. But you can't pretend you aren't more vulnerable. It's just a fact. It isn't fair, but it's a *fact*. And you know I have never asked you to be the good little wife. You know that. I fell in love with your ambition along with the rest of you. And I don't give a damn what other people think. But when I imagine you going up to that man's apartment and what could have happened to you there—" he suddenly stopped. All the anger disappeared from his face and voice. "I can't lose you, too."

Now Kat understood, and remorse replaced her anger. *I can't lose you, too.* He was thinking about Jake, his twin brother who had died in the Pacific in 1943. His loss had left such a hole in her husband's life that Charlie had once told her that if he ever suffered another similar wound, it might not close up this time.

She wrapped her arms around him, silently cursing herself for provoking this pain. She kissed his thick, dark hair. "I'm so sorry." She rocked him gently back and forth, then lifted his face up to hers and kissed him under his eyes, tasting the salt from the tears on his skin. She kissed his cheeks and then, softly, his lips.

He kissed her back gently at first and then with more urgency, his hands tracing the sides of her body, from her breasts to her waist to her hips and then finally to the buttons on the front of her dress. She unbuckled his belt with one hand. They were experts at undressing each other.

They didn't make it to the bedroom or even the living room, but made love standing up in the kitchen, Kat's back pushed against the counter. It started out passionately, as usual, but ended so intensely she was almost gasping for breath. It was as if he wanted to inhabit her. Kat had never been a smoker. But she suddenly understood the desire for a cigarette. It took a few minutes, but her heart rate finally slowed down.

Later, between bites of omelet, Charlie said, "The irony is that Jake would have loved how ballsy you are. He would have cheered as you took on that asshole in his own la di da apartment."

Kat reached across the table and took Charlie's hand. He was right; it had been risky going up to Eugene's apartment by herself, and she had known it. But she couldn't cosset herself, wrap herself in paper like a china doll to make sure nothing ever happened to her. Besides, Kat was just superstitious enough to believe that if she took no risks in her life, she would be hit by a bus crossing the street on an ordinary Tuesday. She wasn't sure how to explain this to Charlie.

"And I thought you liked culinary school."

Kat's attention had drifted. She refocused on her husband and took another bite of omelet. She sighed. "I love it, or I did. Now I just want to finish with it and move on. But I can't move on with Toby's murder hanging over my head."

"I wonder how involved the U.S. embassy will get. What was the fellow's name who came to talk to you?"

Kat realized she had never said. "Bob Braeburn. Do you know him? It seemed like maybe he knew you."

Charlie let out a bark of laughter. "Braeburn? Light hair, self-satisfied?"

"Yes to the light hair. I didn't talk to him long enough to suss out his self-satisfaction. You know him, I take it?"

"Oh yes. Not from Paris, but from Harvard. I lost track of him after graduation. We weren't friends."

"I gathered that. Was he a Crustie?" That is what Charlie and Jake, scholarship students, had called the wealthy students there, the upper crust.

"The crustiest of them all. I heard he was working for the State Department but didn't know he was here."

"I suppose that connection could help if Galland does end up arresting me." Kat was mostly joking, but she filed away the information just in case.

"And what about Eugene?" Charlie asked, not looking at her. "Do you think he could have been involved in Toby's death?"

She thought for a moment. "I don't know. There's something off about him, something cold. But he says he has an alibi—a woman, a prostitute to be precise." She saw her husband's face cloud over.

As Charlie cleared the table and started washing the dishes, she told him about visiting Marie-Hélène and the woman's plans to leave Paris. "I've been thinking about it, and it seems like she's scared. Why else is she running away so quickly?" She told him that Toby had kept a gun, but she didn't mention his friend Gaspard at Les Halles.

Charlie wiped his hands on the towel. "And how can she afford it? Moving to a new country without a job isn't cheap, especially when you're going from France to the United States."

It was an excellent question, and one Kat kicked herself for not having asked.

Chapter Twenty-Four

Kat looked at Charlie before sliding out of bed at five o'clock the next morning. He was facing her, eyes closed and breathing deeply. She lightly traced his full eyebrows with her fingertip in the semi-darkness. Her mother-in-law had warned her that when Charlie got older, Kat would need to trim the wiry, stray hairs that would sprout from his brows like they did in all of the men in her family. Unless he got Irish eyebrows, of course. But since everything else about him appeared to be Italian like his mother, that was unlikely. Kat's father-in-law liked to joke that the only thing Charlie had gotten from him was his last name.

Kat was quiet as she got dressed, but she wasn't worried about waking him. She hadn't known that people could sleep as deeply as Charlie did. "The way you can sleep is a gift," she had told him once. He had replied, "If you call having five siblings who made noise at all hours of the day and night a gift, then I suppose so. We can all sleep like the dead."

In the end, Kat hadn't shared her morning plans with Charlie. She told herself that this outing wasn't dangerous at all. It was broad daylight—well, dim early morning daylight—and she'd be in public places the whole time. She wasn't completely confident that he would see it the same way, but she preferred to ask for forgiveness, not permission. As much as she felt guilty about worrying Charlie yesterday, she chafed at having to discuss all of her movements with him.

The metro wasn't running this early, but she didn't mind the walk, even though it was dark and chilly. Kat wasn't the only person starting the day before sunup this Friday morning. Men and women accompanied small dogs on the sidewalk for their morning tours, and she saw two priests chatting quietly as they crossed the street a block ahead of her. The boulangerie on the corner wasn't open yet, but she could smell the toasty, buttery croissants.

As Kat approached Les Halles, the merest suggestion of dawn edged into the inky darkness. The magnitude of what she was trying to accomplish hit her. There were probably dozens of little shops and stalls both inside and outside the market, not to mention dozens of men named Gaspard. This quest could take multiple visits.

C'est la vie, Kat decided. She would start at the interior of the market and work her way out. She would canvas the entire complex as well as a two-block perimeter at street level. When Toby told Marie-Hélène he went to "Les Halles," he could have meant the market itself or just the general quartier. She had already decided that, barring a miracle, she would miss class this morning.

At each grocer she followed a script. "*Bonjour, monsieur. Je cherche un homme qui s'appelle* Gaspard. Does he work here?" At each place she got shrugs or sorries or just *nons*.

Finally, two hours later, at a grocer that specialized in dried fruits and nuts, the man she asked said yes, there was a Gaspard here. Gaspard Monterac was the man's father who still looked in on the business from time to time. He was in the back. Kat's heart leapt. But when the man came out to greet her, she saw that he was close to seventy years old. Could this be Toby's friend?

Kat greeted the elderly Gaspard. "Do you know an American named Toby Magnusson?"

"From the war?" the man asked, a quizzical expression on his face.

"No, from recently. He died last week, and I want to make sure his friends know. I heard he was acquainted with someone here named Gaspard." She reached into her bag for Toby's notebook and opened it to the page with the self-portrait. She showed Monterac the drawing. "Do you recognize him?"

Monterac leaned in to look more closely. "No, *desolé*."

"That's okay, thank you." She had known this wouldn't be easy.

"One moment, Madame. Could you please open the notebook again?" When she did, Monterac pointed to the drawing opposite the one of Toby. Kat didn't know who it was a likeness of. The man had thinning dark hair and a pocked face. "I can't say for sure, but this looks like Guy . . . Guy . . . Stéphane?" Monterac called his son.

"*Oui?*"

Monterac pointed to the drawing. "Doesn't this look like Guy . . . I can't remember his last name at that grocer across the street."

"Ah yes. Guy Rossi at Marché Gaspard. Ah!" It was like a key fit into a lock in the man's brain. Kat, Monterac, and the son Stéphane all smiled at each other. Gaspard!

The Monteracs described where the store was. They walked by it most days to get home, and they noticed it out of professional curiosity, of course, Monterac said, but also because during postwar rationing it had long lines like everyone else. But the lines persisted later in the day, leading them to guess that it ran out of food less quickly.

"Do you think they were sourcing food from the black market?"

Both men simply looked at her and shrugged slightly. During and right after the war, everyone was trying to buy food off the *marché noir*. That was often the only market around. Father and son Monterac had probably done the same thing.

Kat thanked the men and followed their directions to Marché Gaspard. As she pushed open the door to the shop, she saw that it was a small, traditional French grocery with dry goods lining the shelves. There were a couple of housewives shopping and a sullen-looking woman behind a counter near the front of the store.

"*Bonjour*," Kat said to the woman. "I'm looking for Guy Rossi. Is he here?"

"*Pourquoi*? Can I help you?" The woman's sour expression marred her otherwise striking features.

"He's a friend of a friend, and I need to give him some news."

The woman picked up a small bell from the table in front of her and rang it briskly.

A man emerged from the back, wiping his hands on an apron. Kat recognized the thinning hair that was swept over his head in an ill-fated attempt to hide his balding and the pocked face from Toby's drawing. "*Oui, madame?*"

Kat explained that she was a friend of Toby Magnusson's. Out of the corner of her eye she saw the woman's posture stiffen ever so slightly. "I believe you were friends?"

The man shrugged. "*Non*, I don't know anyone with that name. Do you, Mireille?"

The woman didn't say anything but looked down and shook her head. Kat knew a liar when she saw one.

She flipped through the pages of Toby's notebook and opened it for both of them to see Toby's drawing of Rossi. The woman, Mireille, gave a small gasp, and Rossi couldn't hide a flash of surprise. He reached for the notebook. Kat tried to stifle her reaction when she looked more closely at his hands and forearm. They were covered in dark hair; he was easily the hairiest man she had ever seen, ironic considering the lack of hair on his head. She forced herself to stop staring and reluctantly let him take the notebook for a closer look.

"*Merde*, that's an incredible likeness. What did you say this fellow's name was?"

Kat quickly retrieved the notebook from Rossi's hand and tucked it back into her bag. "Toby Magnusson. Tobias."

"Ahh, Tobias. Yes, I do know Tobias a little. Toby was not a name I'm familiar with."

Kat almost rolled her eyes. "I see. And how do you know him?"

"We met during the war, and recently he came in from time to time to say hello. Sometimes we go for a drink. I was sorry to hear he died. Why are you asking about him?"

Kat thought quickly. "I'm helping his girlfriend gather his friends in Paris for a memorial service."

"Is that so?"

Kat could tell that her lie hadn't been convincing.

"How did you hear he had died?"

Mireille spoke up. "We saw a story in the newspaper."

A man walked into the store and looked sideways at them. Kat saw Rossi jut his chin in the man's direction, ever so slightly, almost like a greeting. The man moved along to do his shopping.

"What's his girlfriend's name again? My wife and I met her once, right, Mireille?" His wife nodded.

"Marie-Hélène."

"Her last name?"

Kat didn't answer. She suddenly felt uncomfortable and thought of Charlie. Had she already gotten herself in another pickle? Surely not. There were other people in the store. But Rossi gave her the creeps.

Rossi took a step closer to Kat. "And who exactly are you?"

"*Je m'appelle* Kasia."

"Kasia. You were a friend of Toby's too?"

"*Merci à vous.* I'll be back to let you know about the memorial service." She turned to go.

"Madame?"

"*Oui?*"

"Did Marie-Hélène tell you that Toby and I were pals?"

"*Non.* I saw your name in his notebook." She patted her bag. "*Au revoir.*"

Chapter Twenty-Five

Jeanette Ketchum had told Kat and Charlie that the U.S. embassy hosted this cocktail party for American journalists in Paris every year, except during the war, of course. "You don't want to miss it. It's a big mix and mingle with the G-men and Army officers. All potential sources. There will likely be some spooks there too, not that they'll ever tell you that's what they do." She sighed. "They'll probably invite American businessmen and their wives too, unfortunately."

"Dull?" Kat had asked.

"The dullest. All they talk about is how their brand of ketchup or canned soup will change the world, starting right here in Paris."

Good luck with that, Kat thought.

"And you, my dear Kasia, will be a frequent topic of conversation I expect. Young, gorgeous, French *and* American? Plus, Charlie Kelly's wife? Don't expect to just blend into the crowd."

When she and Charlie stepped up to the threshold of the event, Kat took in the large room's high ceilings, large mirrors, and ornate gold wall decorations. Clusters of well-dressed people chatted, drinking champagne from coupes and plucking canapés from silver trays presented by waiters in white jackets. Jeanette had said that for some of the stringers and freelance writers who were invited, this meal would be the highlight of their month.

Kat had worn her fanciest dress, a midnight blue frock just a couple of shades darker than her eyes. Charlie looked relaxed next to her in his dark suit, his wavy hair well-coiffed for a change. His plan for this evening went beyond mingling. He was determined to speak with someone at the embassy about the 1944 double murder he was investigating.

Jeanette had been right. The ambient chatter quieted a touch when they walked in, and Kat felt several sets of eyes swing in their direction. Anyone who didn't already know Charlie would be curious to take his measure. The *Tribune* was one of the most prestigious American newspapers with a Paris bureau, and at age thirty-five, he was the youngest foreign correspondent to have earned his position. The people who had already met him—and even those who hadn't—would be curious about his wife. Across the room, a blonde woman in a full-skirted, rose-colored dress caught Kat's attention immediately. She was staring intently at Charlie.

"Mr. Kelly, welcome to the embassy." A handsome middle-aged man with a friendly smile and well-trimmed mustache extended his hand. "I'm George Church, the deputy ambassador. This is my wife, Eleanor."

Charlie introduced Kat, and Eleanor subtly beckoned a waiter over with glasses of champagne.

"Welcome to you both to Paris. You arrived in late summer?" Church asked.

"That's right." The foursome clinked glasses, and Kat took a sip of champagne. The American embassy could clearly afford the good stuff. Kat savored the fizz in the back of her throat before swallowing.

"We're so glad you're in Paris and here with us tonight," Eleanor said graciously.

"The ambassador and his wife had to be unexpectedly back in Washington, so it's our pleasure to host this little get-together," her husband added. "They send their regrets."

Eleanor smiled and inclined her head to the left. "Come, Mrs. Kelly. Let me introduce you to a few people."

"That would be lovely. And please call me Kat."

She gave Charlie a subtle wink and caught his in return as she turned her full attention to Eleanor Church. The woman was likely in her late forties, trim and elegant. Kat knew that the wife of a diplomat had to be something of a diplomat herself, hosting parties and maintaining the couple's social circle, not only for her family's benefit but for the benefit of the United States. Kat knew not to underestimate her.

"Have you spent much time in France, Kat?"

"My father is from Paris, so we came here often. And my grandmother had a cottage in Bretagne, so we often spent summers there."

"Ah, Brittany! Such a lovely part of the country; so untamed."

"Do you ever get out of the city?"

Eleanor guided her toward a tall table where two couples chatted. "We have a weekend home near Fontainebleau that we escape to when we can. Come, let me introduce you."

Kat immediately recognized one of the men. Eleanor introduced her first to Clarence Welch, an American businessman, and his wife Margaret. "And this is Brigadier General Martin Smithson and his wife Patty."

Smithson's face registered recognition, then a shadow of apprehension, and then gratitude when she extended her hand and said only, "It's a pleasure to meet you."

"You as well. We were just hearing from Mr. Welch here about his plans to convert the French into soda drinkers."

"I think you're well on your way," Kat said. "Coca-Cola seems to be very popular at the cafés in my quartier."

"It's true, but French people still drink a tremendous amount of wine."

Kat almost laughed out loud. "They do indeed." If that changed, France would cease to be France and might as well be a new state in the Union.

Eleanor seemed to sense Kat's thoughts and subtly shifted the subject. "Kat is actually half French and half American, isn't that right, dear? So, I expect she could give you some excellent insights on your target market."

Welch looked at her with new interest. "Is that so?"

"*C'est vrai*," Kat affirmed.

"And I'm sure you represent the best of what each country has to offer," Eleanor said.

Spoken like a true diplomat, Kat thought.

Now Margaret Welch spoke up. "And do tell, Mrs. Kelly, what is the best this place has to offer? Our hotel still experiences blackouts, and hot water for bathing appears to be a luxury akin to diamonds."

It was Eleanor Church who answered. "Oh Margaret, be grateful you weren't here last year, not to mention 1945. Paris suffered so during the war and is finally back on its feet. A few little hiccups are to be expected." Kat could tell that the woman's affection for the city was genuine, and she liked her for it.

"Excuse us, please," Eleanor said to the group. "There are a few other people I'd like to introduce Mrs. Kelly to."

Kat spotted Charlie talking with his editor Tom Granderson, Jeanette, and another man Kat didn't know. She would prefer to be in that mix but didn't see a polite way to escape her hostess. "How long has your husband been at the embassy?" she asked Eleanor.

"He came right after the Liberation in August 1944. I joined him a couple months later, and just last year when the new ambassador was confirmed, George was named deputy ambassador. Hopefully we'll be here for a while to come. It does feel like home now. But you never know in this business."

They stopped in front of the woman in the rose-colored dress whom Kat had noticed when they arrived at the party. Kat guessed that she was in her early thirties. She was petite with delicate features.

"Kat Kelly, meet Miranda Braeburn."

"Braeburn! I believe I met your husband yesterday. Bob?" Kat hadn't noticed him at the party, but of course he would be there tonight. She wondered if Charlie had run into him yet and, if so, how that reunion had unfolded.

At that moment, a uniformed server approached Eleanor and whispered something in her ear. She smiled at Kat and Miranda. "I am needed in the kitchen. Kat, be sure to say goodbye before you leave."

Kat turned back to Miranda who said, "Yes, that's right. Bob Braeburn. And you're married to Charlie Kelly."

"Speak of the devil." Kat caught Charlie's eye over Miranda's shoulder, and he circled around to stand next to his wife.

"Charlie," Kat started. "This is—"

"Miranda McFadden," he finished.

The woman blushed so deeply her face almost matched the color of her dress. After a brief silence, she extended her hand. "Miranda Braeburn."

"Ah." He paused. "Of course. It's good to see you, Meems."

Kat looked from Charlie to Miranda and back. Clearly there was some history here. Had Charlie ever mentioned a Miranda? She didn't recall one, although she and Charlie hadn't shared all the details of their romantic pasts.

"How is Jake?"

Kat looked at Charlie, desperate to rescue him, but unsure how. After just a slight hesitation, Charlie responded, "He didn't make it back from the Pacific."

Miranda looked genuinely stricken. She reached out and put her hand on Charlie's arm. "Oh God, I'm so sorry. I can't imagine what that must have been like for you." She suddenly seemed to remember that Kat was there. "You should have seen them in college. We called them the two musketeers. We always said Harvard couldn't handle a third." She smiled at the memory.

For the first time in this exchange Kat felt a stab of jealousy. Miranda Braeburn had spent time with Jake. Kat sometimes felt like she would never completely know her husband because she had missed out on such an essential person in his life.

Charlie put his arm around Kat's waist. "As you've probably gathered, Meems—Miranda," he corrected himself, "was in Cambridge, too, at Radcliffe. And now you're Mrs. Braeburn."

Kat could hear a tinge of disbelief in his voice, and looking at Miranda, suspected that she heard it too. A defensive note crept into the woman's tone. "We got married in 1944. We have two children." Her hand drifted to her belly, and Kat wondered if they were expecting a third.

Then Bob Braeburn himself appeared. "Mrs. Kelly, it's a pleasure to see you again. And, Charlie, old sport, welcome to Paris." Old sport? Kat was almost embarrassed for him. Did anyone actually talk like that? The self-satisfaction that Charlie had mentioned was bubbling to the surface.

The foursome stood in awkward silence for a moment.

"Have you heard of any updates in the Toby Magnusson case?" Kat finally asked Braeburn.

"No, I haven't. But do let me know if the police try to speak to you again. In my position I can have some influence over these matters." He looked at Charlie as he said the last sentence.

"The police?" Miranda asked.

"It's a long story," Braeburn answered his wife. "I'll explain later. Come, we shouldn't neglect our other guests." He nodded at Charlie and made the slightest of bows to Kat. Miranda could barely take her eyes off Charlie as her husband led her away.

Kat turned to Charlie and raised an eyebrow. She couldn't wait to get to the bottom of this story.

"I know, I know," he said. "I'll explain later too."

For Kat, the highlight of the party came when Jeanette introduced her to Ethan Prentice, the editor at the *International Star Herald* who was looking for a food columnist, someone to share French recipes with their American readers. "Jeanette said you were just the person for the job. And only a fool ignores Jeanette Ketchum." Thrilled, Kat agreed to submit a sample column the following week.

As Ethan ambled off, Kat squeezed Jeanette's hand, "*Merci, ma chère!* Thank you for looking out for me."

"I wouldn't have recommended you if I didn't think you'd nail it. I have a reputation to protect."

They found Charlie in a lively circle of men in various states of drunkenness. Clarence Welch, the American businessman, seemed the farthest gone. Kat wanted to ask why he hadn't switched to soda, but she held her tongue. Deputy Ambassador Church and Smithson seemed more sober, but not completely so. As she and Jeanette approached the group, Charlie made room for them. Gesturing to Jeanette he said, "And here's another who was in Paris right after the war. And, Kat, well, she practically grew up here."

Charlie explained that each of these men had been in Paris in 1944, after the Liberation. Charlie for just a week on leave before heading to fight in Germany, Smithson and Welch as Army officers, Braeburn with the intelligence organization—the Office of Strategic Services—and Church at the embassy.

"All roads lead back to Paris!" Church raised his glass. Kat noticed that the men had moved on to whiskey. Soon, the deputy ambassador excused himself to say good-bye to departing guests.

Kat looked around. The party had thinned out considerably. Miranda Braeburn had disappeared. She turned back to the group to hear Bob Braeburn say, "But certainly you agree that we were the good guys during the war."

Charlie responded, "You only had to be a human with a conscience to be a good guy in that war. We may have been better, and thank Christ we were, but we weren't always good."

With that, Kat saw Smithson slip away from the group. Welch appeared interested in the conversation, looking back and forth from Charlie to Braeburn as though he was watching a ping pong match. But he seemed too drunk to contribute.

Braeburn shook his head. "Why can't you just accept that the government knows what it's doing and has the world's best interests at heart? That's what you should be trying to communicate."

"I'm not on Uncle Sam's payroll anymore."

Kat slipped her arm through Charlie's. "Time to go?" he asked. She nodded. She wasn't especially tired, but she needed to hear the Miranda Braeburn story.

Eleanor Church shook her hand warmly as they left. "It was a pleasure to meet you, Kat," Eleanor said. "Come to Fontainebleau some weekend."

Five minutes later, they were in a taxi on their way home. Kat kicked off her shoes despite the cold. Her feet were throbbing. She braced her back against one of the doors so she could swing her feet onto Charlie's lap. He began to massage them. "Spill."

"I told you that I was with someone for a year or so in college. It was Mimi, I mean Miranda."

Kat thought back. Charlie had told her about a girlfriend. But he had made it sound so casual. The way Miranda, Mimi, Meems had looked at him tonight was not casual. How many nicknames did this woman have? Kat was of the firm belief that more than one nickname was overkill.

"I think she must have been in love with you." She said it matter-of-factly and tried to tamp down the small flame of jealousy that meeting Miranda had ignited. She could see why women would be in love with Charlie; it had felt almost instantaneous for her. Surely there had been many.

Charlie sighed. "It's possible."

"So what happened?"

He shrugged. "It just never took off, at least for me. She was pretty, obviously, and sweet, but . . . too traditional. Even my mom thought she was boring."

Kat immediately swung her feet off of Charlie's lap and gave him a scathing look. This was different. "You brought her home to your mother?"

He instantly recognized his mistake. "No! Of course not! Ma came to visit Jake and me sometimes, and one of those times she met Miranda."

Kat was slightly mollified. "And she thought she was boring."

"Yeah, she did." Kat was close to her mother-in-law and liked to think that the woman was looking out for her before she even knew that Kat existed. "And Jake thought she was boring too. And in the end—hell, even in the beginning—so did I."

"She must come from money."

"Another Crustie," Charlie confirmed.

"Did you sleep with her?" Kat wouldn't have been angry, exactly, if the answer was yes. But she needed to know. The community of Americans in Paris was small, and Kat required the full story before she saw Miranda again, which she surely would.

"No!" He was quiet for a minute and then said sheepishly, "But it wasn't for lack of trying. Little did I know there was a lady in Brooklyn who would succumb to my charms so easily." In the dark car she couldn't see the grin on his face, but she could hear it in his voice.

Kat laughed. She couldn't argue with that.

As they drove over the bridge to the Left Bank, Charlie's hand grazed her thigh and then slid under her coat and then under her dress. Kat glanced at the driver. His eyes were firmly on the road. She relaxed back into the seat and closed her eyes. For a few minutes she forgot about Miranda Braeburn and everything else.

Chapter Twenty-Six

Charlie's side of the bed was empty when she woke up at nine-thirty the following morning. Kat tried to remember the last time she had slept so soundly and so late. She had the champagne to thank for that, she supposed, and perhaps the accumulation of almost a week's worth of shocks.

Kat wandered into the kitchen to make coffee and was greeted by a dozen crimson dahlias, her favorite flower, in a tall glass on the table. There was no note, but she didn't need one. Charlie must have woken up early and gone to the Marché aux Fleurs near Notre Dame.

Now he would be at the *Tribune*. He liked to get in a few hours of work on the Saturdays they spent in the city. He would be especially eager to do that today, since he had the 1944 murder investigation to sink his teeth into. He had mentioned the story to both Braeburn and George Church, the deputy ambassador, at the party the night before and had requested help getting the police report. If neither of them came through, he would ask Marcel.

As she sipped her coffee, Kat thought about how she would spend her morning. The smart thing to do would be to start writing the sample recipe column with Annette's chocolate mousse that she would submit to Ethan Prentice. Landing a regular cooking column would be a dream come true. It would give her entrée into every restaurant, grocery, and market in Paris and probably in all of France. Combining her reporting skills and nascent culinary passions should have propelled her to her typewriter *tout de suite*, and it would have . . . a week ago.

Instead, she opened her notebook to the page where she had written "Toby Magnusson" earlier in the week and reviewed the brief notes and questions she had written down. "MH scared? If so, of who? What did Vaughn mean, Toby had it coming?" She still couldn't say with certainty if Marie-Hélène was scared of someone. And while she didn't know exactly why Vaughn thought Toby had it coming, Eugene had intimated that it had to do with his time in Paris after the Liberation.

Now she wrote the names of all the people she knew in Paris who were somehow connected to Toby: Marie-Hélène, Nico, Guy and Mireille Rossi, Eugene, Vaughn, Roy Kasden, and her other classmates. Out of loyalty, she didn't add Chef Durand to the list.

Three names jumped out at her immediately. Guy Rossi, Eugene, and Nico.

Something was fishy at Marché Gaspard. Kat didn't buy for one second that Rossi and his wife didn't know who she was talking about when she asked about Toby Magnusson. It was only when Rossi saw his own picture and knew that he couldn't deny the connection that he admitted to their being friends and said they met after the war. But were they really friends? What if they had a history and Rossi had murdered Toby out of some long-time disagreement or feud?

Kat's visit to Eugene had only intensified her dislike for the man, but she had to admit that she believed him when he said he hadn't killed Toby. It just felt too obvious, too messy, too public. It would have been too risky for him when everyone knew the two men detested each other. Plus, he claimed to have an alibi, which perhaps the police had checked.

Nico had the most obvious motive for wanting Toby dead. And Kat couldn't shake the feeling that Marie-Hélène was scared of something, or someone. Leaving town to escape her estranged husband made sense, and if she suspected that he had killed her boyfriend, it made even more sense. If she continued to reject him, Nico might decide to kill Marie-Hélène too. It was an old story. Just because Marie-Hélène claimed not to be frightened of Nico didn't mean that she wasn't.

Kat squinted into the distance across the kitchen. She was hungry but wanted to remember what Charlie had said or asked when she told him that Marie-Hélène was leaving. It had been a good question.

She remembered now. How did Marie-Hélène have the money to move to the United States without a job or place to live lined up? Neither she nor her family seemed wealthy.

The question suddenly felt urgent, although at the moment Kat couldn't quite explain why. She quickly dressed and dashed out the door. Marie-Hélène had said she was leaving Paris today, but Kat didn't know when.

Ten minutes later a taxi dropped her off in front of Marie-Hélène's building in Montparnasse. The front door was ajar, so Kat slipped right in, making sure to close the door securely behind her.

The possibilities raced through her mind as she took the steps two at a time. The most obvious: Marie-Hélène might have money saved. But that didn't seem likely. Her job probably didn't pay much. The idea that Marie-Hélène had stolen the money seemed far-fetched. That left one possibility. Someone had given her the money, either as a loan, a gift—or as payment for something. Her silence? A plane ticket to Los Angeles was expensive, not to mention rent and living expenses for at least a month or two before she started earning income.

Of course, some generous friend that Kat knew nothing about might have given Marie-Hélène the means to start a new life. But her gut told her that wasn't it. Marie-Hélène always seemed so alone; she had never mentioned other friends or family in Paris. Had it been Nico?

Then she remembered the thick stack of francs Toby had used to pay the bill at Chez Daniel when the two couples went out to dinner. And Detective Galland saying that there was a great deal of cash in his apartment.

Kat raised her hand to knock on Marie-Hélène's door when she realized it was also slightly ajar. She put her ear to the door and heard soft noises from inside the apartment, footsteps probably. Kat took a deep breath, apologized silently to Charlie for doing the dumb thing she was about to do, and opened the door just wide enough to enter the apartment.

Bijou was waiting inside the door, tail thumping on the ground in greeting. Kat gave the dog a pat but didn't say anything. The hallway in front of her was empty except for a suitcase standing closed near the door. Kat walked quietly to the door that led to the living room and peeked inside. An almost fully packed suitcase lay open on the floor by the table. Another noise came from down the hall. Kat held her breath and moved toward the kitchen. Part of her expected to find Marie-Hélène drinking coffee and demanding to know why Kat was in her apartment without knocking. But another part of her knew that wouldn't be the case.

When she got to the kitchen, the first thing she noticed was the sickly sweet scent of wine, a lot of wine. The second thing she noticed was the sharp edges of dark, broken glass scattered across the floor. Red wine was splattered everywhere. The third thing she noticed was Marie-Hélène crumpled face-first on the floor, the back of her head a mass of blood and glass.

And, the fourth thing she noticed, which, in retrospect, should have been the most obvious, was her husband, Charlie Kelly, crouched on the floor next to Marie-Hélène's body.

Chapter Twenty-Seven

For one wild moment, Kat hadn't been able to make sense of the scene in front of her. Her two worlds had collided in the most terrible way. Later, Philippe would ask if she ever thought Charlie had killed Marie-Hélène, and her honest answer was that she hadn't been able to think anything in that moment.

She gasped. Charlie spun around at the sound.

"What's happening?" she asked, barely getting the words out.

"She called me. What are you doing here?"

"She's dead."

"Yes—"

"Was she dead when you got here?"

Charlie stared at her for a moment as if not understanding by the question. "Yes! Kat, yes. Come here." He pulled her to him. She could feel his heart beating quickly; she knew hers was as well. Charlie started to lead Kat away from the kitchen.

"Wait." Kat took a deep breath and tried to memorize the tableau in front of her. She had no doubt that it would invade her dreams, as the scene of Toby's death had, but she needed to understand what had happened here. Marie-Hélène's body was crumpled in such a bizarre way that it barely looked human. A bottle of red wine with a corkscrew in the cork stood on the counter. A second bottle was broken into pieces on the floor; wine spattered around the room. It reminded her of the pools of blood at her feet in the pantry the morning Toby died.

Kat tried to figure out what Marie-Hélène was wearing, but it was hard, since so much of her was stained red with wine or blood. Kat thought it was the violet dress that Marie-Hélène had worn the night they had eaten together at Chez Daniel. Why was she so dressed up on a Saturday morning? Were those the clothes she was planning to travel in?

"Let's go," Charlie said. Kat nodded and scooped Bijou into her arms.

They closed the door behind them, and Kat sat on the stoop holding the dog as Charlie found a phone to call the police. It was starting to drizzle, but Kat ignored it. First Toby and now Marie-Hélène. And somehow she had been the first, or second, person to stumble onto the scene in both murders. What would the police think now?

When Charlie returned, he sat next to her and intertwined his fingers with hers. "She called me," he said again. "Left a message with Florence and said she wanted to talk to me."

"She didn't say about what?"

"No. Just that she was leaving at noon today." Kat looked at her watch. It was 11 AM.

"How did you get in?"

"The dog was barking like crazy. Something felt strange—off. So I tried the door, and it was unlocked."

"When did she leave the message?"

"Early this morning. I picked it up when I got to the office."

"That's good. The police will be able to verify that with Florence."

Faucher arrived first, nodded to Kat, and gave Charlie a long, appraising look. Kat introduced the two men.

He shifted his focus back to Kat. "Madame Kelly. This is the second body you've found in less than a week." Faucher's face was grim, but he was courteous.

When Galland arrived, he barely acknowledged the couple and waved over a uniformed police officer. "Please escort these . . . witnesses . . . to the prefecture for an interview."

At the prefecture, Kat and Charlie were separated. Galland and Faucher questioned her for an hour first.

Kat could see that Galland was testing out a new theory.

"Can you be sure that your husband didn't see Mademoiselle Arnaud after the dinner the four of you had?"

"Yes, I'm sure."

"What time did Monsieur Kelly leave this morning?"

Kat had to admit that she didn't know. Then she remembered the dahlias. "But he went to the Marché aux Fleurs. What time does that open?" She looked from one detective to the other.

Galland just puffed his cigarette, bored, but Faucher responded. "Nine or nine-thirty, I believe."

"So not before that. And you can talk to his secretary. She took the message from Marie-Hélène early this morning."

"Any woman could have left that message. The secretary wouldn't have known Mademoiselle Arnaud's voice," Galland said. Kat was silent. That was true.

"Or perhaps that was how Arnaud and your husband communicated, via message through his secretary."

The idea was so ridiculous and repugnant—Florence complicit in facilitating Charlie's affair, even unwittingly—that Kat just shook her head in disgust.

Galland stubbed out his cigarette. With a satisfied smile he said, "Wives never know what their husbands are up to. And thank God for that, eh, Faucher?" The younger detective didn't respond.

A knot began to form in Kat's stomach. She realized that Charlie was in the same situation that Marie-Hélène herself had been in with Toby's death. There was no hard evidence that he was involved with the murder, but there was also no evidence that cleared him.

Chapter Twenty-Eight

In a few hours, Club Margaux would be packed with locals and tourists grooving along with the celebrated American jazz saxophonist Coleman Hawkins and his band. But now, when she and Charlie stumbled into seats at the bar, the club was blessedly quiet.

"Really?" Philippe asked when he heard their story. "You found another body and now Charlie's a suspect?" He shook his head. "I can't leave you two alone for a minute." He sent out for sandwiches and plied them with drinks.

Kat felt a bizarre combination of exhaustion and adrenaline, and she saw it in Charlie's face too.

"Galland seems certain I did it, although he can't explain why I would have."

They strategized as they ate their jambon-beurre baguettes. Kat brought out the list she had made that morning of everyone she knew who was connected with Toby.

"Okay, first on Toby's list, our classmates: Eugene Sizemore, Vaughn Harris, Roy Kasden, Clark McMurray, and William

Kessler. We know that Eugene and Toby had bad blood, and Vaughn is Eugene's lackey. Clark and William—I suppose it's possible, but I can't see a motive for either of them."

"What about Roy?" Charlie asked.

Kat shook her head. "Toby was always nice to him, and Roy seemed grateful."

"Keep him on the list for now, but star Eugene and Vaughn."

"And then there's Nico," Kat said.

"Who's that?" Philippe asked.

"Marie-Hélène's estranged husband who didn't want to be estranged anymore. She claims he didn't know about Toby, but I'm not so sure. He's in the army." She stopped. "Jesus, I wonder if he even knows that his wife is dead."

"He does if he killed her," Philippe responded.

"Who else?" Charlie prompted.

"Guy Rossi. He and his wife Mireille own a grocery store near Les Halles that Toby visited regularly. Marie-Hélène told me about him and implied that something underhanded was going on. I talked to them, and they were very suspicious of me."

Suddenly Kat felt like she had swallowed a stone, and it must have shown on her face.

"What?" Charlie asked.

"Rossi and his wife must have realized that Marie-Hélène had sent me their way." That's all she could say, but the rest was obvious. Had they killed her to silence her? And if so, to keep her quiet about what exactly?

"You're saying that Rossi killed Toby and then killed Marie-Hélène to make sure she didn't talk."

"Maybe. And if so, that means that Marie-Hélène's death was my fault." Dear God, how would she ever get over this?

"Even if that is how it happened, you are not responsible, Kat. Only Rossi is."

Kat wasn't so sure, but she nodded.

"And it sounds like Marie-Hélène did want to talk." It was Philippe.

Kat and Charlie looked at him.

"Right? She called. She knew she was leaving. Maybe she wanted to get something off her chest."

"The identity of Toby's killer, or something else?" Kat wondered aloud. "But believe it or not, Galland made an interesting point. There's no way to prove that Marie-Hélène made that phone call to Florence. It could have been any woman."

"You're saying I was set up?"

Kat shrugged. "It's possible."

"Why would someone want to do that?" Philippe asked.

Charlie thought for a minute. "I've been asking a lot of questions about the murders of Antoine and Gabrielle Desmarchelier."

"Who?" Philippe asked.

"A doctor and his wife who were murdered soon after the Liberation. The couple was driving home from a party at the British embassy. A witness saw it go down but couldn't identify the men."

Philippe nodded. "I remember that! It was so shocking. It was a robbery, right?"

Charlie nodded and swallowed the last of his whiskey soda. "The wife was wearing a diamond necklace worth a fortune.

There was a rumor that the killers might have been American servicemen. I got a tip from someone in the army brass."

Philippe whistled. "That kind of revelation could make some people pretty nervous. Not only Americans, but any French people who helped cover it up."

Charlie rose. "I need to go see my editor and tell him what's going on. They might need to line up a lawyer. And then I need to talk to my source. If this is a setup, the sooner I can report that story, the safer we'll be. Once it's published, they won't have anything to gain by arresting me. It will be too late." Kat nodded. It made sense. "Are you staying here?" he asked Kat.

"Yes, for a while."

When they were alone, Kat said to Philippe, "I need to find Nico. Marie-Hélène didn't think that he killed Toby. And maybe he didn't kill either of them. But maybe he can help figure out who did."

"But maybe he did kill them and you're just going to start asking a murderer a bunch of questions. Is there a reason that you brought this up after your husband left?" Philippe knew her too well.

"Look, Charlie is right. We need to make some headway ourselves. The police seem to have no interest in actually getting to the truth about either murder." At least Galland had no interest; Kat wasn't sure about Faucher. She couldn't quite get a handle on him.

Philippe drummed his long fingers on the table for a moment, thinking. "Viv!"

"*Oui, patron*?"

"Is your brother still on leave?"

"Yes, he's in Paris."

"Good. I'm giving you the night off so you can help Kat."

"*Bon, d'accord.* I guess that means you'll actually have to do some work around here."

Chapter Twenty-Nine

Vivienne led Kat to La Chausette Rouge, a slim but rollicking club in Montmartre. Barely dressed dancers frolicked on a small stage while men, mostly French soldiers, cheered them on and drank glasses of thin red wine. Kat waited by the door while Vivienne pulled a young man from the front row by his collar. Kat saw that he was quite a bit younger than Viv, maybe only twenty years old.

"Hey, sis!" he said good-naturedly, once they were all outside. He shook hands with Kat and introduced himself as Paul. He had a friendly smile and a sizeable gap between his front teeth.

Vivienne explained that they were looking for a soldier named Nico Girard.

Paul nodded immediately. "I know him. But he won't be here. He and some of the other *vieux* prefer Le Corsaire." He grinned when he said *vieux*. Even though Nico was just in his thirties, that would be old to Paul. "It's quieter there, easier on their old-man ears."

Kat thanked him, Vivienne slipped him a few francs—for a real meal she said—and the two women walked the three blocks to Le Corsaire. "He's my half-brother and a good kid. I'm just so grateful he wasn't born five years earlier. He would have had to fight in the war."

"Has he been abroad at all?"

"Not yet, but he's going soon to Algiers. Better there than Indochina. *Peut-être.*"

Kat wasn't sure.

When they arrived at Le Corsaire, Kat saw that Paul was right. It was quiet, almost depressive. Long and thin, a bar ran along the right-hand wall and a few rickety tables hugged the left-hand wall. The space was well-worn and only about half full. It looked more like a place where people went to drink than to socialize.

Kat spotted Nico at the far end of the bar, hunched over a glass of red wine. There were open seats on either side of him. "That's him."

"Do you think he's dangerous?"

"I don't know, but surely not in public."

Vivienne nodded and squeezed her hand for a moment. "I'm coming with you."

The women walked deeper into the bar. Kat slid onto a barstool on one side of Nico. Vivienne sat at a café table behind her.

At first, Nico gave her only a cursory glance. Then he quickly looked back and studied her. "*C'est vous.*"

"*C'est moi.*"

The bartender arrived, and Kat ordered a glass of white wine.

"Marie-Hélène is dead," Nico said.

"*Oui, je sais.* How do you know?"

"I saw the police at the apartment building bringing out a body. All the neighbors were clucking on the sidewalk, like chickens. Before they even told me, I knew it was her."

"How?"

He pushed his empty glass forward and nodded at the bartender for a refill.

"That one, she ran toward trouble. During the war, with men."

"Including you?"

Nico ran a hand through his dark hair and straightened his back for a moment. "Yes, probably including me. But only because I loved her too much." He looked at Kat sharply. "Do you think I killed her?"

Kat didn't say anything.

He grabbed her wrist. She didn't flinch but felt Vivienne at attention behind her. His voice was low but strong. "I would never hurt Marie-Hélène. Do you understand?"

"Please let go of me."

"Yes, I wanted her to be my wife again, but hurting her would be like hurting myself."

"Let go of me," Kat repeated, this time with more steel in her voice.

"*Desolé.*" He mumbled and turned back to his wine.

"How did you two meet?" Kat asked.

"Here in late forty-two, after she came back to Paris. We met at a bar. I loved her from that very first day, but she was damaged. The war destroyed her. And now she's gone." She saw his eyes fill with tears.

Could all this sadness be an act? It was a good one, if so.

"The war destroyed her?"

"Some people can bury what happened deep inside and never let it come up. For Marie-Hélène, it was always on the surface. For a while I helped her forget."

Kat remembered how Marie-Hélène said that both Nico and Toby had made her feel safe. Safe from what?

"What about Toby?" she asked.

"What about him?"

"Would you hurt him?"

"I might have, but someone beat me to it." He took a sip of wine. "The American was no good."

"How do you mean?"

"I know his type. So slick, thought Paris and France were his for the taking."

Kat wasn't sure exactly what Nico meant. "What was his for the taking? French women?"

"*Évidemment.* But not just that. I don't know what he was involved with, but he wasn't just learning to make soufflés."

"How do you know that?"

"She told me. He got her mixed up in something, and she was frightened." *Yes*, Kat thought, *she was.* "Maybe that's what got her killed."

"Nico, did you know that Marie-Hélène was planning to leave Paris?"

He nodded. "I barely tried to stop her. You see? That is how much I loved her. For once in her life, she got it right. Leaving was the best thing for her."

"Did you give her money?"

Nico looked confused. "No, she didn't ask. I don't have a lot, but I would have."

"I don't understand how she could afford to pick up and move all the way to California with no money and no connections there. Is there someone in Paris who could have given her the money?"

"*Je ne sais pas.* Did you ask her uncle?"

"No, not yet. But it didn't seem like he had a lot of money to spare." She stood to leave. "*Merci,* Nico. I'm sorry for your loss."

"Madame. Do you think the police will come after me? Surely a neighbor will tell them she was married."

"I think their attention is elsewhere at the moment." *Unfortunately.*

"One more thing."

"*Oui?*"

"Do you want Bijou? I have him now but can't keep him permanently."

Kat thought about the sweet little dog and was tempted. But she and Charlie were barely home. There was no room in their lives. "No, I'm sorry. Good-bye and good luck."

Chapter Thirty

All day Sunday, Kat kept expecting the police to knock on the door and take Charlie away. But no knock came. Charlie spent the day at the bureau, looking for leads in the 1944 murder case.

Kat felt at loose ends. How could she have been so wrong about Toby? She prided herself on her instincts about people, but had she been so blinded by his charm and talent that she hadn't picked up on any other signals? Enough people were telling her that he was mixed up in something that it was now impossible to ignore. But what was it?

Kat paged through Toby's notebook for what felt like the hundredth time. She saw the classroom notes and the sketches and the incomprehensible list of cities, dates, and numbers. The cities were all French, mostly in the south—Nice, Marseille, Carcassonne, Moulins. Kat remembered that this was where Annette and Jacques Roche were from. The last city on the list was Périgueux, a town near Bordeaux.

Could these all be places Toby had visited? If so, the dates didn't make sense. They began in early August and stretched into November; in fact, the last one was tomorrow. Kat found a calendar and cross-checked the dates. They were all weekdays. Toby hadn't missed class any of these dates.

And what about the two- or three-digit numbers after the cities? They seemed totally random, and she gave up trying to make sense of them.

Kat stood up and walked around the kitchen. She needed to do something to be useful. She wanted to go back to the quartier around Gaspard and poke around there. But it was Sunday, and most of the shops would either close early or be *fermé* altogether.

She also wanted to see Harold again—not to ask him directly if his brother was a criminal, obviously. He didn't seem to know much about Toby's current life in Paris, but maybe he could tell her more about his brother's time in the city during the war.

If Harold was available, a dinner party would be perfect. Not only would she hopefully get some information, but she could also keep her mind and hands busy all day preparing food. She put on her coat and hat and left the apartment to make phone calls and buy provisions while her neighborhood shops were still open.

At seven o'clock, their small party was complete—Kat and Charlie, Harold, Jeanette, and Philippe. Philippe was often at their place for dinner on Sundays, since the club was closed.

Kat prepared gougères and, inspired by Madame Poitrine, fromage fort to start, then a veal roast with a simple sauce, pommes Anna—that gorgeous, buttery, layered potato dish that could be tricky to get just right—and a green salad. She would make Annette's chocolate mousse for dessert, of course.

Soon after he arrived, Kat took a deep breath and told Harold that Marie-Hélène had also been murdered. He suddenly looked unsteady on his feet, and Charlie led him to the sofa.

"I just can't believe it. Who would do such a thing? It must be the same person, right?"

Kat shrugged. "It seems like it must be connected."

"I hope the police sort it out soon," Harold said.

"Have you heard anything else from them?" Kat asked.

"I spoke with Detective Galland again and apologized for coming on so strong when we first met. He assured me that he's working very hard to find Toby's killer. Now, as awful as his girlfriend's death is, maybe that will lead them to his murderer."

Kat didn't say that the police had been convinced that it was Marie-Hélène who had killed Toby. Certainly her death would change their theory about that. Unless they just pinned it on Marie-Hélène to be done with it.

Then Jeanette and Philippe arrived. This was the first time Harold had met either, and Kat watched him closely for any signs of surprise, disapproval, or distaste that one of their dinner companions was a decidedly untraditional woman and that the other wasn't white. But Harold seemed genuinely friendly to both and particularly interested in Philippe's background.

"Did you ever go back to America when you were growing up?" Harold asked.

"Every two years or so. We'd make the rounds, seeing Kat and my uncle and aunt in New York, my grandparents in New Jersey. Sometimes my father and I traveled to Virginia to see relatives." Kat remembered that her aunt Margaux would stay with them in Brooklyn while her husband and son went south. Kat had asked her father why Margaux didn't go with her family, and he explained that her presence could put Philippe and his father more at risk. Being part of an interracial couple wasn't easy anywhere, but in Virginia it could be downright dangerous.

Better not to rub people's noses in it, he said. Margaux had barely slept while they were away.

Philippe continued. "He always looked forward to seeing his family. But as the visits went on, he became more and more tense, especially when we were down south. He always said he could breathe again when we got back to Paris."

"Do you think you'd ever want to live in the States?"

Kat looked at Philippe, curious. He shook his head. "Paris is my home. But don't misunderstand, things aren't perfect here either. The war showed that."

"How so?" Jeanette asked. This was the benefit—or downside, depending on your perspective—of being friends with journalists. Someone always had a follow-up question.

"When Pétain came to power, a shocking number of people supported him and his capitulation to Germany. Yes, some did it because they thought it would bring peace, and they couldn't bear more war. But many genuinely liked what he represented: a return to 'God, Family, and Country' over 'Liberty, Equality, and Brotherhood.' Many French thought that the country had gotten too decadent. Pétain would bring people back to the church, they thought, to France's 'traditional values.'"

"Thankfully, it didn't work out that way," Kat said.

"There were just enough people who wanted to defend what France is and could be, not just what she was. But it wasn't all some rosy, heroic story. The French police, the *French* police mind you, rounded up Jews for deportation. The Nazis were impressed by their zealousness."

"Imagine impressing the goddamn Nazis with your zealotry," Jeanette said.

Over veal and potatoes, they talked a little about the mess of French politics after the war, although Kat doubted that Harold would have much interest in that. Charlie told the story of another Charles, Charles Gray, a suave American diplomat in Paris after the Liberation. Unlike the dour American ambassador, Gray fit in well in Paris. He was cultured, clever, and spoke perfect French. Diplomatic, just like a diplomat should be, Charlie said. He was instrumental in acting as a bridge between the French and the Americans.

"But after a disagreement, some Frenchman challenges Gray to a duel. Says, name your weapon." Charlie refilled everyone's wine glass as he spoke. "Gray couldn't believe it. A duel! So nineteenth century! But to refuse would be impossible, shameful. But no matter how important this guy was at the embassy, the ambassador was not going to allow his deputy to fight in a duel. It was either the duel or the job."

Kat had never heard this story. Maybe the current deputy ambassador, George Church, had told it to Charlie the other night at the party.

"So what did he do?" Harold asked.

"He did the only thing he could do. He named his weapon." Here Charlie grinned and paused for effect. "Tanks." They all laughed, and Kat felt a release of tension in her body. The wine was probably helping too.

For most of them, with the exception of Philippe, stories of Americans outfoxing the French could be deeply satisfying. Even Kat admitted that the French were so *proud*. Although they owed the Americans so much, both militarily and economically, they clung to a sense of superiority that could become tiresome after a while. Not that they didn't have much to feel superior about: their food, wine, and general joie de vivre for starters.

Then Kat remembered the murders of the doctor and his wife and the other mayhem that American soldiers were rumored to have caused in Paris after the war. If even a fraction of that was true, maybe the French were right to hold a grudge. She also thought about Clarence Welch and his fellow businessmen, eager to claim the French market for their products, traditional culture be damned.

Charlie cleared the plates, and Kat brought out the chocolate mousse and another bottle of red wine. It was getting late, and she was getting impatient. She wanted to nudge the conversation toward Paris after the war in the hopes that Harold would reveal something about Toby's time in the city that could be a lead. Charlie knew her plan, and she kicked him under the table to hurry him up.

"So, Harold, now's the time in the evening when we tell our war stories," Charlie said with a friendly smile. "What's yours?"

Harold told the group that he landed on the beaches of Normandy on D-Day and then marched into Paris soon after General Leclerc and the French troops.

"To the French, it was very important that they get to Paris first, to officially liberate it, even though they never would have gotten to that point without the Americans," Harold said. "I guess old Ike bought that line, because he okayed us coming in after. I'll never forget those days. It was incredible. Pure adoration."

Philippe looked down and scratched his eyebrow but said nothing. He knew the plan too.

Harold continued. "People had been hiding champagne from the Krauts and popped the corks when we arrived." He paused, like he was replaying the scenes in his head. "We threw boxes of cigarettes into the crowds on the streets like they were candy. They loved us, especially the ladies." He winked at Charlie. "Right?"

"I was only here for a week before continuing on to Germany, and it was a few months later. I think some of the bloom was off the rose by then."

"It's true that the mood turned pretty quickly," Jeanette said. "After a few weeks, the French women I talked to felt that a lot of the GIs got too accustomed to that attention."

"That could be. I was already engaged to my wife, so that wasn't my scene. My brother, on the other hand . . ." He smiled ruefully. "Toby was always a lady's man."

"How long was Toby in Paris after the war?"

"Let's see, I was here the longest, for four months. Toby overlapped for two of those."

"Toby did love Paris," Kat said. "I guess that started when he was here then?"

"It must have," Harold agreed.

Kat tried another tack. "And not only did he love Paris, but he seemed to love French people. His French was pretty good, and he seemed to enjoy making friends here. His girlfriend of course." They were all silent for a moment, but Kat forged ahead. "Did he make any friends in Paris after the war?"

"He was always very outgoing, but I don't know of anyone he stayed in touch with." He raised his glass. "To Toby."

They all followed suit. "And to Marie-Hélène," Kat added.

Over dessert, Kat tried to think of additional questions for Harold; how could she draw more information about Toby from him? For a brief moment, the thought flashed through her brain that he was being deliberately obtuse. She studied him as he listened to Jeanette describe a story she'd written about a recent murder trial. If he did know more about Toby's past or present misdeeds, why would he share them with her? Surely, he would want other people to remember his brother well.

But now was not the time to be timid. She took another sip of wine and at the next gap in conversation plunged ahead. "I just remembered one friend Toby mentioned, a fellow named Guy Rossi. Do you know him?" She'd had a little too much wine to be subtle and saw Charlie roll his eyes across the table. She pasted a neutral expression on her face and waited for Harold to respond.

He shook his head. "No . . . that name doesn't ring any bells for me." Kat sighed, defeated at last. Then Harold changed the subject. "How about the other journalist in the room? Do you have anything interesting cooking, Charlie?"

Charlie lied smoothly. "Just the usual political shenanigans in the Assemblée and the threat of yet another transportation strike."

Harold shook his head. "I can't wait to get back to America."

Chapter Thirty-One

After counting down the minutes to the end of class on Monday, Kat slipped a gray cloche over her dark hair. It wasn't going to disguise her, but she hoped that if Madame or Monsieur Rossi caught a glimpse of her out of the corner of their eye, they wouldn't recognize her.

The week since Kat had found Toby's body had been both the longest and shortest of her life. Despite the horror she had experienced finding Toby and Marie-Hélène dead, she admitted to herself that she was enjoying the frisson of excitement that came with piecing together the clues about what had happened to them. It was the same thrill that came with reporting pieces for the *Tribune*, like quenching a deep-seated thirst to know the real story. Not just to know it; to be the one who revealed it.

Marché Gaspard was in the middle of a block of five shops. Kat started with the store at the end of the block, a wine shop. When Kat showed the shopkeeper the self-portrait Toby had drawn and asked if the man had seen him at Gaspard, he looked at her with disbelief. "You think I'm keeping track of who comes into all the stores on the block? I probably wouldn't even be able to tell you if he was a customer here. Business is good these days." And he was right; there was a steady stream of customers coming in the door.

The people at the next two shops Kat visited also couldn't help. But finally, at the last shop on the block, Kat got a nibble. It was a chocolaterie, and the middle-aged woman who worked there was standing at the door surveying the street when Kat entered. As Kat approached the door, the woman returned to her spot behind the counter. Kat caught an immediate whiff of sugar, with an undercurrent of chocolate, and was momentarily distracted from her mission. So much chocolate in one place!

"*Bonjour*, Madame." Kat nodded politely as she marveled at the chocolate truffles, coins, and mendiants on display. "The selection here is amazing!"

"We are one of the first chocolate shops in Paris to be fully stocked again." The shopkeeper beamed with pride.

"And how is that possible?" Kat asked.

"My brother-in-law is a chocolatier in Brussels. We get all our product from him."

Kat chose a selection of six truffles. The woman wrapped them in a beautiful box with a gold ribbon.

"Actually, *madame*. I didn't come in to buy chocolates at all—this was a lovely surprise! I'm looking for my cousin. He came to Paris in August but hasn't been in touch with his family for over a month. We heard he was working in this quartier, and I told my aunt I would ask around." Kat showed the woman Toby's self-portrait. "This is a good likeness of him."

The woman, who had introduced herself as Madame Cheverny, looked closely at the drawing. "*Oui . . . oui*, I do think I remember seeing him a few times. He's a good-looking fellow."

"Yes, yes he is." Kat caught herself before she said that he "was" good-looking.

"In fact"—Madame Cheverny squinted her eyes like she was watching a movie on a screen far away—"I'd often see him going into Gaspard, the grocery. Usually late afternoons. Quite often, actually. Once or twice a week."

"Ah, *vraiment*? *Merci*! I haven't been to the grocery yet. But, how can you be so sure what time of day it was?"

Madame Cheverny looked at Kat and winked. "Dearie, we don't get many customers in the afternoons. Chefs come in the morning, or I'm packaging up deliveries. But in the afternoons my only entertainment is looking out those windows to see who's coming and who's going."

Three cheers for neighborhood busybodies.

"Yes, he'd arrive in the afternoon and go into Gaspard. I couldn't see when he left because that's always around the time when a delivery truck parks in front of the shop. Even if I crane my neck like this"—she demonstrated—"it's hard to see people coming out."

Kat stifled a laugh. This woman was positively wasted as a shopkeeper. The CIA—that new agency that had replaced the OSS—could do with a spy like her.

"I wonder why my cousin was so often at that grocery. Maybe he was friends with someone there? I'll go there now to ask."

"Pfft, good luck with that, dearie. I don't mind saying that those are two snakes in the grass at Gaspard."

"How do you mean?"

"Rossi and his wife Mireille have been raking it in since the Boche were kicked out of town."

"Do you mean the black market? That was pretty common, no?" Kat didn't want to sound judgmental; who knew how this woman had survived the war?

"Sure, sure, we all did what we had to do. And, yes, somehow Rossi had more stock on his shelves than anyone else." Madame Cheverny shook her head. "But something else is happening there now. I can't put my finger on it."

Kat waited.

"Why do so many men go there? It's usually women who do the marketing, isn't it?"

Kat nodded; that was true.

Now Madame Cheverny nodded with authority. "Yes, that's it. Men stop in there all day. So I don't know that you'll get much from Rossi and his wife. I'm sorry your cousin has gone missing. But if he was mixed up with them . . ." She didn't finish her thought.

"Have you considered calling the police? About the goings-on at Gaspard?"

"To say what? That they get a lot of male customers?"

Good point. "Madame Cheverny, *merci beaucoup*. You've been so helpful."

"Anything else you need to know about this neighborhood, you know where to come, dearie," the shopkeeper said with a wink.

Kat left with her box of bonbons and saw a delivery truck parked in front of Gaspard. Painted on the side were the words "Spécialitiés de Périgueux" and a drawing of a duck.

Périgueux. That had been one of the cities in the list in Toby's notebook. She knew she should leave the area before checking, but she couldn't wait. Kat quickly pulled the notebook from her bag and flipped to the correct page. Périgueux was marked with today's date and the number seventeen. It was the final entry on the list.

"Mrs. Kelly."

Kat started. She pivoted to her left where the voice had come from to see a familiar face. It took her just a moment to place it. She quickly tucked Toby's notebook back into her purse. "Mr. Braeburn! You startled me." She smiled, but looked over her shoulder. Could the Rossis see her from the store?

"I apologize. How are you? I was just finishing lunch in this area when I saw you across the street."

Kat turned slightly so her back was to the store.

"Have you had any more contact with the police? Do let me know if they're giving you any trouble."

Kat didn't want to go into that now. She wanted to get off this block before anyone from Marché Gaspard spotted her.

"I was just doing some shopping."

"Are you headed into the market?" Braeburn gestured to Marché Gaspard.

"No, no. I was just trying to remember if I bought everything I needed, and I have. So I'm headed home. Will you walk with me to the metro?"

Kat exhaled as they began walking, but just then the door to Gaspard opened and out walked Mireille Rossi. Her hair was curled, and she wore cherry-red lipstick. And she almost walked right into Kat and Braeburn.

Her eyes met Kat's, and she pursed her lips. But all the shopkeeper said was, "*Pardon.*" She walked around the couple and crossed the street.

Kat closed her eyes briefly and then recovered herself. They continued walking.

"Have you heard anything from the police, any developments in Toby's case?" she asked.

"In fact, Galland hasn't returned my phone calls. I wonder if he's trying to avoid telling me that he has nothing."

Or, that he's going to pin it on a dead woman and pin that murder on my husband.

Braeburn continued. "I think he's getting desperate. No one at the embassy likes an American's death going unanswered for. But unfortunately, not every murder is solved."

"Tell that to Toby's brother, Harold."

"I have, just this morning. I advised him to go home when his brother's body is released and leave it to the French police. We'll keep him apprised."

"Do you think he'll listen?"

"Hard to say. He strikes me as the stubborn sort."

They were at the entrance to the metro. "It was nice to see you again, Mr. Braeburn. I enjoyed meeting your wife on Friday."

"I'm sure the feeling was mutual." Kat wasn't sure at all if that was the case. "Speaking of spouses, I spoke to Charlie today. Could you give him a message for me?"

Kat had been so distracted worrying if the Rossis would see her that it took her until now to realize that this meeting was a little too cute, a little too coincidental. Could he possibly be going to say something about Charlie and Miranda? Surely not, but she instinctively braced herself for the awkwardness. Despite everything that had happened since the embassy party, she hadn't quite been able to banish the thought of Charlie and Miranda together from her mind. She wondered if Bob Braeburn was experiencing the same thing.

She raised an eyebrow "Yes?"

"Tell him he's barking up the wrong tree."

"Excuse me?"

"This story he's working on about the doctor and his wife. He got some bad information." After a split second of relief, she was immediately on guard.

"Did you tell Charlie that?"

"Yes, but I didn't get the sense that he believed me. Following this story would be a waste of his time." Braeburn's face was pleasant but firm. "Will you tell him that?"

Kat forced herself to smile. "If you know many journalists, you probably know that they don't just take someone's word for it when they deny there's a story, not even their wife's. Say hello to Miranda for me." Kat turned down the steps and into the metro.

Chapter Thirty-Two

Even though Club Margaux was closed, Kat knew Philippe would still be there, either reading at the bar or writing in his office. She didn't know exactly what he was writing. Whenever she asked, he replied in a lofty air, "My memoirs." She didn't know if she should take that response seriously.

Today, when she arrived, he moved out into the bar area and offered her a drink. Kat loved the club when it was empty like this.

"Just a small glass of white, please." Kat was restless, pacing. Maybe the wine would calm her down. She wondered how Charlie had gotten on today. She would need to tell him about Braeburn's warning, since that was certainly what it was. She used the club's phone to call Florence and ask her to tell Charlie that she was at Margaux.

Kat told Philippe about her visit to the Rossis' neighbors. She was trying to make sense of what Madame Cheverny had told her about Toby, the deliveries, and the men who frequented the grocery store.

"Philippe, is the black market still happening?" She thought about Jacques and his altercation at Les Halles, the high-quality coffee they served at Café du Vent. She was pretty sure the answer was yes.

Her cousin stood behind the bar, checking the levels in each liquor bottle—actually working!—and making a list of what would need replenishing soon. "Maybe a little coffee here and chocolate there. But not so much, certainly not like before when the *marché noir* was the best option for nearly everything. But think about it. Certain things—drugs, liquor, cigarettes, weapons, even people—have always moved thanks to an underground economy, which is the same as saying black market, *n'est-ce pas*?"

Kat nodded. There would always be a market for things like that, especially in a big city like Paris. "How much do you know about it?" No one who owned a club could be insulated from at least brushing up against that world.

"I know the outlines. Why?"

"What if Toby was mixed up in something like that, with the Rossis? There could surely be a motive to kill him somewhere in there, couldn't there?" Her conversation with Madame Cheverny and the delivery truck from Périgueux—the last city on the list in Toby's notebook—made this scenario seem likely. And if the arrangement had started during the war, it could explain Eugene's comment about Toby skirting the rules.

Philippe nodded. "I suppose."

"But who can I talk to that would know for sure? I can't go to the police."

Philippe thought for a moment, then lowered his voice. "There is one person—"

"Why are you whispering? There's no one here."

Philippe grimaced. "Second nature. This is someone you talk about sotto voce." Kat was immediately intrigued. "I don't even know his real name. He's called Le Pêcheur."

"The Fisherman? Who is he?"

"I don't know. I don't know if anyone knows. But he has Paris."

"What do you mean, *he has Paris*?"

Philippe sighed, like telling her this was against his better judgment. "Supposedly, Le Pêcheur has final say over most of the criminal activity in the city. He's the boss."

"He would know about what's going on at Marché Gaspard?"

"If it's a very small operation, maybe not. But if it's anything beyond that, then yes, I think so."

"But, if he knows, doesn't that mean he has a hand in it?"

"I would be very surprised if he would work with an American."

Kat nodded. This was promising. "Where can I find him? I'll go tonight."

"No, no; it's too dangerous."

"So you don't know where to find him?"

"Well, probably, but—" The shrill ring of the telephone behind the bar interrupted him.

Philippe picked up the receiver. "Le Club Margaux." As he listened, he looked at Kat, frowning. She moved from the table and rested her elbows on the bar.

"D'accord, merci mon chèr. À demain." He replaced the receiver and looked at Kat. "That was Marcel. It's not good."

"Tell me."

"Apparently this Galland fellow is dead set on Charlie. He's their man, at least for the second murder."

Just then Charlie walked in, briefcase in hand, and asked for a glass of red wine. Philippe shook his head and handed him a whiskey with one ice cube. "You'll probably want something stronger."

Kat filled him in on her day, including her run-in with Braeburn, and Philippe relayed the phone call they had just received from Marcel.

"Braeburn called me at the office, said that looking into this story was bad for national security. And then he called my editor and told him the same thing."

"Jesus," Kat said. "What did Tom say?"

"I don't know what he said to Braeburn, but he told me to work faster." Kat had always liked Tom Granderson, Charlie's editor, and this response confirmed it. He wasn't backing down from official pressure.

Charlie took a stack of files out of his briefcase and spread them on the bar.

"What's this?" Philippe asked.

"I had the idea that if there was talk about an American or Americans pulling the trigger in these murders, then it wasn't exactly a secret. While no one was punished for it, it's possible that the Army pushed out the killers on another pretext. My source got me the files of everyone who was dishonorably discharged after being in Paris during the Liberation."

Kat picked up one of the files. "What were they discharged for?"

"All sorts of things. Theft, disobeying direct orders, other crimes against the locals."

Suddenly Kat's eye caught on one typewritten name. She reached for the file and gasped. Vaughn Harris.

"I know this one; he's in my class at L'École."

Charlie swiveled the file so he could read it. He grimaced. "Discharged for underage prostitution."

Kat read. "He was caught paying for sex with a fourteen-year-old and warned. After the fifth time he was discharged. The fifth time! Doesn't seem like the Army ran a very tight ship."

"I remember this," Philippe said. "Well, maybe not this specific case. But there was a lot of pressure from the local French authorities on the U.S. Army to stop soldiers from paying minors for sex. The girls would wait for customers next to their barracks."

Kat shuddered.

Philippe continued, "Of course some people argued that, since the girls were going willingly, it shouldn't be a crime."

"But they were basically children," Charlie said. "And probably so poor that they had no other options."

So Vaughn had been dishonorably discharged. She quickly looked through the rest of the names. No Eugene Sizemore.

"Eugene told me that he, Vaughn, and Toby were in the same unit. Surely Toby knew what happened. That could explain their visceral dislike for each other. Maybe Toby was blackmailing Vaughn?" Kat's mind raced. Could Vaughn have killed Toby and also Marie-Hélène?

"That could be a motive for Toby's murder," Philippe said. "But it doesn't seem like it had anything to do with the murder of the doctor and his wife."

Kat dragged her focus back to Charlie. "Tell us again what happened that night in 1944."

Charlie explained that Antoine and Gabrielle Desmarchelier had been driving home from a party at the British embassy. It was after the Liberation, but there were still few cars on the road. Anyone who drove was clearly wealthy. A witness from the third floor of an apartment building saw three men with guns stop the car. The couple were pulled from the vehicle. The doctor handed over his wallet. One of the men pulled a necklace from the woman's neck, and then two of the men opened fire and killed the couple. The diamond and sapphire necklace the killers took was worth many thousands of francs.

"And they never recovered it?" Kat asked.

Charlie shook his head.

"Did the thieves take the car?"

"No . . . no they didn't. I guess they thought it would be too noticeable."

Kat thought for a minute. "So the official story was a robbery gone wrong? That the thieves stopped the car to rob the occupants, but something happened and they ended up getting killed."

"Correct."

"It doesn't make sense," Kat said. "The thieves just lucked out that the woman was wearing incredibly valuable jewelry?"

"What are you thinking?" Charlie asked.

"Maybe someone at the party they were at saw her wearing the necklace."

"And then left to pick up their buddies and their guns before coming back to the party to follow them home?" Philippe asked.

Good point. "Right, not very likely. What family do the couple have left?"

"He was in his mid-forties, and she was in her late thirties; they didn't have any children. I spoke to Dr. Desmarchelier's parents and brother, but they couldn't shed new light on anything." Charlie paused to finish the last of his drink. "I considered whether it was a targeted attack against Desmarchelier. Had he done something during the war that this might have been revenge for? Or did someone hold a grudge against him? But there's no evidence of that."

"And what about Madame Desmarchelier?" Kat asked.

"What about her?"

Kat looked at her husband, slightly exasperated. "Did anyone have a grudge against her?"

Charlie looked at her for a long while and then grinned. "You got me."

Kat shook her head in mock disappointment. "Remember the ladies!"

Then she asked, "Does Madame Desmarchelier have any surviving family?"

"A sister. I'll set up an appointment for tomorrow."

"In the meantime, do you think we should talk to Braeburn about the police? As disagreeable as he's being, I'm sure he doesn't want to see you arrested."

Charlie looked dubious. "Not sure we can count on that. He never liked me."

"And he probably doesn't like that his wife is still in love with you."

Charlie winced slightly.

"Wait a second. What did I miss?" Philippe asked.

She gave him an "I'll tell you later" look. "Okay then, what about George Church, the deputy ambassador? Maybe he could help take the pressure off."

"It isn't a bad idea, but not yet," Charlie replied. "We can only play that card once."

Chapter Thirty-Three

Kat and Charlie arrived at a posh address off the Avenue Montaigne at nine o'clock sharp the next morning to meet Madame Louise Beauvais, Gabrielle Desmarchelier's sister. Kat had barely slept the night before, thinking of Vaughn, his dishonorable discharge, and how that potentially changed everything, giving him a motive to kill Toby. She wanted to talk to him but wondered if she should take the information to Faucher. Perhaps he actually cared about solving Toby's murder. Galland seemed to only have eyes for Charlie.

A servant opened the ornate wooden door and ushered them into a spacious courtyard, paved in pearly gray cobblestones and lined with tall shrubs. He led them through the home's front door and gestured toward a sweeping staircase. "*S'il vous plait.* She is on the first floor."

Kat admired the intricate ironwork on the banister and the shining marble of the steps. They reminded her of the staircase that led down to the kitchen classrooms at L'École. She was missing school again but knew that this interview was more important.

A maid in a black-and-white uniform met them at the top of the stairs. She led them into a bright and spacious sitting room. The furniture and the art on the walls were clearly expensive, but the overall effect was light and modern, not stuffy.

They crossed the sitting room into a small parlor with a writing desk at the window overlooking the quiet courtyard below. A slim woman of about forty rose from the desk. Madame Beauvais shook their hands, perched on the blue velvet divan, and gestured to her guests to sit in chairs opposite her. She asked if Kat and Charlie wanted anything to drink, and when they declined, she dismissed the maid with a nod.

"How can I help you?"

Charlie began. "As I explained on the telephone last night, I'm with the *New York Tribune*, and I'm investigating your sister and her husband's murders. We have some new information that might help."

Madame Beauvais looked at Kat. "And you? Do you work for the paper as well?"

"I'm helping Mr. Kelly with this story." It wasn't a lie.

"Well, I'm glad someone is finally taking the case seriously. The fact that the police never solved it is appalling. The whole family is still in disarray over it."

Kat looked at Charlie, and he nodded. They had agreed that she should take the lead on the questions since Madame Beauvais might be more comfortable speaking with a woman about her sister. Plus, Kat's French was better. "Madame Beauvais, your sister and her husband were coming home from a party at the British embassy that night. Do you know how they happened to be there?" Falling back into the role of professional journalist was so effortless that Kat had to restrain a smile.

"My brother-in-law's brother ran in diplomatic circles in those days, and he often secured invitations for them to various functions at the British and American embassies. Gabrielle and Antoine were in-demand guests. They spoke English, Antoine was debonair and charming at these events, and my sister . . . well . . . she was very beautiful." She shrugged her shoulders as if to say, *What more would she need to be?*

"You said that your brother-in-law was charming at these events. Do you mean he wasn't usually?"

Madame Beauvais shifted on the sofa, uncrossing and recrossing her ankles in the opposite direction.

"I suppose he was, although you know, after fifteen years of marriage I'm not sure Gabri was charmed by him anymore. It happens."

Kat felt Charlie glance in her direction, but she kept her focus on the interview. "And the necklace. Was that something your sister wore often?"

Madame Beauvais laughed thinly. "Of course not. It was worth a fortune. And she was a fool to wear it that night. Showing off, I'm sure."

"For whom?"

"The diplomats' wives, the British and Americans. You weren't here then?"

Both Kat and Charlie shook their heads.

"The British and the Americans, and of course some more fortunate French, were the only ones with enough to eat and cars to drive. My sister and I, our families, were among the fortunate. But it still rankled. The French were like the poor cousins, in our own city. In Paris!" After four years, she was still incredulous. "And of course she looked like a diamond herself in that necklace. As I said, she wanted to impress the women." She paused a moment. "And the men." Her left eyebrow arched slightly.

Kat's instincts told her this wasn't an idle comment. She waited to see if Madame Beauvais would add anything else, but she didn't. "Anyone in particular?"

Madame Beauvais hesitated, as if she was making up her mind about something. Then she nodded, cocked her head, and looked squarely at Kat. "My sister was having an affair."

Now they were getting somewhere. It could be nothing—it seemed like everyone in Paris had affairs—but at least it was a thread to follow.

"Did you tell the police this when they were investigating the crime back in 1944?" Charlie asked.

"Of course not. Embarrass my parents and sully her name? For what? The police assured us it was a random crime. But over the years I have started to wonder."

"Wonder what?" Charlie asked.

Madame Beauvais thought for a moment before speaking. "I suppose it's possible that the thieves got the best surprise of their lives. Maybe they wanted the car or Antoine's fat wallet. And then they couldn't believe their luck when they saw what my sister was wearing."

"But?" Kat prompted her.

"*Mais, je ne sais pas!*" She opened her hands as if to say, *how could I know?* "It just seems improbable."

"Do you know who your sister was involved with?" Kat asked.

Madame Beauvais shook her head. "Just that he was American and official, at the embassy or in the military. She never told me his name, just called him '*mon américain*.' She was enraptured. She told me she was planning to leave Antoine."

"Was her lover also married?"

"I don't know, perhaps. I can't be sure, but I felt that he didn't take the affair as seriously as she did. I think that was why she wore grand-maman's necklace. To show off her value. She told me he wanted to see her in it."

"Did anyone ever discover what happened to the necklace?" Charlie asked. He already knew the answer to this question, since there was nothing in the police report Marcel had slipped him about the necklace being recovered. But it was always smart to cover your bases.

"*Non*. The police tried to trace it. It was the best clue. They checked all the usual places where stolen jewelry would be sold in Paris and throughout France. But it seemed to vanish."

"Do you happen to have any letters or journals from your sister? Anything from that time?"

"No journals. Gabri didn't have the patience for anything like that. There are a few letters that she wrote me when I was in Cannes that fall, but I would have to find them. I read through all of them again after she died. I don't think there was anything relevant."

"We'd still like to see them, if possible," Charlie said.

"Of course. I will look for them today and send them over to you."

Kat and Charlie stood and thanked Madame Beauvais. As they shook hands she said, "Despite my sister's silliness and mistakes, she didn't deserve to die like that, gunned down in the street like in a gangster film. Good luck with your investigation."

After they left the Beauvais home, they hurried to the metro. Kat felt a charge; they finally had a new lead to pursue.

"It wasn't random! They knew she'd be wearing the necklace. It was a setup. I don't know why I didn't see it before. You saw it though," Charlie said.

"And, Charlie, this may sound crazy, but what if the necklace was just a bonus, a cover?"

"And that killing them was the plan all along?"

She nodded. "And, maybe, she was the real target."

"I need to make some phone calls." At the Concorde stop near his office, Charlie took the steps two at a time. Kat rushed to keep up with him. She would walk him to his office and then figure out what to do with the information she had about Vaughn Harris.

"Thanks for coming with me today, Kat. I think she was more open with you there. You're good at this, you know." He slowed down enough to give her a quick kiss on the cheek. "Thank you."

"Of course." She squeezed his hand. They were going to figure this out together. They turned the corner and stopped abruptly. Galland was leaning casually against the exterior of the *Tribune* bureau. Faucher was pacing in front of the door. Galland ran his hand through his hair and approached them first.

"Ah, Monsieur Kelly, *finalement*. Come with us please. We need to talk about the murder of Marie-Hélène Arnaud."

Chapter Thirty-Four

All afternoon, Kat tried to push down a rising sense of panic. As Galland had led Charlie to their car, hand on his shoulder, Faucher had turned back to her, standing in front of the door to the bureau. He had seemed about to say something before Galland barked his name.

Kat didn't know how to interpret the look he gave her, but she didn't have time to think about it. She had raced up the stairs to talk to Charlie's editor. Tom Granderson was livid.

Granderson had lined up a lawyer for Charlie. He told her that the police could hold Charlie for two days without charging him. After that, they would need to either release him or formally arrest him.

"It's political posturing. They're trying to get us to kill that story. And I'll be damned if we'll give in to that. These goddamn Frenchies don't know who they're dealing with." Usually Kat liked that he had no qualms about swearing in front of her. But she wasn't in the mood to appreciate it at the moment.

Granderson continued. "And I have an urgent message in to the embassy."

The embassy. Kat remembered that Louise Beauvais had said that her sister was involved with someone official. "Who did you call there?"

"I started with that fellow Braeburn. He tried to warn us off the story before, but now that Kelly has been arrested it's entirely different. If he isn't responsive, I'll go to the deputy ambassador, the ambassador, and hell, the president himself. Don't worry, sweetheart. He'll be out before you know it."

Kat was torn. The embassy might be their best chance at getting Charlie released. But if the police were responding to political pressure themselves—to scare Charlie into getting him off the story—it might be where the pressure was coming from in the first place. "I need to go," she said.

As Kat walked briskly down the colonnade on the Rue de Rivoli, she tried to put her thoughts in order. The murders—Toby's, Marie-Hélène's, and the Desmarcheliers—were like three pieces of yarn that had become hopelessly tangled in her brain. She didn't know which string to start pulling first, but somehow she was sure that tugging on one would eventually make them all unravel. If she could prove that someone else had killed Marie-Hélène, they would have to let Charlie go. And finding Toby's killer could lead her to Marie-Hélène's. And, if she could figure out who killed the Desmarcheliers, there would be no reason for anyone to threaten Charlie anymore.

In the middle of the Pont Royal Bridge she stopped and looked over the river toward the Ile de la Cité. The water was dark and murky. The damp November chill seeped through her coat, but she barely noticed. She thought about who was on—and off—the suspect list for each crime. Kat now considered Vaughn Harris a possibility when it came to Toby's murder, although she wondered if the police had already checked his alibi. After all, they had questioned him. But if they didn't know about his crimes during the Liberation, and Toby had, they wouldn't know what to ask him.

As much as she detested Eugene, and knew that he detested Toby, he at least had an alibi that satisfied the police. And she didn't doubt that the police would have happily rung him up for killing Toby. Arresting an American for killing an American was much tidier than arresting a French person.

The Rossis. Somehow Toby was mixed up in something there, potentially having to do with the black market.

And then there was Nico. Kat had to admit that he was the most likely person to have murdered both Toby and Marie-Hélène. What was more common than a love triangle gone wrong? But yet she believed his grief for his wife was genuine.

Her brain circled back to the Rossis. She closed her eyes as she remembered mentioning Marie-Hélène's name to them. God, what had she done? She shook her head and made herself focus.

Gabrielle's lover was the only concrete lead she had for the Desmarchelier killings. How was she going to untangle that thread?

Tonight, she would make Philippe take her to Le Pêcheur, whoever he was. Surely, now that Charlie was in custody, Philippe would see that, despite the risks, they had to act. Despite Tom Granderson's confidence that Charlie would be released soon, Kat couldn't take the chance. If he was arrested, there was always a chance he'd be convicted. She turned around to look toward the obelisk rising from Place de la Concorde. That was where the guillotine had done its vicious work during the French Revolution. While executions didn't happen in public anymore, they still happened. And they still happened by guillotine.

Chapter Thirty-Five

By midnight, the dampness in the air had developed into a thick mist that settled onto the streets. Kat wrapped her arm through Philippe's as they walked from their taxi toward Club du Sud. After reluctantly agreeing to her plan that afternoon, he had sent her to Le Bon Marché with a stack of francs to buy an evening gown. Shopping was the farthest thing from her mind, but he insisted that if they were going to call on Le Pêcheur, she had to look the part. She chose a long sapphire gown that clung to her torso and featured wide, off-the-shoulder straps. It was belted at the waist and then flowed to the ground. She washed and curled her dark hair and carefully applied makeup. Philippe looked dapper in his tuxedo, long, lean, and confident.

An hour before, as they were about to leave Club Margaux, Philippe had held out a small rectangular object for her to take. She looked at him blankly. He pressed his thumb to the side of the object, and a sharp, silver knife sprang out.

"A switchblade?" She laughed. It felt good to release some of the tension that had been building inside her all day. "Are you serious? A, where am I supposed to put that? And B, who am I supposed to use that on?"

Philippe wasn't laughing. "Put it in your garter or your bra or wherever; I don't really understand what's going on under there," he said, gesturing at her gown. "They'll probably search your purse. And you'll know if you need to use it. These are not regular people we're going to see. They're dangerous. We're hoping that they'll be on our side, but there's no way to know."

"Do you have a weapon?"

Philippe shook his head. "They'll search me."

"So I'm responsible for both of our safety?"

"Basically."

"*Formidable*," Kat said sarcastically. She slid her dress up her thigh and tucked the small switchblade under the top of her garter belt. Then she was serious. "Philippe, just point me in the right direction. You don't need to go with me. I'm already responsible for Marie-Hélène's death. If it's as dangerous as you say, and something happens to you, I'll never forgive myself."

Philippe helped her on with her coat. "You're not responsible for Marie-Hélène's murder, and there's no way I'm letting you go in there alone. If I did, Charlie would murder me when he got out of prison. I'm more worried about him than Le Pêcheur." Kat knew that was a lie, but she accepted it. She didn't want to go alone.

In the taxi, Kat asked, "How do you know that he'll be here?"

Philippe spoke in a low voice. "I don't, not for sure. But if he's out in Paris tonight, he'll be at Club du Sud. It's his club."

"Does he know you?"

"I'm sure he knows of me. Club Margaux is small potatoes compared to what he operates. But it's his job to know everything about everyone. He's got eyes and ears throughout the city."

"Usually that would terrify me, but now I'm hoping his eyes and ears can help us clear Charlie. Why do they call him Le Pêcheur?" She mouthed the last word so the taxi driver wouldn't hear her.

"His father was a fisherman in Marseille, so the story goes."

There was a cluster of people around the entrance to the club, smoking and hoping the sentry at the door would let them in. They were well-dressed, but Kat immediately pegged them as Americans.

"Act like you belong here," Philippe said, and Kat straightened her shoulders and put on an air of bored self-confidence.

Philippe skirted around the people who were waiting and went directly to the large man at the door. The man's hair was slicked back, and he wore a white scarf loose around his neck over his tux. "*Bonsoir*," Philippe said.

The man looked closely at him. "*Bonsoir*, Monsieur Washington. *Bienvenue* to Club du Sud." He opened the door for Philippe and Kat.

Philippe raised his eyebrows at Kat as if to say, "See?"

Kat had been to several clubs in Paris before, but none quite like this. Jazz clubs like Philippe's tended to be dark and somewhat serious. The Folies, Moulin Rouge, and their kin were raucous performances of forced frivolity. Fun, yes, but a show mostly for tourists. Club du Sud oozed glamor. A large band played swing music on a spacious stage that hugged one wall, and the dance floor was full. Besuited servers swirled between the tables filling coupes of champagne and dropping off cocktails. But the real entertainment was watching the guests. Women wore dazzling gowns with fur stoles thrown casually across their chairs. Everyone laughed and flirted and buzzed from table to table. Kat couldn't see any tourists. It felt more like a private club than a public space.

"Who are these people?" she asked Philippe.

"Businessmen, socialites. You can't throw a pebble without hitting a collaborator. These are the people who don't face consequences. And most of those Americans at the door aren't getting in, no matter how rich they are."

"Did Le Pêcheur collaborate with the Nazis?"

"It's hard to say. This is where the high-ranking German officers spent their evenings, drinking and dancing with their French girlfriends. But the rumor was that Le Pêcheur funneled any information the servers and maître d' overheard to the Resistance."

"So they were spies."

"Of a sort, I suppose."

Kat thought about Annette at Café du Vent. She and Jacques had served Nazis at their café in Moulins. But really, what choice had they had? They would have had to close their café to avoid it, and then how would they have supported their family? Kat wasn't sure if they had tried to help the Resistance with any tidbits they picked up, but she didn't think so. If they had been caught, they would likely have been shot or deported.

When they reached the host, Philippe whispered something in his ear. The man looked surprised but quickly recovered his serene expression. He looked at Kat. "*Un moment, s'il vous plait.*"

Kat watched as the maître d' made his way to a discreet table half hidden by a large, leafy plant. If she had been seated there, she would have been disappointed; it was easily the worst seat in the house. Now she wondered if that was by design.

Kat could make out a man and a woman seated at the table, but nothing more.

The maître d' returned. "Madame, your purse." Kat opened the tiny clutch for him to inspect.

"Monsieur, please step through here." He gestured to Philippe to join him in the coatroom.

The door closed, and thirty seconds later both men walked out. Philippe offered her his arm, and they followed the maître d' to the half-hidden table.

"He searched you?"

Philippe nodded.

The maître d' deposited Kat and Philippe in front of the table. The man—Le Pêcheur, Kat assumed—was middle-aged and well-built with broad shoulders and a neck that verged on thick. His face was handsome in a crooked sort of way. It looked like his nose had been broken, possibly more than once. He studied them as they walked to his table, and Kat imagined that she could hear Philippe's racing heartbeat. Or maybe it was her own.

It was harder to tell how old the woman was. She could have been anywhere from thirty-five to fifty. Beautiful wasn't the right word to describe her; she was what Kat's mother would have called striking. With a strong jaw and sharp cheekbones, her face was all angles. She didn't look at Kat or Philippe but sipped a cocktail and gazed lazily around the room. Kat thought she looked bored.

"Monsieur Washington and Madame . . . ?"

"Kelly. My name is Kat Kelly."

"The foreign correspondent's wife."

It wasn't a question, but Kat responded anyway. "*Oui.*"

"Welcome to Club du Sud. I'm Michel." So that's what Le Pêcheur called himself. Kat wondered if that was his real name. "Please, join us. What would you like to drink?" He didn't introduce his companion but gestured to the chairs at the table. "Champagne?" He beckoned to a waiter.

"*Merci,*" Kat said.

"How can I help you?"

Philippe gave Kat a nod. All afternoon she had thought about what to say to this man, but she hadn't come up with any clever strategy. Why would he help her? He was a criminal. Appealing to his sense of justice didn't seem promising. Philippe thought he might help her out of professional courtesy for him. She hoped her cousin was right.

"Thank you for seeing us. It's a long story; I'll keep it as short as I can." She started with Toby's murder, then Marie-Hélène's, and Charlie being detained by the police.

Michel listened attentively. The woman next to him seemed to stare off into space. Kat was curious about her. She wasn't the type of girlfriend Kat had expected for a man as powerful as Le Pêcheur. She would have thought he would prefer a younger, more conventionally beautiful woman at his side. It made her like him a little bit more.

The waiter returned with two coupes of champagne. The table fell silent until he departed. Kat and Philippe both left their glasses untouched. They would need all their wits about them tonight.

"I'm sorry for your troubles, Madame, but I am not sure what you want from me. No murder is a small crime, but people are killed all the time over petty grievances or jealousies. And sadly, the police get it wrong all too often in this city. Probably everywhere."

"It isn't just that they have it wrong; I think Charlie is being set up."

"By whom?"

She shook her head. "I'm not sure. But Charlie was investigating the 1944 Desmarchelier murders."

For the first time, the woman looked mildly interested in the conversation at the table. Her eyes flickered toward Kat.

Kat quickly continued. She hadn't been sure what order to put all of this in. "And I think there might be a black market connection with Toby's death."

"I see. How so?"

She told them about the Rossis, Marché Gaspard, the deliveries to their store, and the list in Toby's notebook. She told them that they may have been worried that Marie-Hélène would talk and murdered her because of it.

"What kind of goods do you think they're dealing in?"

Suddenly the music changed to a high, seductive melody. Kat's eye was drawn to the stage. Six women in sparkling brassieres and flowing harem pants were undulating in unison to the music, their hips and bellies moving in a way Kat had never seen before. The club's guests had ceased their dancing and chatting and were as enraptured by the performance as Kat was. She tore her attention back to the table. *"Je ne sais pas."*

"And the Desmarcheliers?" It was the woman who spoke. She still didn't make eye contact with Kat.

Kat hid her surprise and took a deep breath; Charlie probably wouldn't want her to reveal what she was about to reveal. But doing so might be the only way to help him. "Charlie got a tip that an American or Americans were involved in the murder. It was only once he started investigating that the police became very interested in him for Marie-Hélène's murder and possibly even set him up to find her body."

"Does he know where the necklace ended up?" It was the woman again.

"No, just that it vanished."

Michel and the woman exchanged glances. Then he sat back, and she sat forward. Her whole body had transformed. She no longer looked bored, but calm and in control.

"*Merci, madame.* It is good to see a woman taking matters into her own hands. I quite like that."

Kat was confused, and she could tell that Philippe was, as well.

"Who are you?" Kat couldn't help asking.

"Your friend," she looked at Philippe, "would call me La Pêcheuse. But you can call me Marina. We cannot tell you anything about the murders of your friends, but we are interested in what's going on at Marché Gaspard, aren't we, Michel?"

"*Oui*, Madame."

"To thank you for sharing that piece of information, I will tell you what I can about the murders of the Desmarcheliers. It isn't much, only that Americans were involved and at least one of them had enough power that he couldn't be touched."

"You don't know who?"

Marina didn't answer. "We will be in touch. *Bon soirée.*"

Braeburn's image flashed through her mind. "Did he work at the embassy?"

"*Bonne soirée.*" It was Michel this time.

Philippe stood, but Kat didn't follow. While she now could be certain that a powerful American was involved in the killings—probably Gabrielle Desmarchelier's lover—she didn't feel closer to clearing Charlie. "But Charlie has less than two days. I need more to go on."

Michel's face was impassive, and Marina resumed her bored stare off into space. She was like a robot that had been switched off.

Philippe gently grasped Kat's arm and tugged her to her feet.

Chapter Thirty-Six

They exchanged nods with the man with the long white scarf as they left Club du Sud.

Philippe waited until they turned the corner outside the club before speaking. "*Merde! Une femme!*" They could still hear occasional snatches of music. The band had resumed playing swing. The mist swirled around them, and now the night felt unseasonably warm to Kat, or maybe it was just the adrenaline flowing through her body. They stopped on the quiet side street to catch their breath.

"I don't understand. Is she Le Pêcheur?" Kat asked.

Philippe bent over slightly and put his hands on his knees. He inhaled deeply and exhaled loudly, like he had just run a race. "I'm not sure."

A woman dripping with diamonds and her companion turned the corner from the club, laughing loudly, their voices piercing the still night air.

"Who can you ask?"

Philippe looked at her like she was crazy. "No one! I'm not going to start talking about the Fisherman now. It's bad enough that I went to see him . . . her. It's like inviting attention you don't want." He took another deep breath and appraised Kat. "Look at you, cool as ice."

She didn't feel cool inside; she felt like she was burning up with impatience. "I think what we did was draw attention to the Rossis. But I'm not sure how that will help Charlie." She wanted to go back into Club du Sud and demand that Marina help them.

She saw a figure approaching from the opposite direction, a man wearing no coat but a scarf and hat that covered most of his face. He didn't look polished enough to be going to Club du Sud, and the evening certainly wasn't warm enough to be coatless. She held a bit tighter to Philippe's arm, but the man passed them without looking their way.

Before she could suggest returning to Club du Sud, Philippe said, "Come on, let's go back to Margaux."

"Pansy."

Kat whirled around. It was the man who had just walked by; he was now standing right behind them. He wasn't wearing a hat and scarf like she had initially thought, but a mask over his face. Since her eyes focused on the mask, it took her a second to realize he had a small knife in his hand.

Philippe caught on instantly and raised his hands. "Here. I'll give you my wallet. There's no need to hurt anyone."

"I'm not here for your wallet."

Kat couldn't be sure, but his voice seemed familiar.

"What do you want?" Philippe asked.

The man jutted his chin at Kat. "Her."

Philippe stepped in front of her, and she suddenly remembered the switchblade tucked under her dress. But for a split second, she stood frozen with fear, unsure if she should take it out. That instant was just long enough for the man to lunge at Philippe. Kat screamed. Her cousin dodged the knife but tripped and landed hard on the ground.

The man kicked Philippe in the kidneys. Kat turned to run back to the club for help. But the man scooped her up with one arm and held her close, her arms pinned to her sides. "Oh no, you're coming with me."

It had been maybe sixty seconds since they were first accosted, but it felt like a lifetime to Kat. The man's grip around her was unyielding. Her face was close to his ear, and he smelled rank and sour. She turned away and managed to let out another yell, although it came out as more of a yelp because of their attacker's hard grip around her. Kat glanced down to see if she could bite the man's hand or arm. It was too far away from her mouth. But she did get a look at a sliver of the man's hairy flesh between his glove and his shirt.

Philippe was writhing on the ground, curled into a ball to protect his soft middle. The kicks didn't stop. Kat struggled in the man's arms, but then the point of his knife in her neck stopped her.

She saw the man raise his heavy foot as if to stomp on Philippe's head. "No!" she shouted.

Just then, the attacker's head jerked back. His knife clattered to the ground, and his arm flew from around Kat's shoulders. She barely looked to see what had happened, just rushed to crouch down next to Philippe. Blood trickled from the corner of his mouth. His immaculate tuxedo was covered in dirt. He groaned quietly, and she whispered in his ear. "It's okay. It's okay now."

She turned back and saw the man who had attacked them tussling with the doorman from the club, the doorman's white scarf lying on the ground. Kat dashed to grab the knife; it was easier to access than the switchblade in her garter. She was now prepared to use it if she had to.

But what she really wanted was to unmask the bastard.

The doorman landed a punch to the attacker's face, but the mask must have protected him because he barely seemed affected by it. Just then, Kat saw Michel and another man turn the corner. Their attacker must have seen them too, because he gave the doorman a vicious blow to his groin, then ran off in the opposite direction.

Michel rushed to the doorman lying on the ground. "Pascal, *ca va*?"

Pascal winced but nodded. "*Ca va, ca va*."

Then Michel crouched in front of Philippe. "Let's bring him inside," he said to the third man.

"He needs a hospital!" Kat was terrified.

Michel shook his head no. "There's a doctor in the club."

They helped Philippe into Club du Sud through a back door. His feet barely touched the ground, but he was able to hold his head up. His eyes caught Kat's, and he gave her such a look of disapproval—*see what you dragged me into?*—that she almost laughed, despite her worry for him. It reminded her of playing together as children at their *grand-mère*'s cottage in Bretagne. She would lead him on adventures that their parents had specifically forbidden. The cousins didn't often get caught disobeying, but when they did, his doleful expression temporarily shamed her. Yet she always had a new adventure to lead him on the next day, and he always followed.

Now she had led him into something truly dangerous. If Michel and the other men from Club du Sud hadn't arrived when they had, her cousin would likely be dead. She wasn't sure what she was going to do next to try to clear Charlie, but whatever it was, if there was any potential danger, she would do it on her own.

They laid Philippe on a couch in an office. Kat held his hand. He was conscious, and some of her fear began to subside. Pascal left to fetch the doctor. "Do you know who that was?" Michel asked.

It had all happened so quickly. Kat took a moment to think about the man's voice and body. He had spoken in French, and it wasn't accented like an American's. She thought she had heard the voice before but still couldn't connect it with a face. Then she remembered his hairy wrist. "I can't be certain, but I think it was Guy Rossi, owner of Marché Gaspard."

But why attack them now? He was connected to Toby . . . and probably Marie-Hélène . . . and the black market. But the Desmarcheliers? She had lost track of all the strands. Then she remembered his words.

"I think he was going to kill Philippe, but he was going to take me with him. Why?" She looked at Michel.

He shrugged and excused himself. Kat hoped Marina would come in so she could talk to her more, but in this she was disappointed.

After a doctor examined Philippe, treated his wounds, and pronounced him bruised and battered but not in any life-threatening danger, Michel put them in a taxi. Before sliding in after Philippe, she paused. "Please, is there nothing else you can tell me?"

"Stay away from Guy Rossi."

Kat sighed. She didn't need that advice.

"Have you been to Place de la Concorde?"

"Of course." It was one of the most trafficked squares in Paris at the base of the Tuileries gardens, and just a short walk from Place Vendôme, home to the Ritz and the Ministry of Justice.

"You don't need to go far."

Kat sat down next to Philippe. She wasn't sure what Michel was trying to tell her, and she was tired of all these cryptic messages. She just nodded.

"Be careful."

She nodded again as Michel closed the taxi door behind her.

Chapter Thirty-Seven

Kat was there when Claudine unlocked the door at Café du Vent at eight o'clock the next morning. The woman looked as exhausted as Kat felt. She had dark circles under her eyes, and once again, her usually immaculately styled hair was only haphazardly pinned up. For a moment Kat forgot the murders and the fact that her husband was in police custody. "*Ca va*, Claudine?"

"*Oui, oui, ma belle*. Just overwhelmed. We have been so busy that I need to hire someone to help. I just haven't had the time." She gave Kat a quick smile. "Do you want a job?"

Kat considered telling Claudine about Marie-Hélène's murder and Charlie being a suspect but dismissed the notion immediately. It was too big a story to tell at this early hour and after such a long night. "Right now all I want is a café crème and croissant, *s'il vous plait*."

It had been close to three o'clock in the morning by the time Kat got Philippe home. Luckily Vivienne had still been at Club Margaux. The two women had gingerly supported him up the stairs to his apartment and then into bed.

Philippe had stirred just as Kat was leaving his room. She turned back and saw his eyes open.

"I'm sorry," she said quietly.

"Pfft. I've been through worse."

She had to get closer to hear him. "Really?"

"No."

She kissed him on the cheek. "Sleep."

"And you?"

"I'm going to sleep too."

As she had undressed that night, she set the switchblade on the bedside table, furious at herself for hesitating to use it. She wouldn't make that mistake again.

She knew she needed to sleep to prepare herself for wherever the next day took her, and her body was exhausted. But her brain refused to rest. She relived the agony she had felt as Philippe lay on the ground, receiving blow after blow, the fear that he had been seriously hurt, and the relief that he hadn't.

Despite never seeing the man's face, Kat was certain Guy Rossi had been their attacker. His voice, his build, and the glimpse she had caught of his skin convinced her. Without going into details of where they had been or why, she would tell the police; certainly this would help Charlie's case. But she knew better than to mention their new acquaintances at Club du Sud.

She also knew that she should be scared. Rossi had wanted *her* tonight; Philippe had just been in the way. Instead of fear, her visceral reaction was anger. They—whoever they were—weren't just going after her husband now, but also her beloved cousin. She had finally fallen asleep, more determined than ever to get the bastards behind this.

Annette walked into Café du Vent just as Kat was eating the last shards of croissant. They exchanged waves before Annette went behind the bar to greet Claudine. Kat remarked that they looked more like sisters than sisters-in-law, although Annette seemed calmer and more put together than Claudine these days. Kat wondered if Claudine had gotten more than she bargained for with the upgrade in food. Kat hurried to finish her coffee, hoping to escape before Annette could ask her about her article.

She succeeded, and after leaving Café du Vent she found a pay phone to call Charlie's editor.

"Any updates?" she asked.

Tom Granderson sighed. "It's the damnedest thing. Through one side of its mouth, the embassy says they're going to try to get Charlie out of this mess. Through the other, they remind me that there's no teeth to the Desmarchelier story."

It's like they were holding Charlie hostage in exchange for the story. "Who did you speak to?"

"That Braeburn fellow, who was no help. I have a message in to George Church, the deputy ambassador. The ambassador himself is still in Washington."

"Let me know if you think it would be helpful for me to call on Church. I met him and his wife at the embassy party just a few days ago, and he seemed reasonable."

"Will do."

Thirty minutes later, Kat lifted the heavy knocker at a modest but attractive home near Parc Monceau in the eighth arrondissement. She had gotten the address from Florence, who seemed to be able to get any piece of information Kat or Charlie ever needed. It was a quarter after nine. The sky was steel gray.

It hadn't rained yet today, but Kat could smell it in the air. It was only a matter of time. She knocked again, and seconds later, Miranda Braeburn opened the door.

Coming here was a gamble—several gambles in fact. First, Kat had wagered that Bob Braeburn wouldn't be home. He seemed like a go-getter, and she expected that he would be at the office well before nine. If Granderson hadn't gotten anywhere with Braeburn, she doubted she would. Braeburn certainly didn't have warm feelings toward Charlie, the man that his wife had once been—and maybe still was—in love with.

But Kat couldn't help but wonder if his reticence to help went beyond that. He clearly wanted the story about the Desmarcheliers killed. He had told Kat as much himself. But was it because he thought it would somehow jeopardize national security, like he had said? Or was it for another reason?

Second, she hoped that Miranda *would* be home.

And, third, she hoped that Miranda could—and would—help her.

Upon seeing Kat, Miranda Braeburn was momentarily speechless but quickly recovered herself. She was wearing a pale green dressing gown, her face was bare, and her hair pulled back simply from her face. She looked tired but lovely.

"Mrs. Kelly! What a surprise."

"Please call me Kat. I'm sorry to come unannounced."

"It's fine, but Bob already left to take the children to school. Are you here to see Bob?"

"No, actually, I'm here to see you."

"I see. Please, come in." She led Kat into an elegant but unstuffy sitting room. She gestured for Kat to sit on the couch and picked up a stuffed bear and toy train from the floor and placed them on a sideboard. Miranda sat in a chair opposite Kat. "I'm sorry I'm not dressed to receive anyone. I haven't been feeling well. I'm expecting." Her hand drifted to her belly as she confirmed Kat's earlier guess.

"Congratulations," Kat said with genuine warmth.

"Thank you. I always wanted a lot of children. This will be number three. You . . . you and Charlie don't have children?"

"Not yet." She thought of both Smithson and Harold Magnusson proudly pulling photos of their children from their pockets, but she quickly moved on. "May I call you Miranda?" The woman nodded. "Miranda, I'm short on time, so I'm going to get right to the point. I need your help."

"What's going on? You wouldn't be here if it wasn't serious."

"Charlie is being held by the police on suspicion of murder."

Miranda sat back. "How ridiculous! Charlie would never murder anyone."

Kat privately disagreed that there wasn't *anyone* Charlie would murder but kept that to herself.

"I can't believe it. Who are they saying he killed?"

"A woman we were friends with. It looks like he was set up to find the body. He's working on a story that someone is desperate to stop."

"What is the story?"

"He's investigating whether there was a cover-up in the murders of a French couple, the Desmarcheliers, in 1944."

A wave of recognition passed over Miranda's face. "I remember that! Bob was here then, and he wrote to me about it. It was so shocking. The police never solved the crime, did they?"

"No. And Charlie got a tip that could reopen the case. But someone isn't happy about it." Kat took a deep breath. And here was the biggest gamble of the morning, that this pregnant woman would agree to take Kat's side over her husband, the father of her children. "And Bob could help him, but he won't."

"I don't understand."

"Charlie's editor called Bob to ask that he put some pressure on the detectives in this case. There is no evidence, not a scrap, that Charlie killed Marie-Hélène Arnaud. He found her body, but that can easily be explained."

"How?"

"The secretary at the bureau took a message from someone claiming to be Marie-Hélène asking Charlie to come to her apartment to share a tip. That's why he was there."

Miranda nodded and stood up. "Come to the kitchen with me."

Kat followed her and saw the remains of family breakfast, crumbs on the table and dishes stacked next to the sink.

"Would you like some tea? I still need to tidy up. The mess weighs on me." Miranda wiped the table with a cloth and shook the crumbs into the sink.

"Do you have any help? With two children and a third on the way, that is a lot to manage."

"We have a housekeeper, but she's visiting her family in Nantes for two weeks. Tea?" she asked again.

"No thank you. I don't have much time. The police are allowed to hold Charlie for another twenty-four hours without charging him. I think they will wait until the last possible minute in the hopes that he or his editor agree to drop the story. But if they do charge him, it will be much more complicated to get him out. I need to find information that proves he's innocent or find a way to make the pressure stop—today."

Miranda nodded, and she turned to the sink.

Kat stood next to her. "Please, sit. Let me do this."

Miranda looked like she was about to protest, then changed her mind. "I'm so tired all the time," she said as she sat down. "It's always like this during the first trimester. You'll see someday."

Kat started the water and began to wash. This would take her all of five minutes.

"So you're coming to me to put pressure on Bob?"

"Yes." *Just like your husband came to me to ask me to use my influence on Charlie.*

"And why do you think I would help?"

Kat rinsed the final bowl and placed it in the dishrack. She turned off the water and leaned against the counter, facing Miranda. "Charlie told me you were friends in college."

Miranda said nothing for a moment. "How long have you been married?"

"Almost four years."

"I've been married for nearly twelve, and if you think Bob is going to listen to me on this subject, of all subjects, you're fooling yourself."

"Surely he doesn't think you still have feelings for Charlie."

Miranda blushed and gave a little laugh. "You don't beat around the bush. I can see why Charlie likes you. I always knew he wanted something different, someone less . . ."—she searched for the right word—"traditional. It turns out I was a much better match with Bob than I was with Charlie. It only took me ten years to figure that out." She looked away for a moment before meeting Kat's eye again. "Or maybe it took until meeting you. I don't know."

"A better match how?" This wasn't what Kat had come for, but she couldn't help asking.

Miranda reflected for a moment. "Bob needs me; Charlie didn't."

Kat nodded; she understood. She wanted to tell Miranda that neither she nor Charlie had ever needed the other, which meant they could be together just for the pleasure of it. But she didn't know if that was true anymore. Now that he was gone, Kat felt like she needed him desperately.

"Bob never liked Charlie from the beginning. He and Jake were so different than the other boys at school. Their self-confidence was intrinsic. It didn't stem from their family name or how big their house on the shore was. They were charming and funny and seemed naturally brilliant, but I knew from being with Charlie that they studied very, very hard. I think I was a little in love with both of them, but Charlie was the only one who was interested." She shook her head. "How did he die?"

"In the Pacific in 1943. The ship he was on was torpedoed." Charlie had later discovered that the ship's captain had misinterpreted orders and sailed in the wrong direction. The entire crew had died because of his incompetence. The world had discovered that there were a thousand ways to die in a war. Most were a waste.

"I can't imagine Charlie without Jake."

Kat looked at her sharply. Had Miranda meant to zero in on Kat's biggest insecurity, that she'd never truly know her husband since she hadn't known his brother? Jake had been Charlie's first other half.

Maybe coming here had been a bad idea. Kat forced herself to regain focus. "Can you help me?"

Miranda shook her head. "I'm sorry, but no."

Kat nodded and pushed herself away from the counter. "Thank you for seeing me." Without waiting for a response, she left the kitchen and walked toward the front door, almost tripping on a baby doll. She picked it up and placed it on a nearby table.

"Kat, wait."

Kat didn't turn back. "I need to go."

"Please believe me when I say that my going to Bob wouldn't help. But . . ."

Now she faced her. "But what?"

Miranda looked as if she was making up her mind about something. "I don't know if this will help either, but I will tell you just in case. Usually Bob takes all his official calls at the office, but Saturday he got a call here. I remember because it was so early, around six. We had been at the embassy party the night before, and for once the children were still asleep."

"Go on."

"I followed him to the study because I was worried. He shooed me out." She made a sweeping motion with her hand. "But as I was walking away I heard one thing he said."

"Tell me."

Miranda nodded. "Something like, 'Clarence, it was years ago. Surely we can contain whatever he digs up.'"

"Clarence," Kat repeated.

"Clarence Welch, I think. Do you remember him from the night before?"

"Yes. He's in Paris to spread the soda gospel. Why would Clarence Welch care about who killed the Desmarcheliers in 1944?"

Miranda shrugged. "Perhaps because any hiccup in French–American relations could damage his business prospects? That's all anyone is worried about these days."

Perhaps, Kat thought. *But perhaps not.*

Chapter Thirty-Eight

It was ten o'clock. It still wasn't raining yet, but Kat could feel the clouds above her getting even more swollen. She had only the flimsiest of straws to grasp at, but it was time to present them to the detectives. Maybe, just maybe, they would have the imagination—and decency—to at least pursue one of them.

At the prefecture, Kat asked for Galland. Faucher came out instead and shook her hand.

"Madame Kelly. I am sorry, but I cannot let you see your husband."

"I'm not here to see Charlie. I have new evidence to share with you and Detective Galland."

Faucher raised an eyebrow. "You have been investigating?"

"Just talking to people." Which was how one investigated, she thought. But she let that go.

"Very well, come in." Faucher led her back through the maze of desks to the same room she had sat in with Harold the week before.

As she took off her coat, she asked, "Has Toby Magnusson's brother been back?"

"Yes, and we were able to update him with some progress."

"Oh?"

"Madame Kelly." Galland stood in the doorway to the room. He didn't look pleased to see her. No faux friendliness this time.

Kat stood up, determined to be polite—at least at first. "Detectives, thank you for seeing me. As I mentioned to Detective Faucher, I've discovered a few things that might be interesting to you."

"Is that so? Please, do tell," Galland said, sarcasm in his voice. He closed the door, and he and Faucher sat across from Kat. Galland lit a cigarette, sat back, and looked at his watch. The message was clear: She was wasting his time.

Kat wasn't under any illusions that the detectives would listen to her, realize Charlie was innocent, and release him into her arms. But she hoped that they would be intrigued enough by what she would share that they would start tugging at the same threads she was trying to unravel. There was no denying that the police would likely get farther, faster than she could on her own.

She also remembered that Jeanette had said that Galland was a good detective, when he wanted to be. Maybe he would want to be this time, although his body language wasn't promising.

Kat started by telling them about Guy Rossi and Marché Gaspard, the probable locus of a black-market ring that Toby had likely been involved with. "And last night my cousin and I were attacked on the street. Philippe was beaten, and I was held at knifepoint. I am certain it was Rossi."

"You saw his face?" Galland asked.

Kat hesitated. Was she going to say she recognized his arm hair? "Yes."

"Where were you, and why didn't you report this attack to the police?" Faucher asked.

"I'm here telling you now."

"Did he hurt you?" Faucher asked. She saw Galland subtly roll his eyes at his colleague's concern.

She shook her head, impatient. "No, I'm fine. And that's not all."

She told them about Vaughn Harris's dishonorable discharge from the Army in 1944. "He had been soliciting underage French girls. Toby was in the same unit, so he must have known about it. What if Toby was blackmailing Vaughn and then Vaughn killed him and Marie-Hélène too?" She didn't quite believe this scenario; why would he kill Marie-Hélène? But she had to try everything in her arsenal. She felt like a court jester, desperate to find the funny dance or joke that would please the king, or in this case, inspire the king to leave the prefecture and actually investigate who had killed Toby Magnusson and Marie-Hélène Arnaud.

Galland shook his head dismissively. "Harris has been cleared. Anything else, Madame?" He looked at his watch again.

Kat was starting to get desperate. "Yes. I think someone set Charlie up to discover Marie-Hélène's body."

Finally, she saw a spark of interest on Galland's face. "Is that so? And who would do that?"

"Charlie is investigating two murders that happened here in Paris in 1944. Someone doesn't want him to find out the truth."

"What do you mean? What murders?" Faucher asked.

"Antoine and Gabrielle Desmarchelier. Ever since he started looking into this story, the American embassy has been pressuring him to let it go. They approached him, his editor, and even me."

"Why would the Americans care who killed the Desmarcheliers?" It was Faucher again.

Kat was more than happy to throw the U.S. embassy under the bus if it meant Charlie could come home. "Charlie got a tip that Americans were involved in the murders."

"Madame Kelly—" Galland tried to interrupt her.

But she continued, raising her voice and rushing out the next words before Galland could stop her. "And just this morning, I learned that it was Clarence Welch, an American businessman, who wants the story killed."

"Enough!" Galland said with a roar. He rose, his physical presence seeming to take up half the room. "Madame Kelly, let me explain something to you. Most of life is not a wild conspiracy theory. And most of the time murders are committed by the most obvious person. Your husband was found, by you I might add, with the dead body of a beautiful woman. I am sorry to say that the most obvious answer is that Monsieur Kelly was having an affair with Mademoiselle Arnaud, she broke things off, and he killed her. If you hadn't surprised him at her apartment, he would simply have left, and no one would have been the wiser."

Kat opened her mouth to protest, but Galland held up his hand and continued in a more measured tone. "So, despite spending your time playing girl detective, the only real piece of evidence you have uncovered is your husband's guilt. Bravo, Madame." He quietly applauded before walking to the door. Without looking back he said, "Faucher, show her out."

Kat stood up as well, fighting back her fury and desperation to say in a firm, but even tone, "You haven't arrested Charlie yet.

There must be a reason for that. You know you don't have anything on him."

"Rest assured, *madame*, it is imminent."

For a split second, Kat wanted to sink back into the chair and put her head in her hands in defeat. All she had in her quiver were long shots, and none of them had found their target.

She took her coat and hat and slowly followed Faucher to the building's entrance, fighting back tears. She was failing Charlie, and she couldn't think what to do next. She needed to pull herself together.

Faucher held open the door to the prefecture for Kat to exit. As she walked by him, he said in a low voice, "The river," and jutted his chin across the street.

Kat looked at him in surprise and then nodded. Faucher disappeared back into the prefecture.

She crossed the street to the *quai*, found the nearest staircase, and walked down. It felt ten degrees colder down here. The wind whipped by her and agitated the murky gray-green water. She wrapped her scarf more tightly around her neck and stood against a wall to avoid the brunt of it. She would be able to see Faucher when, if, he walked down the stairs.

As tempting as it was to just crawl into bed, curl into a ball, and hope that Granderson's influence would win out in the end, she couldn't give up. She knew that if *she* was in police custody, Charlie would beat down the doors of the chief of police, the Paris mayor, and the Pope if he happened to be in town.

What routes hadn't she exhausted at this point? The image of George Church came into her head. Yes, that would be her next stop, and she would go in person. Maybe he could help.

Then she saw Faucher walking down the steps to the riverbank. He looked around for a moment before spotting her against the wall.

To her surprise, the first thing she blurted out when he walked toward her was, "Charlie did not kill Marie-Hélène. And I'm not just being naive."

"Come," He started toward the Pont Neuf.

She caught up with him. "Do you believe me?"

He didn't answer right away. "I have been in the room while Galland questions your husband. We have asked him in every way about Mademoiselle Arnaud."

"And?"

"And nothing. There seems to be no attachment, no reaction."

"So you believe him."

"Some people are very good liars."

Kat almost smiled. Charlie was a terrible liar. It was one of the things she liked best about him.

Faucher continued, "But, yes, I believe him."

Kat felt a rush of relief. At least one of the detectives was on their side. "Why doesn't Galland?"

"That is a good question."

"Detective, why are you here? Talking to me?"

He stopped and gazed toward the water. She faced him as he spoke. "I can offer you no assurances about your husband. Detective Galland is senior to me, far senior. I have only been a detective for a few years and have virtually no influence over him, as you have seen. And he seems convinced that your husband is guilty. I do believe he will charge him tomorrow."

Kat's heart sank. "Is that what you wanted to tell me?"

"I wanted you to know how dire the situation was. But I also wanted to share that we discovered something important in the case of Toby Magnusson."

"Tell me."

"Before the death of Mademoiselle Arnaud, we went back to L'École and questioned the staff again. The first time, the housekeeper, a Pole, barely spoke, and we assumed she knew nothing. But this time, she admitted that she had seen Monsieur Magnusson the morning of his death . . . with a woman."

The surprise took her breath away. "A woman!" She thought back to that day she had translated for Harold at the prefecture. After Toby's brother had left the room, Galland said he suspected the killer was a woman, committing a *crime passionnel.* In the days since, she had found herself so mistrustful of the detective that she had ignored that initial observation.

"Yes, outside of the school. The woman followed him in."

"But the housekeeper didn't recognize her?"

He shook his head.

She thought for a moment. "Did you ever get any results from the fingerprint analysis?"

"*Non*; there were too many sets on the knife and around the room for them to be of use." He inclined his head towards her. "Just as you had suggested there would be in our first interview." She appreciated his remembering that.

"So how are you going to figure out who it was?"

"At the moment, we are not. Galland claims that he doesn't believe the housekeeper or thinks she was mistaken. He seems sure that the crimes were connected."

Now Kat understood. "And that Charlie was responsible for both."

Faucher nodded.

"But doesn't this bolster Galland's original theory that Marie-Hélène killed Toby?" Kat still didn't believe that was how it happened, but it seemed like the conclusion Galland would immediately jump to.

Faucher shrugged. "This explanation is more convenient."

"It's so ridiculous," she said with disgust in her voice.

He smoothed his mustache with his fingers. "I have to go back."

"Why are you telling me this?"

"I am not at liberty to look into this more, but you seem . . . resourceful."

She felt a flicker of pride. "*Merci*, detective."

He only nodded, turned and began walking back towards the prefecture. Then he stopped and faced her. "Madame Kelly?"

"*Oui*?"

"Be careful."

Chapter Thirty-Nine

Kat decided to push off talking to George Church. She couldn't be sure that the deputy ambassador would even see her. And if she could get a solid lead on who had killed Toby, that would surely lead to who killed Marie-Hélène, wouldn't it? She rehearsed how she would describe Mireille Rossi to the housekeeper at L'École de la Grande Cuisine. Faucher said the housekeeper was a Pole. Kat thought the woman's name was Eva, but she couldn't quite remember.

At the school, Madame Poitrine corrected her. "*Elle s'appelle* Ida, Ida Klaczko. She's likely in the pantry now. Shall I fetch her?"

Ida, not Eva. "No, no, *merci*. I'll go down myself, if that's alright?" Kat's own class would still be in session for another hour. She didn't want to see any of her classmates today to explain why she'd barely been in class this week. But this conversation with Ida Klaczko should only take a few minutes.

"*Allez-y.*" The concierge gestured to the stairs.

When she pushed open the door to the pantry, Kat saw the woman wiping down shelves in one of the refrigerators with a rag.

"*Bonjour, mademoiselle.*"

Klaczko started slightly and turned. She was young, with creamy skin and dark hair. "I'm sorry to startle you. My name is Kat Kelly. Kasia, actually. My grandparents are Polish."

Klaczko closed the refrigerator and stood to face Kat.

"Where are you from?" Kat asked with a smile.

"Cracow, but I have lived in France for ten years." The woman had a soft Polish accent but spoke good French.

From her last name, Kat thought that Klaczko was probably Jewish. Like many Eastern European Jews in the years when Hitler had been unleashing his terrible campaign, her family had probably migrated to France thinking it would be safer. But they had been wrong. Once the Germans occupied France, thousands of foreign-born Jews were deported to concentration camps, including children. All of this had happened with the full knowledge, cooperation, and sometimes even the leadership of the wartime French government and police.

Kat immediately thought of a half-dozen questions to ask the housekeeper, about her background, her family, and how she had survived during the Occupation, but she forced herself to stick to the subject at hand.

"I'm sorry to bother you while you're working. But I was friends with the man who was killed here last week, and I wanted to ask you a few questions."

Klaczko nodded slowly. "Fine." She placed her rag on the large table in front of the refrigerators.

Kat looked around and saw a few stools pushed against the wall. She picked up two and carried them over to the table. She sat down, but the housekeeper did not.

"I have told the police everything I know."

"I know, and thank you for speaking with me about it again. I don't know about you, but I find that sometimes the police don't always know the right questions to ask." Kat had a hunch that this young woman was no fan of the police. Klaczko nodded slightly and sat down.

"Detective Faucher said that you saw Toby Magnusson with someone the morning he died, outside the building. Is that right?"

"*Oui*. I was across the street coming to work when I saw him approach the entrance. There was a woman standing at the door. I didn't recognize her or think anything of it."

"Did it seem like she was waiting for him?"

"That's what it seemed like. As soon as he arrived, they began speaking."

"Can you describe what she looked like?"

"At first I couldn't see her clearly because she had a scarf over her head."

"But then?"

"Then when I crossed the street, I saw her face. I don't know how to describe it, though. There was nothing special about it."

"Could you tell if she was older or younger?"

"Perhaps in her late thirties."

Mireille Rossi was likely only thirty-five years old, possibly even a bit younger, but that was close. "Could you see any of her hair under her scarf?" Mireille Rossi's hair was jet black. There would be no mistaking that.

Klaczko thought for a moment. "Yes, a bit in front. Please, I walked by her very quickly, but I think it was not quite blonde and not quite brown, like *miel*."

The color of honey. Rossi's hair was certainly not that. Could she have been wearing a wig to disguise herself? But why wear a scarf over a wig?

Klaczko continued. "And she followed him into the building."

Kat considered what other details she could ask about. "Did he hold the door for her?"

The housekeeper looked toward the ceiling and squinted like she was trying to remember. "No. She went in after him."

Kat had never seen Toby not open a door for a woman.

"Did you follow her in?"

"*Non*. I smoked a cigarette first. Madame Poitrine does not like me to take breaks during the workday."

"Ida—may I call you Ida?" The housekeeper nodded her assent. "And please call me Kasia or Kat. Did you ever see Toby's girlfriend? Her name was Marie-Hélène. Sometimes she waited for him after our class finished around midday." Marie-Hélène also had dark hair, and Kat didn't believe that Marie-Hélène had killed Toby, but she felt she needed to cover this base. What if her death was revenge for Toby's? There were still so many possibilities that Kat's head swam.

"*Non*, not that I can recall. I'm sorry."

"*D'accord, pas de probleme*. Ida, when they were outside, did you happen to hear anything that either of them said?"

"I heard a little, but I didn't understand. He spoke English and she mostly did too."

"Mostly?"

"I can't say for sure, but it seems like she spoke bad English. Sometimes she said a phrase in French, but I can't remember what." Although Kat had spoken with her mostly in French when they were alone together, she knew from their group dinner that Marie-Hélène spoke excellent English.

"Ida, when the police spoke to you the first time, did you tell them that you saw Toby with a woman that morning?"

Ida looked down and shook her head.

"Why not?"

"I told them I didn't see anything so they would leave me alone."

"Why did you change your mind?"

"Madame Poitrine said there was nothing to be afraid of. That nothing I would say would make me lose my job. She is very kind, except for not allowing smoking breaks."

Kat smiled. "Is there anything else you remember about that morning, Ida?"

Ida shook her head.

"Even if it's just an impression."

Ida spoke slowly. "He seemed angry, like he didn't want to talk to her and was ignoring her. She was following him, trying to get him to pay attention."

"Interesting." Kat supposed there was no way, short of laying hands on the woman, that Toby could have kept her from following him into the building. "Thank you so much, Ida. How long have you been working at L'École?"

"A year."

Kat nodded, struggling to keep her instinct to ask more questions in check. She failed. "How old were you when you moved to Paris?"

"Fourteen."

"And did you go to school here?"

"For a year, but then no. I tried to do my studies on my own. And then after the war I went to work."

"What about now? Is there any opportunity for you to finish high school? Would you like to go to university?"

Ida looked wistful. "University is a dream. I don't know if I would have to finish high school first. I am so old now."

"Thank you again, Ida. I'm glad we met." Kat slid off her stool; Ida did the same. Kat reached out to shake hands.

Ida gave her a shy smile. "*Merci, madame.*"

"Please, call me Kat."

"*D'accord,* Kat." Kat walked to the doorway, about to head out to the hall.

"Oh, Ida, one last thing. Do you think you would recognize the woman if you saw her again?"

Ida hesitated for only a split second. "*Oui.*"

Chapter Forty

As Kat climbed the steps to the Guillaume publishing office, she hoped that Marie-Hélène's uncle would be there. She realized she didn't even know when Marie-Hélène's funeral was. It might even be today.

She also wasn't quite sure why she was here. Based on her conversation with Ida, she was now convinced that a woman had killed Toby. And as much as she didn't want to believe it, she couldn't rule out Marie-Hélène. Her hair wasn't the color of honey, but Ida hadn't seemed entirely sure about that anyway.

And Kat still had the nagging question about how Marie-Hélène had planned to pay for her escape from France. Because that was how Kat thought of it now. An escape. It was so hasty and so soon after Toby's death. It just felt . . . off.

Whether or not it was the right one, this was the thread Kat was tugging.

Kat knocked on the door and heard a flat voice, "*Oui, entrez.*"

Kat opened the door to see Etienne Arnaud behind what had been Marie-Hélène's desk. If the desk had been covered in papers before, it was now positively overflowing. And if Arnaud had looked harried before, he now looked positively at loose ends. His hair was disheveled, and there were large pouches under his bespectacled eyes.

"Madame Kelly, *bonjour*." He approached Kat to shake hands.

"Hello, Monsieur Arnaud. I wanted to come by to express my condolences. I'm sure that you and your wife are devastated."

"We are. Please, have a seat." He gestured to the sofa. "Would you like a coffee? It isn't like before, but it still does the job."

"*Oui, merci*." A coffee was exactly what she needed right about now.

Monsieur Arnaud disappeared into the adjoining room, saying he would be back momentarily. Kat assumed there was a kitchenette there or at least a hot plate, and soon she heard espresso being poured into a cup. "Sugar?" he called.

"Yes, please."

Marie-Hélène's uncle returned carrying two small cups and handed one to Kat. He dragged a chair across from the sofa and sat down opposite her.

"How are you and Madame Arnaud doing?"

He ran his hands through his hair and shook his head. "It's just so hard to believe. Marie-Hélène was like a daughter to us ever since her parents died soon after she finished school. First to hear that she was leaving France. That was shocking enough. But now this? Who could have wanted to hurt her like that?" He looked at Kat intently as he asked the question, as if he truly expected an answer.

"I don't know," Kat said. Suddenly she realized that he might know that Charlie was in custody, that the detectives suspected her own husband of killing his niece. A lump of anxiety formed in her throat. "Have you spoken to the police?"

"Barely. They informed us of her death and asked a few cursory questions, but that was Saturday. I asked if they had any suspects, and they said they were looking closely at someone but didn't say who. I've left messages at the prefecture since then, but they haven't responded to me. I will go there tomorrow."

Kat hoped her relief didn't show on her face. She still wanted to ask him about Marie-Hélène's travel, but another question came to her first. "Do you think it's possible that Nico, Marie-Hélène's husband, killed her?"

"Ah, you know about Nico. Not many of her new friends do, I don't think."

Kat nodded. "I met him after Toby died."

Arnaud blew a little air out of his lips. "Who can say? He certainly was no great husband to Marie-Hélène, leaving her for so many years. But even though he's a career soldier, he never seemed like the type to me." He shook his head. "I would be very surprised." Kat nodded, glad that he confirmed her impressions about Nico.

"They were married in 1942?"

"Yes, when she came back to Paris during the Occupation, so late 1942."

"And you were here that whole time?"

"Yes. She left the city when the Nazis showed up in 1940, but she came back after things got even worse back home."

"Do you know a couple named Guy and Mireille Rossi?"

Arnaud thought for a moment and then shook his head. "No, I don't think so. Who are they?"

"They own a small grocery store near Les Halles and were acquaintances of Toby's."

"I don't know those names. Why are you asking me so many questions?" He didn't say this unkindly or with suspicion, more like curiosity.

"I'm a journalist by training, and it's in my nature, I'm afraid. And, well, I can't stop thinking about her and Toby's deaths. The police . . ." She trailed off.

He finished the sentence for her. "The police seem incompetent."

She gave a brief, sad smile. "Yes, they do." She leaned forward and clasped her hands on her knees. "Now, Monsieur Arnaud, this is what I really wanted to ask you about. I know that you were surprised that Marie-Hélène was leaving Paris."

"Not just Paris, but France. Europe! I understand why she didn't want to go home again. Too many bad memories. But, why not Lyon or Nice? Or even London. She spoke English well, and I could have helped her find a job in publishing."

"Yes, and she didn't have a job lined up yet in America. It was all so sudden. Do you know how she expected to support herself in California?"

Arnaud looked surprised. "*Mais, non* . . . I thought perhaps her husband was giving her money."

Kat shook her head. "I don't think so. As far as you know, she didn't have a lot saved?"

"I can't say for sure, of course, but unfortunately I couldn't pay her so much here." Kat had suspected as much. "We're a small firm, and work was nonexistent during the war, of course.

We're getting back on our feet, but no one goes into publishing for fame and fortune. Especially not fortune," he said with a flash of a grin. Kat could tell that it was a well-practiced joke. His face suddenly turned serious again. "What are you thinking?"

"I don't know. It just feels like a missing piece of the puzzle." Kat's mind raced. She wondered again if Marie-Hélène had somehow gotten access to Toby's money. She would need to ask Harold about that. She thought about what to ask Arnaud next.

"You said that Marie-Hélène left Paris when the Germans invaded, but that things got worse at home."

He shook his head sadly. "In 1940, she went back to live with her brother in their family home in the Free Zone, which of course wasn't really free." Kat understood this. The French-led Vichy regime had governed that half of France, but under the watchful eye of the Germans.

"It seemed like a quarter of the population was trying to outdo the Germans in repression and cruelty, to prove that they were the good children. Another quarter was fighting back in small and large ways. And the final half was just keeping their heads down and trying to survive."

"Which was Marie-Hélène?" Kat knew it was a sensitive question.

"She was never political. I think she was keeping her head down. But her brother Albert was different."

"How so?"

"He wasn't a communist, but definitely more left. He was a schoolteacher, and even as a boy, he had a soft heart. He took care of people, of animals, of plants. We always said he was on the side of life." Kat noticed that Arnaud was speaking of his nephew in the past tense.

"What happened?"

"Marie-Hélène never told me this story, but she did tell my wife." He hesitated, then looked squarely at Kat. "If she were still alive, I wouldn't tell you this. She was petrified of people knowing."

"I understand."

"In the summer of 1942, it was becoming increasingly dangerous for Jews in France. There was a big round-up in Paris in July, and even in the Free Zone it seemed inevitable. In August, it was summer vacation, but Albert had kept in contact with his students. Two were Jews who had come to France from Belgium in 1939. It was more dangerous for foreign Jews, *comprenez*?"

Kat nodded. She thought of Ida Klaczko and her family.

"It was a terrible time, and Albert agreed to hide his students in their cellar."

"Without their parents?"

"It was only the children," he confirmed. Kat imagined the children's mother sensing the imminent danger and begging the teacher's help. It made her heart hurt.

Arnaud continued. "Marie-Hélène was not happy about it, I don't think. She was more practical, less idealistic, more afraid. But Albert insisted, and the children lived in their cellar for three weeks." Arnaud took a handkerchief out of his pocket, removed his glasses, and polished the lenses. Kat waited without speaking.

"And then they were betrayed," he said, finally returning the glasses to his face.

Kat had known it was coming, but the ache in her chest grew stronger.

"The French police—not the Germans—the French police," he said the last two words like he couldn't believe it, "got a tip. They came and brought Albert and Marie-Hélène in for questioning. Albert had built a clever hiding place in the cellar, so they didn't find the children."

Kat thought about how frightened those children must have been. How frightened Albert and Marie-Hélène must have been.

"The police separated my niece and nephew. They told Marie-Hélène that if she admitted what they'd done and told them where the children were, the children would only be deported to a Jewish homeland the Nazis were establishing in Eastern Europe. Many people believed that lie or at least pretended to. They told her that the children wouldn't be harmed and that she and Albert would be free to go with only a warning." Arnaud stood up and walked to the window, where he looked out at the street. He was silent a long time.

"She told them," Kat guessed.

Arnaud nodded, his back to Kat. "And, of course they had lied. They deported the children and Albert. They violated my niece and cut her face with a knife." He traced his jawline with his finger, and Kat remembered the fine scar she had seen on Marie-Hélène's face.

It was almost worse than she had imagined. "What happened to Albert?"

He turned back to Kat. "After the war we went every day to the Lutetia, where French people from the camps returned to. His name was never on a list of the dead, but he never arrived."

"And the children?"

Arnaud opened his hands as if to say, "Who knows?" He sat down again. "After that Marie-Hélène came back to Paris. She was broken and brittle. But she met Nico, and that seemed to help. For a while at least."

"Did you spend much time with Toby?"

"*Non*, not much. We met him two or three times. He was very tender with Marie-Hélène, and that made us glad."

Kat stood up. "*Merci*, Monsieur Arnaud. I won't take any more of your time. Thank you." She put out her hand to shake his; he clasped it with a small bow.

"Remember, if you are looking for a job after L'École, I have one waiting for you."

He was the second person who had offered her a job that day, after Claudine at Café du Vent. Kat smiled. "You're very kind. And I'm sorry I didn't ask this before, but has there already been a funeral for Marie-Hélène?"

"Yesterday. We spent a couple of days deciding if she should be buried here or with her parents in Moulins. But we decided on Paris since she had such bad memories of her hometown."

Kat's blood began to buzz. "Moulins?"

"*Oui*, that's where our family is from. It's a town about three hundred kilometers south."

"Monsieur Arnaud, did Marie-Hélène ever find out who betrayed her and Albert?"

"Yes. But I do not know his name. All I know is that it was a chef."

Chapter Forty-One

Kat sat at a window table at Café du Vent with Ida Klazcko. Kat's back was to the stairs, but it was more important that Ida have an unobstructed view of the people walking up from the kitchen. Kat looked for Philippe and Marcel, who had come into the café just after her and Ida. They were seated closer to the bar.

The women ordered coffees from Jules and then sat in silence. Nerves shot through Kat's body like bolt after bolt of lightning. What if she was wrong? In her own desperation to keep her family safe, she might be making a grave error that publicly affected someone's life. But Ida would be here to corroborate, she reminded herself, shaking away the doubts.

When Kat had left Etienne Arnaud just a couple of hours before, the rain had pounded her umbrella as she walked to the metro. But she had barely noticed. Her mind catapulted back to the night she and Charlie had gone out with Toby and Marie-Hélène. How Marie-Hélène had left so abruptly. Before that, they had been enjoying themselves. Marie-Hélène seemed to have thawed, charmed by Charlie, Kat thought. Claudine had brought the desserts, and then Jacques had visited the table.

But Marie-Hélène had excused herself before Claudine led the chef over to meet them. She had gone to the toilets downstairs, where the kitchen was. She might have easily passed Jacques on the stairs as she was returning to her seat. That was when she had rushed out of the café.

After paying her metro fare, Kat had realized she didn't know where she was going. She sat on a bench on the platform and let a train pass her by. Back to the police? But what evidence did she have? None. Only hearsay and what Galland would call coincidence: Marie-Hélène, Jacques, and Annette all being from Moulins, Marie-Hélène betrayed by a chef, Marie-Hélène becoming upset when she—maybe—saw Jacques at Café du Vent.

Kat could easily fill in the gaps of the story, though. Marie-Hélène thought she had left her rape, her betrayal, and the loss of her brother behind in Moulins. Then in Paris, she came face to face with the man who had betrayed her to the police.

Marie-Hélène had told her that, before he died, she and Toby were beginning to share the difficult parts of their past. If she had told him about Jacques and how he had informed on her, how that had led to her rape, Kat was certain that Toby would have been enraged. Had he stormed over to Café du Vent and threatened the Roches with exposure?

"He broke my trust, and it was unforgivable." That is what Marie-Hélène had told Kat about Toby. And she had broken up with him.

If Toby had confronted Jacques and Annette, perhaps Marie-Hélène was upset about it. She had kept the story to herself for so long. And just when she shared it with someone she thought she could trust, he flew off the handle and threatened to make it public, the last thing Marie-Hélène wanted. Kat admitted to herself that this was all conjecture. But she didn't believe it was a coincidence.

Kat began pacing on the platform as a train squeaked to a stop on the opposite side. This would explain Toby's murder, but did it explain Marie-Hélène's? Despite having hidden the crime for years, was she planning to reveal what Jacques Roche had done? Perhaps it was her who had called Charlie that morning. Maybe she had decided that since she was leaving Paris, she was ready to unburden herself to a journalist.

While she didn't know all of the answers, Kat felt sure she finally knew who had killed Toby. When the next train arrived, she got on and rode it to L'École.

Now, at Café du Vent with Ida, she felt like she couldn't wait a second longer. As Jules passed by their table she said, "*Excusez-moi*. Is Annette downstairs?"

"*Oui.*"

Kat forced a smile onto her face. "I'm not sure if you heard, but I'm writing a story about her, and I realized I have a couple more questions. Would you mind asking if she could come upstairs when she has a moment?"

"*Bien sur.*" He bowed slightly and went downstairs.

Kat looked around at the cafe. Aside from Philippe and Marcel, there were several other tables occupied. This would be public indeed. "Okay, Ida, if you recognize her when she comes over to our table, just tap my foot with yours like we discussed. *D'accord*?"

Ida peered under the table, checking where Kat's feet were. "*D'accord.*"

Kat heard the click of low heels walking toward their table. "*Bonjour*, Kat." Annette said warmly. She turned to Ida.

Kat waited, looking at Ida. The young woman gazed at Annette with a puzzled look on her face, and Kat felt nothing on her feet, just as she had expected. Her heart broke a little. Because if it wasn't Annette . . .

"This is my friend Mademoiselle Ida Klaczko. Ida, this is Madame Annette Roche. She makes the wonderful desserts here."

"*Bonjour, mademoiselle.* Kat, my brother-in-law said that you had more questions for me."

Suddenly Kat felt a stab of pain in her big toe. It took her a moment to realize that Ida had stomped on it. Her eyes were wide and set on something, or someone, behind Kat.

"*Bonjour*, Kat. *Ca va*?" It was Claudine. Kat looked at Ida for confirmation, and the housekeeper nodded.

Kat stood up and saw Philippe and Marcel stand up as well. After going to L'École and convincing Ida to come with her to hopefully identify the woman she had seen with Toby the morning of his murder, they had swung by Philippe's. Despite his bruises from the night before, he was in the club, ordering Vivienne around from a chair.

"Please take him away. My sympathy ran out an hour ago," Vivienne had said, rolling her eyes at Kat.

Kat had obliged, but only after she had explained the situation to Philippe and asked him to call Marcel. She knew she needed a member of the police there to arrest the woman Ida had seen. She also knew that there was a chance it was Annette. But her gut told her it was Claudine.

"Claudine, this is Ida. She's the housekeeper at L'École."

What little color Claudine had in her cheeks drained from her face.

"What's going on?" Annette asked. "Claudine?"

Kat saw that Marcel and Philippe had moved closer to their table. The restaurant was so quiet Kat could hear a spoon stirring a cup of coffee. The other patrons had stopped eating and talking and stared at the scene unfolding in front of them.

"Claudine?" Annette looked at her sister-in-law. Kat thought she could read worry and confusion on the pastry chef's face. Claudine was frozen. When she didn't respond to her sister-in-law, Annette looked at Kat. "What's going on?"

"Annette, did you know what she was going to do?"

Kat's question seemed to break the spell Claudine had been under, and she answered for her sister-in-law. "No, of course she didn't know. I didn't know myself what I was going to do. I was just going to talk to him."

"Claudine, stop!" It was Jules's voice. Kat hadn't realized he was there. Marcel turned to face Jules and held out his arms to prevent him from approaching his wife.

"No, it's over now, Jules. I am not a very good criminal," Claudine said with a sad little laugh. And Kat saw that it was true. She had thought that Claudine's fatigue and dishabille had come from the pressure she was under at the café. But, actually, she was falling apart under the weight of her guilt.

"Oh, Claudine. What did you do?" Annette asked. "We would have figured it out."

"How? That man threatened to expose Jacques, and you, and that would have ruined everything. After ten long, hard years when this café barely earned a *sous*—so much debt!—we were finally, finally going to be secure, secure enough to take care of Mélisse and pay for her school. And then that man was going to ruin everything."

Kat needed to know the details. And she needed to hear Claudine say that she had killed Toby. "That night when the four of us came in, Marie-Hélène recognized Jacques." It wasn't a question, but Claudine nodded her head yes.

Kat continued, hoping what she was saying was true. "Then a couple of days later Toby came in, angry."

Claudine said nothing.

"And he threatened you." Kat continued, willing Claudine to pick up the story herself. She had a feeling that Claudine wanted to confess. The secret was eating away at her.

Finally, Claudine nodded. "*Oui*. He threatened to tell the world that the new chefs at Café du Vent were collaborators and informers if they didn't surrender themselves to the police."

Annette looked at Kat, stone-faced. "So naive, the American. So eager for justice." She said it with a sneer in her voice. "What would the police do at this point?"

Kat ignored this and said to Claudine, "So you waited for him at L'École."

"*Oui*. Just to talk to him, to beg him, to make him see reason." Her face hardened. "But he was so arrogant, so haughty. He wouldn't listen."

"You followed him in."

A tear slipped from Claudine's eye. "I told him about Mélisse. I still thought I could talk him out of it."

"But when you saw that you couldn't . . ."

"I tried so hard!" The tears came faster now. She wiped her nose with the back of her hand. "But my pleas meant nothing to him. I was nothing to him, like an annoying insect. I told him that of course what Annette and Jacques had done was reprehensible"—she glanced sideways at Annette—"but it was so long ago. What good could come of dredging up the past?"

"And what did he say?"

"He said that Marie-Hélène would never be able to escape the past; at least this way someone would be punished." Claudine shuddered. "He looked so angry. It was like he needed to save her from her fate, even years after it happened. And I knew he wouldn't let it go. So I picked up a knife from the table. At first just to scare him. And he laughed at me. He laughed."

"Arrogant fool," Annette said under her breath.

"What did you do then, Claudine?" Kat asked.

Claudine's eyes gazed at something far away, like she was replaying the terrible scene in her mind. "I stabbed him," she said simply. "It was like I didn't have any control over my body. I was just trying to protect my family. Do you understand?"

Kat didn't reply but asked her own question, "What about the towel?"

"I couldn't believe what I had done. I almost called for help. Maybe he could be saved! But then I saw it was too late. I couldn't stand to leave him exposed like that, so I covered his face." She looked at Kat now, with a beseeching expression on her face. "Please . . . you have to understand. I never meant to hurt him."

Marcel stepped forward to address Claudine. "Madame, *je suis* Detective Arsenault. I have a question for you. How did you leave the building with no one seeing you?"

Claudine was silent. She seemed to be in another trance. So Kat answered. "Jules went to culinary school there, and when you visited, he had shown you where the back exit was."

Jules nodded, probably without realizing it. The other patrons watched the scene in rapt silence.

"Claudine," Kat said, "how did you know what had happened in Moulins?"

At that moment, the door to the café opened and a man stepped gingerly inside, clearly confused at the spectacle in front of him. Philippe walked over, whispered to the man, held the door for him to exit, and flipped the sign to *Fermé*.

"That day he came in here, the day before . . . before he died, I heard him talking to Jacques. Yelling at both of them. I asked Annette about it afterward, and she told me."

"You told her everything?" Kat asked Annette.

"*Oui*. I am not ashamed. You don't know what it was like, trying to survive, feed your family, not be targeted. Jacques would do it again, would tell the police where the Jews were hiding. And if he wouldn't, I would. We were obeying the law."

"There is a difference between keeping your head down and denouncing your neighbors. You could have said nothing and saved three people's lives, not to mention kept Marie-Hélène from being raped."

"You don't understand," Annette shot back.

"You're right, I don't." And in this case, Kat felt that no matter how many questions she asked, she never would.

"And what about Marie-Hélène?" Kat held her breath.

"What about her?" Claudine asked. "I was sorry, of course, for what happened during the war. But I couldn't change that. And what her boyfriend was doing now was going to destroy us."

"Did you kill her to keep her from exposing you after Toby's death?" As she asked the question, Kat realized that Marie-Hélène must have suspected all along who had killed Toby, or at least why he had been killed. Not only had she lost her love, she had probably felt responsible for his death. Just when she started giving up her secrets.

Confusion clouded Claudine's face. "She is dead?" She looked from Kat to Marcel. Neither responded. "*Mais, non*! I didn't know!" Claudine looked terrified now. "I did not kill her. Why would I? She kept quiet all of these years, yes?" she asked Annette.

"She never breathed a word of it."

Claudine looked at Kat, with a pleading expression on her face. "You must believe me."

Kat ignored her. "Annette, you weren't going to try to stop Toby from exposing you?"

Annette shrugged. "I knew it wouldn't last here. Everyone became so sanctimonious in Moulins after the war, like they hadn't also supported the Vichy government or informed on their neighbors." She said it like it was the most normal thing, and perhaps it had been. "People stopped coming to our café, there were whispers about prosecution, that we were collaborators. I became afraid to walk down the street alone. Suddenly everyone was a *résistant*. So we went to Nice, but we had no family, no roots. Paris should have been the perfect solution. We were with family, and no one knew us here. But I knew we were cursed."

You cursed yourselves, Kat thought.

Marcel spoke. "After this discussion, this seems irrelevant, but *mademoiselle*," he nodded at Ida. "Is Madame Claudine Roche the woman you saw with Toby Magnusson at L'École de la Grande Cuisine the morning that Monsieur Magnusson was murdered?"

Ida nodded and said with quiet authority, "*Oui*."

"Madame? Do you have anything else to say?"

Another tear slid down Claudine's cheek, and she looked at Jules. "I'm sorry. Tell Mélisse that I'm sorry."

Jules looked shell-shocked but reached for his wife.

"*Monsieur*, your wife must come with me." Marcel grasped one of Claudine's arms and walked her outside.

Kat was left in the restaurant with Annette, Jules, Ida, and Philippe. It was like the customers at the tables had been frozen, watching the tableau. Now they melted into lively chatter. Several stood up, mid-meal. Kat saw a man place a few coins on the table, disgust in his eyes. At that moment, Jacques appeared at the top of the stairs and looked around, wiping his hands on his apron. "No orders?"

"Let's go," Kat said to Ida and Philippe.

Chapter Forty-Two

Finally, one of the threads was completely untangled. Kat turned the solution of Toby's murder over in her head. She couldn't help but feel for Claudine, so desperate to protect her family and her business. Then she thought about what Marie-Hélène had experienced in Moulins during the war, the deportation and likely murder of her brother and those two children. Claudine hadn't only been protecting her family but also her brother and sister-in-law who had knowingly sent people to their deaths.

Kat knew she should push Toby's murder and what had preceded it out of her mind now. She didn't have time to think about it. It didn't get her any closer to either proving that someone else had killed Marie-Hélène or convincing the police that Charlie was being set up because of his story about the Desmarcheliers. Those were the two strands she needed to work out now.

But she couldn't help but revel in the satisfaction of solving the case and solving it before the police. She allowed herself to enjoy the feeling of triumph and, yes, pride for a moment. But then she moved on. She had to refocus.

She believed Claudine when she said that she hadn't murdered Marie-Hélène. Her reaction when Kat had told her the woman was dead was too genuine. But it was still possible that Toby's death had somehow precipitated Marie-Hélène's. The Rossis were the obvious answer, but she couldn't just barge into Marché Gaspard and accuse them. She needed to find another connection—and fast. It was five o'clock. She had until ten o'clock the following morning, assuming that Galland intended to wait until the last possible moment to charge Charlie, in the hopes that he or Granderson would cave to the pressure.

"Philippe, can I come make a few phone calls?" Ida had left them as soon as they'd exited the restaurant. Kat thanked her profusely and assured her that she'd let Madame Poitrine know how helpful she had been. Philippe had walked silently alongside her as she was lost in thought.

"You don't have to ask."

Kat looped her arm through his and rested her head briefly on his shoulder as they walked. The excitement she had felt just moments ago had already dissolved. She thought about everything that had happened over the past week, Toby's death, Marie-Hélène's death, Charlie's detainment, the attack on Philippe just the night before. As hard as she tried, she felt like she was failing her husband.

"It's going to be okay, Kit Kat. I promise we'll figure this out."

She gave a faint smile at her childhood nickname.

With a glass of red wine by her side, Kat began working the phone at Club Margaux. Her first call was to the *Tribune*, where she began by asking Florence for three phone numbers. Then she asked to be transferred to Tom Granderson.

"You got it. Just have him transfer you back to me when you're done and I'll have those numbers for you."

"Thank you, Florence." While she waited for Granderson to come on the line, she considered setting the paper on the trail of the Rossis and their likely black-market dealings. But she quickly realized that the *Tribune* would never discover anything fast enough to help Charlie.

"Kat."

"Hi Tom. Do you have any updates?"

"I'm sorry to say that I don't, Kat. That Galland fellow is the most stubborn detective I've ever spoken to, and Church said he'd look into it, but I haven't heard a peep back. But I do have a damn good lawyer lined up for Charlie if he gets charged tomorrow."

Even if Charlie was later found innocent, being charged and tried could keep him in prison for months. And, if the fix was in, there was no guarantee that he'd be found innocent, no matter where the evidence pointed. Punishment for murder in France could be the guillotine. Kat closed her eyes, tamping down her frustration and panic. "Promise me you won't give up, Tom."

"Not on your life. I've got more calls to make."

He transferred her back to Florence, who gave Kat the three phone numbers she had asked for.

The first number Kat used was for George Church's office. His secretary put Kat on hold while she checked if the deputy ambassador was available. Kat was prepared to argue if the secretary came back and said Church couldn't speak with her. But she didn't have to.

"Mrs. Kelly, this is George Church. How are you?"

"Deputy ambassador, thank you for speaking with me. I'm not well. I know you've heard that Charlie is in police custody."

"Yes, of course. I'm keeping close tabs on the situation."

"And?"

"And, well, unfortunately that's all I can do right now. The police have every right to keep Kelly in custody for forty-eight hours before they charge him. I spoke with Detective Galland, and he assured me that your husband is being treated well."

"Did he give you any indication that they were going to charge Charlie?"

Church hesitated for a moment. "No, but that probably isn't information they would share with me."

Kat couldn't understand why Church wasn't outraged. Why was he so calm? "But surely you could pressure them to release him now! Charlie is innocent!"

"Mrs. Kelly, I know this is upsetting, and I'm very sorry that you and Charlie are having to go through it. But let me be frank. This is a very sticky situation for us. The police claim to be quite certain that your husband killed this woman, Mademoiselle Arnaud. Relations between our countries are at an exceedingly delicate spot. For the embassy to bluster in making demands would likely have the opposite effect you're seeking."

Kat closed her eyes. He could be right, but doing nothing felt like too dangerous an option. She decided she needed to level with him. "Mr. Church, I'm not sure how much Tom Granderson told you. But we believe Charlie is being set up because of a story he's investigating about the murders of a French couple in 1944, Antoine and Gabrielle Desmarchelier."

"Yes, I'd heard that's a theory."

"The pressure would be coming from the American side, since the lead Charlie was following suggests that Americans were responsible for the murders."

Church snapped, "Who told him that?"

Kat was taken aback. It had been Smithson, but she wasn't about to reveal Charlie's source. Surely he would realize that. "I don't know," she lied.

His voice was calmer. "Mrs. Kelly, this is a serious accusation. Let me look into it on my end and see if there's anything I can do to verify it."

She breathed a sigh of relief. "Thank you. And, Mr. Church . . . ," she closed her eyes. Should she give him the name?

"Yes?"

"You might want to speak with Clarence Welch."

"What does Welch have to do with this?"

"Apparently he was adamant that the story be killed."

Church was silent for a moment. "I see. Thank you for this information. Where can I reach you?"

She gave him the number at Club Margaux, thanked him, and hung up. She couldn't be sure that she could trust him, but she felt like she had to take the chance. He was the most powerful person she had access to, the one most likely to be able to actually help.

Kat drummed her fingers on the bar and thought about the other two phone numbers she had. She picked up the phone again and put it down. She felt like a chicken with its head cut off, running this way, then that, talking to one person and then chasing a lead in the complete opposite direction. She needed a plan. "If I were going to write a story about this, what would I say?" she murmured.

Philippe was sitting on the other side of the bar, reading a book. Vivienne was bustling about, readying the club for the evening's poetry reading. She hadn't made the snide comments to Philippe she usually would. Kat supposed that his injuries from the night before gave him a pass—for a day at least.

"What was that?" Philippe asked.

Kat looked up. "I was talking to myself. If I were writing a story about all of this, how would I organize it? What would the holes be? I need to find those holes and fill them in."

Philippe closed his book. "Talk me through it."

Kat began pacing behind the bar. "Toby is murdered, we now know by Claudine Roche. Before his death, Toby was involved in a black-market ring that also involves Guy and Mireille Rossi—let's just assume that for now. Other accomplices are unknown. Charlie starts investigating the 1944 Desmarchelier murders, after getting a tip that Americans were involved. Then Marie-Hélène is murdered. Charlie is arrested. Let's say, for the sake of argument, that he's arrested because someone doesn't want him investigating the Desmarchelier murders."

Philippe prompted her. "And why would someone want to stop that investigation?"

"There are at least two possibilities," she said. "First, someone doesn't want to sour Franco-American relations. Second, someone doesn't want their guilt to be exposed. And then, to continue the chronology, last night after we visited La Pêcheuse you were attacked by Guy Rossi. I'm certain."

"Who are your suspects in Marie-Hélène's murder?"

"Guy Rossi, first." Kat put her elbows on the counter and looked at Philippe. "And last. I don't have any other suspects! But it could have been whoever is trying to set up Charlie."

"That's an extreme way to set someone up."

"I know. Maybe they were killing two birds with one stone. Taking care of Marie-Hélène because she knew something and turning the police onto Charlie."

"So you're saying that Marie-Hélène knew something about the Desmarchelier murders?"

"Am I?" Kat ran her hands over her face and through her dark hair. "Is that even possible? It's all so mashed up together in my brain."

"But it sounds like you know the big hole."

Kat nodded. "Who killed the Desmarcheliers?" She started pacing again. The more she thought about it, the more obvious it seemed. Would a businessman like Clarence Welch really get Charlie arrested just to protect French feelings toward American products? The relationship between the United States and France had experienced plenty of bumps. One more wouldn't doom it. Right? Surely only whoever had killed the Desmarcheliers would go to such extreme lengths.

Kat looked at her watch; it was just after six o'clock. She ignored the second number, for Clarence Welch, and dialed the third.

Chapter Forty-Three

Brigadier General Martin Smithson stood up as she approached his table in Le Petit Bar at the Ritz. As she had crossed in front of the column at the center of Place Vendôme and walked down the long corridor from the entrance of the Ritz to LPB, she hoped—again—she wasn't making a mistake.

If you included all of the soldiers in Paris in 1944, there had probably been thousands of Americans in the city at one time or another. Gabrielle Desmarchelier's lover hadn't been a common soldier, but someone high up in either the military or diplomatic circles. Bob Braeburn and even George Church had been in Paris then at the embassy. Clarence Welch had been an Army officer. And so had the man standing in front of her. The first three all had reasons for wanting to keep Charlie's story quiet that didn't include murder.

If this were a mystery novel, it would be Martin Smithson, the man who had started it all by giving Charlie the tip, who was the guilty party in the end—the most unlikely suspect. But Kat couldn't believe that Smithson would put himself or his family in jeopardy by opening a can of worms that had been so long buried. He could have just told Charlie he didn't know anything. Kat prayed that her instincts were right.

"Mrs. Kelly, what would you like to drink?"

"Please call me Kat. Nothing. I can't stay long." On the phone Kat had explained the situation to Smithson and practically begged for his help. Did he have anything that could help shed light on who had killed the Desmarcheliers? He had asked her to meet him.

"I understand. I'm glad you called. I found something yesterday that I wanted to give Charlie. When I heard he was in custody, I wasn't sure what to do with it. I was going to get it to his editor, anonymously, tomorrow. But I have a feeling it's in good hands with you."

"What is it?"

Smithson handed her a large, flat envelope. She looked at him as she opened it, but he didn't say anything. There was a single piece of paper inside, stamped with U.S. Army letterhead at the top. She pulled it out and read it quickly. A jolt of recognition passed through her body. Her heart thudded in her chest, and she took a deep breath to calm herself.

"Where did you find this?"

"I asked my assistant to bring up a couple of boxes from the archives. I wasn't sure there would be anything in there about the killings, but I knew there was a chance."

"And this was all you found?"

He nodded. A single piece of paper that someone had forgotten to destroy. A single piece of paper that implicated three men.

Kat put the paper back in its envelope and tucked it into her bag. "Can I take this?"

Smithson nodded.

"I don't understand why you're doing this."

"Doing what?"

"Any of it. Why did you tell Charlie this rumor in the first place? Why put yourself at risk sharing this with me now? If anyone found out you were the source, you could be drummed out of the Army."

"Perhaps. Though I suspect I could cash in enough chips to save my job."

She persisted. She needed to understand. "But what about the Army? It doesn't bother you that when this comes out it will tarnish its reputation?"

"What tarnished its reputation is the fact that American soldiers were involved in not only the cold-blooded murder of civilians but in covering it up."

She still couldn't figure out his angle. Her puzzlement must have shown on her face since he gave a rueful laugh. "Is it so hard to believe that I want to do the right thing?"

"Unfortunately, yes."

"I grew up a Quaker. That probably surprises you, right?" It did surprise Kat, considering that Quakers are pacifists. "As much as I would like for there to be world peace, I was always too practical—or maybe too jaded, even from a young age—to practice what my faith preached. I always believed that the world needed someone to keep order, and that could be us, the Americans." Smithson paused and took the last sip of his drink. "And that's what we want the world to believe, too. We swoop into conflicts, beat the bad guys, and ask people to trust us. I've been in the Army for twenty-five years now, and I'm not naive. War is complicated. People would say, there are always bad apples."

Kat interjected, "But a bad apple isn't just a bad apple. It spoils the whole barrel."

He looked at her intently. "Exactly. We're only the good guys if we act like the good guys."

It reminded her of what Charlie had said at the embassy party, what he had said that had so riled up Church, Welch, and Braeburn. That he rejected an unthinking devotion to the cult of might makes right. Smithson reminded her of Charlie, and now she understood their connection.

"Thank you," she said. She stood up, as did he, and they shook hands.

Kat zipped home on the metro, still stunned by the contents of the letter Smithson had given her. It changed everything.

She had promised Philippe she'd be back to Club Margaux by nine o'clock, and she knew he would send out a search party if she didn't show up. But she had just enough time to quickly clean up and eat something. She felt like she'd lived several days in just this one and several weeks in the past seven days. And she needed to think about how to handle the information Smithson had given her. It was more complicated than she had expected—and proved again that you never knew who you could trust.

Kat unlocked the big wooden door on Rue du Bac and stepped inside. Lying on the floor in front of the building's mailboxes was a large envelope about an inch thick, addressed to her and Charlie. She carried it up the stairs to the second floor.

In the kitchen, she found an apple and some cheese. She opened the large envelope and pulled out a stack of papers and a note card embossed with the initials LB. Louise Beauvais, Gabrielle Desmarchelier's sister. A short note read:

These are the letters I have from my sister in the last year of her life. I read them again and don't see how they can help you, but I hope I am wrong.

Kat hoped Louise was wrong too. Between bites, she skimmed the letters. Gabrielle was not a lengthy writer, nor a particularly eloquent one. She mostly shared day-to-day details with her sister. Who she had lunch with—no names that Kat recognized—her frustration at not being able to find the clothes she wanted because of fabric shortages, complaints about the servants. There were few details about what it was like to live in Paris under Nazi occupation. But Kat supposed that, for a wealthy couple like the Desmarcheliers, that affected their life less on a quotidian basis.

For the first time, Kat wondered about Antoine Desmarchelier. Wasn't it rare for such a wealthy man to be a practicing doctor? Perhaps he had married into the wealth, but surely he didn't need to work. Gabrielle barely mentioned her husband, except to call him a boring stick in the mud.

About halfway through the letters, in August 1944, just after the Nazi occupation ended, Gabrielle's tone changed. She had met someone, she told her sister. Here Kat read faster, eager to find some clue. Gabrielle had been very careful. She never mentioned the man's name or specific profession. She alluded to the fact that he was prominent, but like Louise, Kat couldn't discern what his job was.

In these last dozen or so letters, Gabrielle wrote of almost nothing besides "her American." Weekends away, a growing closeness. She mentioned that the man was married but was dismissive of the fact. "Our love could overcome a meteor; a wife is a trifle." She didn't mention her husband in this calculation. As the letters went on, the affair came to read more like an obsession. She began complaining about her American's lack of consideration and attentiveness. But rather than souring her on him, it seemed to make her even more determined to win him.

The last letter was from the morning of the last day of her life. Gabrielle told her sister about the party at the embassy that night and that she'd be wearing their grandmother's necklace. "I know you won't approve," she wrote. "But I am determined to outshine everyone tonight, especially her." Kat assumed "her" was her lover's wife, but she couldn't be sure. Gabrielle signed off by saying, "Everything will be different tomorrow."

Kat wondered what she meant by that. Had she been planning to tell her American's wife about their affair? In the hopes of pushing him to commit? Surely that could be enough to incite some men to murder.

Kat sighed. These letters confirmed much of what Louise had told them and what Kat and Charlie had suspected. But there was nothing specific that pointed to the identity of who her lover was.

Kat set aside the first half of the letters and set to work reading the second half, after the American was introduced, more closely. Surely there would be some detail that could help.

And there was. It was in the third to last letter that she found it. Kat's breath caught in her throat, and her pulse started to pick up. She read the sentence again. Gabrielle was describing a weekend away with her lover. And suddenly Kat knew who it was.

Equal parts excited and nervous, she pulled on her coat, laced her shoes, and checked her watch. It was already nine. Philippe would be worried if she didn't get to Club Margaux *tout de suite.* She folded the incriminating letter and put it in her dress pocket, better than her coat in case it somehow fell out. Without a doubt, this letter was Charlie's ticket home.

Kat hurried down the building stairs and pushed open the wooden door that led to the street. The air had turned frigid in the past ninety minutes. She wished she had put on gloves. She held her hat to her head as she quickly walked down the block toward Boulevard Saint Germain. Usually there would be more people out at this time of the evening, going to or from dinner or out to a club. But the weather must be keeping people indoors.

She knew almost everything now, including who had killed the Desmarcheliers and who was pulling the strings in the background. She couldn't wait to tell Philippe.

She was thinking so intently about the letter in her pocket and what she could do with it that she didn't remark on the man exiting the backseat of a car parked at the curb just a few feet in front of her until he was directly in her path.

"Mrs. Kelly, fancy meeting you here."

Before she could say a word, Harold Magnusson put his arm around her and pushed her into the back seat of the car.

Chapter Forty-Four

Kat would have been lying if she said she had suspected Harold Magnusson all along. In the days since Toby's death, she had gradually accepted that she had known her friend only on the most surface of levels, that he had a secret life and a past far different from the shiny veneer he gave his war story.

Frankly, she had barely given any thought to Harold. He had fooled her with his avuncular Midwesterner act. Granted, there had been flashes of steel, like when they met with the police his first day in Paris, but she had explained that away by remembering that he was simply an uncouth American.

So when Smithson had shown her that letter buried deep in the archives from a low-level soldier to his commanding officer reporting the rumor that two American brothers from Chicago had committed murder, she was shocked—at first. But with that information, many of the pieces of the puzzle locked together, and she saw how it all worked. Especially when she saw who the letter was addressed to.

"Let's go," Harold told Mireille Rossi, behind the wheel of the car. She put the car in gear, and the vehicle lurched down the street. Harold grimaced. "Just go easy, Mireille."

Kat saw Mireille's eyes in the rearview mirror. She looked terrified. Of what, Kat wondered—Harold or driving through the streets of Paris?

"You don't look surprised," Harold said to Kat, a gun pointed at her torso. She couldn't tell him about the letter she had seen from Smithson, of course. But damn. She had forgotten to look surprised.

"Where are you taking me?"

"It hardly matters. You won't be there for long."

Kat watched as they approached the river. Chances are they were headed to Marché Gaspard. Suddenly they made a sharp left turn, throwing Kat and Harold to the right side of the car. Kat saw headlights swerve in front of them, narrowly avoiding their vehicle.

"Jesus, woman!" Harold shouted.

"I told you I don't know how to drive," Mireille said through gritted teeth.

Kat almost wished for a car accident. She might have a chance of escaping in the confusion.

Harold sighed deeply and said in a voice he might use to calm a child, "We're almost there. It's going to be fine. Just go slowly."

They sat in silence for a moment until Kat said, "I found out who killed your brother." Had Harold even heard about that?

"Yes, and I'm grateful. The police told me. It was just like Toby to get killed trying to avenge a woman. But maybe he was trying to make up for '44. Do you know what I'm talking about?"

Kat tried her best to play dumb. Surely the less she knew, the better her chances of survival—if they made it to Gaspard in one piece. "No." She knew immediately that she hadn't been convincing. Acting had never been her strong suit.

Without warning, Harold reached out his hand and slapped her hard across the cheekbone. Her head smacked back against the car door, and she tasted blood on the inside of her mouth. She touched her cheek where he had hit her and felt blood there too. He must have been wearing a ring.

"Let's not play games, Kat. Do you know what I'm talking about?"

What the hell, Kat thought.

"Killing Madame Desmarchelier?"

Harold shook his head no. "I loved my brother, but I would never expect Toby to be able to kill a woman." He said it like this was some sort of failing. "Unfortunately for you, I don't have the same scruples."

"So he killed Doctor Desmarchelier?"

"Actually, Toby didn't kill anyone that night. The charming Guy Rossi took care of the doctor. Toby was just the lookout."

"What do you want with me?"

"You aren't enjoying our chat?" Harold asked.

"Not particularly." Her cheek was still smarting. Kat had always wondered in a macabre way if she'd be able to hold up under torture. She thought grimly that she might be about to find out. This slapping business, though, she could withstand. She had always despised a bully. "What do you want?

"Just a little information. You know about 1944. How do you know, and who else did you tell?"

Kat made quick mental calculations. Could she parlay her knowledge of who was behind the Desmarchelier killings—and likely part of the black-market ring operating out of Marché Gaspard—to her advantage? She tried another tactic first.

"The police are expecting me tonight. I made an appointment with Detective Galland to share what I know. They're going to come looking for me."

Harold laughed. "I guess you haven't figured everything out. Galland is as crooked as an Englishman's teeth. He'd kill you himself if it was to his advantage."

Kat slumped back into the seat. All this time she had assumed that the detective was some combination of incompetent and opportunistic. In fact, he was much more dangerous. If he was in Harold's—and Harold's accomplices'—pocket, Charlie would never get out of jail.

"Look, I'm not going to lie to you. You're not going walk away from this, and your wop husband is going to rot in jail knowing that you were the victim of his nosiness."

The car jolted to a stop in front of Marché Gaspard. In the rearview mirror, Kat saw Mireille close her eyes in relief. Harold spoke to Kat. "Now you're going to get out of this car like everything is normal and walk up to the grocery entrance. Got it? I'll have this gun in my pocket the whole time, and my finger is on the trigger."

Kat quickly scanned the sidewalks. There were a few pedestrians; Les Halles was gearing up for another night of feeding Paris. But she didn't see how she could enlist anyone's help or make a break for it with Harold's gun in her side. She nodded her assent.

Mireille Rossi hurried to unlock the shop, and Harold pushed Kat inside.

"Go park the car," Harold said to Mireille.

"I can't!" she cried.

"Jesus Christ, you're useless. Give me the keys." He handed Mireille the gun. "Just hold this on her. I'll be back in two minutes. Lock the door behind me."

Kat expected to see Guy Rossi waiting for them inside, but the store was empty.

"Sit down." Mireille gestured with the gun to the stool behind the cash register. She was shaking, and Kat saw an opportunity.

"Mireille, please. Call my cousin Philippe at Club Margaux and tell him where I am. He'll bring help."

The woman just looked at Kat.

"You know this isn't right. Too many people have died. If you help, the police will go easy on you."

"You heard what he said. The police are in on it."

"Not all of them. Philippe knows who to go to. Why are you helping Harold?"

Before Mireille could respond, there was a sharp rap on the door. Mireille peeked out, checked that it was Harold, and let him in. Kat felt her chest tighten with fear, but she pushed it away. She needed to be smart and brave.

"She give you any problems?" He took the gun from Mireille.

Mireille shook her head, her face cold. "Just running her mouth."

"No surprise there. Let's go." Harold pushed Kat through a door into a back room. It was a large space with a small kitchen at one end, a door to what was probably a closet of some sort, and floor-to-ceiling shelves with stock lining the other walls. In the kitchen section there was a table and two chairs, likely a place where the shop owners took their breaks, drank coffee, and ate simple meals.

"Where's her husband?" Kat asked.

"What do you care?"

"He attacked Philippe and me last night."

"If he hadn't done such a poor job of it, this would all be over."

And I would probably already be dead, Kat thought.

With the gun, Harold waved her toward the closet. "Open the door." Kat did as he said and saw that it was a tiny space, filled with brooms and mops. "Take everything out."

Her bravado fell out of her like water being poured from a bucket—all at once. Was he going to lock her in here? Harold must have sensed her anxiety, and he laughed harshly. "I've got to soften you up somehow, and I'd rather not have a mess to clean up afterward."

The space was probably two feet square. Very slowly, Kat lifted out the contents of the closet.

"Look, you don't need to get in there. We can end this right now if you tell me what I need to know. Who gave you the information, and who else did you tell?"

"I didn't tell anyone." That was true. She hadn't had time.

"And who told you?"

"It doesn't matter who told me because by now he'll have told others too. You'd have to kill too many people."

Harold waved that away. "I'm remarkably efficient. Well?"

Kat was silent. She couldn't have her last action on earth be betraying Charlie and his source. Besides, if she could stall a little longer, perhaps she could think of a way out.

Harold sighed. "Get in."

She didn't move.

"Get the fuck in there." He shoved Kat into the closet.

As she braced herself so she wouldn't crash into the wall, Kat's mind seemed to be thinking a million thoughts at once. She remembered meeting Harold for the first time at L'École, going with him to the police station, having lunch with Marie-Hélène, him coming to their apartment—their apartment!—for dinner. Shouldn't she have noticed something?

Harold had his hand on the door to close it, when suddenly, like a combination lock falling into place, she knew, and the words slipped out of her mouth. "You killed Marie-Hélène."

Harold shrugged as if to say, so?

"She knew, didn't she? She knew what happened back in 1944."

Harold grimaced. "Dumb broad. She told me that Toby had come clean with her the day before he died."

Kat remembered that Marie-Hélène had said that the couple had finally opened up about their pasts. What should have brought them closer together had gotten both of them killed, Toby by Claudine and Marie-Hélène by Harold.

Despite her predicament, Kat felt the thrill of solving the puzzle. She kept going, riffing. "And she was blackmailing you. That's how she thought she had enough money to go to America on short notice with no job."

"She asked for $100,000. It was laughable. I told her I'd be back with the money, and she actually believed me. She was opening a bottle of wine, like we were celebrating."

"And you hit her with another bottle."

"Strangling is my preferred way to kill a woman. No blood to clean up. But in this case, I knew I'd be leaving the mess for your husband to find."

"Who called his office and pretended to be Marie-Hélène? Was it Mireille?"

"I'll leave that for you to ponder for the next few hours. Otherwise you might get awfully bored." He motioned with his gun for her to get fully in the closet.

Kat tried one more gambit, just to keep him talking and the closet door open. "I know who you're working with, who set up those murders in 1944."

Harold looked at her thoughtfully for a moment. "This is one of those cases where knowledge isn't power." He closed and locked the closet door. She heard his muffled voice call. "Don't worry, you won't suffocate. There's a quarter inch of space under the door for air."

Chapter Forty-Five

The mention of suffocation was enough to make Kat struggle to catch her breath. It was pitch black in the closet. Harold must have turned off the light in the kitchen. She felt in front of herself; the wall was impossibly close, like she was standing up in a coffin. Her heart fluttered in her chest like a bird trapped in a too-small box.

In and out. In and out. Kat focused on her breath, and after a few minutes, she succeeded in harnessing it. And then she realized how uncomfortable she was, standing upright. She braced her feet against the opposite wall and leaned back. Somehow Harold had found the one form of torture that Kat was likely to crumble in the face of.

How long would he keep her in here? He had said a few hours. Was it possible that she only had a few hours left to live? While Philippe would surely be missing her by now, no one knew she was here. No one was coming to her rescue. Barring some miracle, Harold would come back. She would continue to refuse him, and he would kill her. A shiver went through Kat when she thought about that phrase "barring some miracle."

Almost worse than Harold coming back was Harold not coming back and her dying of thirst standing up in a closet.

Kat tamped down the rising panic that came with that vision and tried to think concretely. Assuming Harold came back, she had two options—to talk her way out or to fight her way out.

Talking would always be her first choice. Perhaps she could promise to lead him to her source as a way to buy time. But that might only lead to more softening up and perhaps in a messier way. *Think, think!* She commanded herself. What else could she say that would convince him to let her live, even a little longer? The truth was she couldn't think of a single thing. "Face it, Kelly," she said out loud—it was surprisingly comforting to hear her own voice—"you've got no leverage."

That left fighting her way out.

She made a mental list of what she could use as a weapon. Her shoes had heels, but they were thick and sturdy, not sharp. They could do in a pinch, but Kat wasn't sure she could get enough purchase in the closet to land anything more than a glancing blow when Harold opened the door.

Again, she had nothing. Her feet and legs were aching from staying in the same position for so long. Would it be possible to sit down? Kat sank down into a crouch. Her rear made it to the floor. Her legs were fully bent and tucked into her body. And she felt something hard dig into her ribs.

Dear God, it was the switchblade Philippe had given her the night before. She had completely forgotten about it. Kat quickly stood up and fished it out from the waistband of her garter belt. Last night she had been too scared to use it. Now she couldn't wait to get her chance. Harold had his gun, but she would have surprise on her side.

"Come on, come on, come on," she whispered, willing Harold Magnusson to come back and open the closet door. She didn't want to kill him. She didn't want him dead, just injured enough so she could escape and get help. She wanted him alive and arrested and imprisoned for all of his crimes. But she would kill him if she had to.

She was ready. But still he didn't come. She had no idea how long she had been imprisoned for; it felt like hours. She practiced flicking the knife open and closed.

Kat found herself feeling faint and fought against it. To keep herself alert, she imagined what her parents were doing at this very moment back in Brooklyn. It would probably be after dinner, and her father would be grading essays at his desk in their living room on Henry Street. Her mother would be curled up on the couch reading a novel. Then she thought about Charlie. Hopefully he was asleep, his mind at ease.

If she wasn't able to get herself out of this mess and share what she knew with Faucher, Galland could easily fabricate evidence against Charlie to lock him up for the rest of his life or worse. The thought sent frustration running through her body again. It was time to be more proactive. She banged her fist against the wall, hard. And then again and again. She yelled. "Harold! I'm ready to talk!" She didn't know if he was at the store. But if he was, it was time to get this over with. "Harold! I've got to get out of here!"

She heard the door to the back room open and footsteps enter. She flicked open the knife and waited, ready, for Harold to open the door.

She was surprised to hear muffled voices and put her ear to the door.

"Fellas, as you can see there's no one here." It was Harold. Who was he with?

"But what are you doing here?"

She recognized that voice and began banging on the closet door. "Help!"

A moment later, the door flew open. Kat stood poised, knife in hand, just in case. But, after a quick glance around the room, she exhaled and retracted the blade.

"Kat!" Philippe held her forearms and looked closely at her. "Are you okay? Your face is bleeding." Kat touched her cheek.

"It doesn't matter. What's going on? How did you find me?"

Harold's arms were pinned behind his back by Pascal, the doorman from Club du Sud. Michel, La Pêcheuse's right hand man, was next to him, a hand tightly gripping Mireille's upper arm.

"When you weren't at Margaux by nine-thirty, I knew something was wrong. Then she called and told me where you were." He nodded in Mireille's direction.

Harold tried to break in Mireille's direction. "Bitch!" She flinched, but Pascal's grip on Harold didn't waver.

Kat looked at Mireille. "*Merci*. You did the right thing."

Philippe continued. "I went to Club du Sud for help, and then we came here."

Kat walked closer to Harold. His eyes were cold as he looked at her. She flicked open the knife again. He was lucky there were witnesses around. "I was going to stab you when you opened the door again. I want you to know that. I wasn't going to be your victim."

He just glared.

"Let's go," Kat said. "We need to take him to the police where he can confess to killing Marie-Hélène."

"Fine, I'll go," Harold said now. Kat wondered why he was suddenly being so accommodating.

"First, tell us more about the operation you were running here," Michel said.

"Fuck you," Harold said.

"I see you're a tough guy." Michel nodded at Pascal, who walked behind Harold and dealt swift blows to his lower back. Harold yelped and fell to his knees, gasping for breath.

"I request again that you tell us more about the operation you were running here."

Harold looked up at him and struggled to his feet. He used the back of his hand to wipe a stream of drool off his chin. He cleared his throat and shook his head. "Take me to the police, and I'll tell them everything." Now she understood. Harold had a better chance of surviving an encounter with the police than with La Pêcheuse's men. It was time to go.

But before Kat could say anything, she heard Mireille, speaking quietly at first. "It started after the Liberation. Throughout the war, and after, my husband sourced food and some wine to sell on the black market. It was small, just a little extra money to support us. Then he met Harold; I don't know exactly how. He got us things to sell—more food, bullets, soap, whiskey. It became a big business."

"What about now?" Kat asked. She wanted the whole story. "The supply chain is mostly back to normal."

Mireille shrugged. "There's always something to sell."

"Heroin?" Michel asked.

Mireille looked down, and nodded, almost imperceptibly.

"Where are you getting your product?"

"It comes from Indochina to smaller cities in France so it won't attract as much attention. Then it comes here by truck with food deliveries." The list of cities and dates in Toby's notebook. Everything was falling into place.

"How did Toby get involved?" Kat asked.

Finally Harold spoke, glaring at Mireille. "I noticed that, despite the fact that we were dealing in more highly valued product now, the revenues coming my way were shrinking. Toby wanted to go to chef school here, so I set him up, and he began checking on the business."

"Were you taking more than your share?" Kat asked Mireille.

"Rossi got greedy. He was a pig."

"Was?" Michel asked.

"He's dead," Kat said. "I'm sure of it." Neither Harold nor Mireille contradicted her. "He was double-crossing Harold, and he couldn't even kidnap me properly."

"And he was a pig," Mireille repeated.

After a moment of silence, Michel asked Harold, "This operation, it's a big one?"

"It isn't small."

"And you have protection?"

Harold didn't answer, so Kat piped up. "They have protection from two places. A well-placed detective, Maurice Galland." She looked at Harold to confirm. He didn't say anything. Suddenly she remembered the meeting at the prefecture when she translated for Harold and the detectives, when Harold had been so rude. "You already knew Galland, didn't you? That day, when you played the tough guy, you were just putting on a show for me and Detective Faucher."

"Who else gives them protection?" Michel asked.

"A well-placed American," Kat responded. She knew who this was but would keep the information close for now. She couldn't play all her cards. "Killing the Desmarcheliers was a side job, a favor, let's say. But with good payment. Madame Desmarchelier's necklace. I bet that's what let you expand your business back home."

Harold looked at her, contempt in his eyes.

"Okay, that's enough. Let's get out of here," Kat said. Michel pushed Mireille to Philippe, who put a hand on her shoulder to lead her out of the back room, into the store, and then outside. Kat followed them out. She relished the sensation of the cold night air filling her lungs. The clouds had cleared, and she could see a few stars. She drank them in. She turned around, expecting to see Michel, Pascal, and Harold following them.

"*On y va*," Philippe said. "Let's go."

Kat shook her head. "We need to take Harold to the police. Why aren't they coming out?"

Philippe opened his mouth to speak, but before he could, a single shot cracked through the night air. It came from the direction of Marché Gaspard. Mireille tried to run, but Philippe held on strong.

The shot rang through Kat's body. This couldn't be happening. If they had killed Harold, she would have nothing to take to the police, nothing to free Charlie. She whirled around and started back to the store.

"Kat, stop!" Philippe grabbed her arm. "That was the price. They wouldn't help me unless I promised they could take Harold."

Kat stared at Philippe, aghast. How could he? "Then it was all for nothing! Charlie will never get out now. You might as well have left me in that closet!"

"We have her," Philippe jutted his chin at Mireille. A small crowd was beginning to gather in front of Marché Gaspard, drawn by the sound of the gun. "Come on, let's go!"

They began walking briskly in the direction of the Marais. Kat scoffed, anger welling up inside her. "It's all hearsay, goddammit! Galland will make mincemeat of her."

"Then we take her to someone else. And you'll talk, right?" He looked at Mireille.

She hadn't said a word, just walked in between Philippe and Kat, Philippe's hand around her upper arm.

"You'll talk to cut your losses and get out of this mess. You probably know a lot and didn't have much say in the whole operation. Am I right?" He looked at Mireille.

Kat saw in her face that Mireille had made a decision. "I will tell them what I know. It was all my husband and Harold. They forced me to help. I was frightened."

"And what about Marie-Hélène?"

"I heard Harold say that she was blackmailing him and he would take care of her."

Kat nodded. It was a start. But she had one more card to play.

Chapter Forty-Six

Braeburn, Welch, or Church. Kat had suspected that one of these men had been Gabrielle Desmarchelier's lover. One of them had arranged her and her husband's murder. One of them had offered protection to the Rossi- and Magnusson-fronted black-market operation. And one of them was behind the pressure campaign to keep Charlie in jail. It was Gabrielle Desmarchelier's letter to her sister that confirmed which one it was.

Now it was eight in the morning, and Kat stood across the street from a stately home in the 8th arrondissement, not far from the American embassy.

When she had left Club du Sud with an injured Philippe in the taxi the other night, Michel had asked her if she had ever been to Place de la Concorde. He had said, "You don't have to go far." He was right. The American embassy was only a two-minute walk away.

But now she was waiting in front of someone's home. Detective Faucher stood next to her.

After convincing the officer on duty to wake Laurent Faucher, and not Maurice Galland, in the middle of the night and ask that he come to the station, Kat had slept for two hours on a bench at the prefecture.

Philippe had offered to come with her here this morning, but she told him to go home. Faucher was with her, and she trusted him. Mireille was in police custody. And Charlie—if all went well here, hopefully Charlie would be released this morning. There was just this one last thread.

As they waited, Kat saw Faucher's eyes linger on her cut cheek. She knew a bruise was forming. "You are very lucky," he said again. "You shouldn't have put yourself in such a situation."

"This was one situation I didn't have any say over."

Faucher didn't look satisfied. "And tell me again how you escaped?"

"Philippe, my cousin." When they had told the story at the prefecture, they had omitted the part about Michel and Pascal. Mireille knew enough about the Parisian underworld to keep her mouth shut about their involvement.

"All by himself?"

"Yes. And then Harold Magnusson disappeared." This wasn't a complete lie. Kat was certain his body had disappeared.

Kat stamped her feet to keep warm. She could see her breath. But at least it wasn't raining. The sky was a crystalline blue. "Detective, did you know that Galland was compromised?"

Faucher squinted at the front door across the street, as if willing it to open. Finally he said, "I had no evidence. While he has made decisions in other cases that I wouldn't have made, nothing was ever as egregious as this one. Of course, it was proper that we investigate Monsieur Kelly, but the lack of motive and any true evidence was obvious."

"You didn't believe that Charlie and Marie-Hélène were having an affair?"

Faucher looked at her square in the eye. "Never."

She couldn't explain why, but Kat felt her face redden slightly. She changed the subject. "What's your war story, Detective?"

"Did anyone ever tell you that you ask a lot of questions?"

"Only every day of my life." They both grinned, any awkwardness gone.

"I was already in the police department, but still in uniform. Of course, I could have stayed in Paris. It isn't popular to say now, but in those days, the police walked a thin line between protecting the people and collaborating with the Nazis. Too often, police officers decided that collaborating was the best way to protect." He said the last word with a touch of sarcasm. "I left in early '42 and went to Algiers with the Free French force."

"And then you fought?"

"*Oui*. In Corsica and then Italy."

"You were able to rejoin the police after the war?"

"Of course. I was a hero." Again, he placed special emphasis on the last word. "People who fell over themselves to placate the Germans were now tried-and-true *résistants*. I was celebrated."

"They didn't resent that you did the honorable thing?"

"Probably, but they had no choice. I had made enough connections with the Gaullists that it was untenable to deny me my former role." Faucher craned his neck to look at the front door of the house. "What time does this man go to work?"

Now, it was like he had willed it. The door to the house they were watching opened, and a man stepped out with a briefcase. Faucher looked at Kat for confirmation, and she nodded, suddenly charged with adrenaline.

Faucher jerked his head, and two uniformed police officers from opposite corners of the block converged on the man, each taking him by the arm. The man seemed not to have noticed them until the moment they grasped him. Now he looked indignant.

Kat followed as Faucher crossed the street. "Monsieur George Church?"

"*Oui.* What is the meaning of this?"

"You are under arrest for the murders of Antoine and Gabrielle Desmarchelier."

Church shook his head back and forth, as if trying to wake up from a dream. "That's preposterous! Let me go!" He turned angrily to the police officers restraining him. That's when he saw Kat; she could see surprise—and a flash of fear—register on his face. "Mrs. Kelly! What's going on here?"

"What's going on is that the police know you were Gabrielle Desmarchelier's lover and that you ordered her and her husband's murder. They also know that you get a cut of the profits from Guy Rossi and Harold Magnusson's black-market operation. I'm no detective, but I think you're in pretty big trouble."

Church scoffed. "You have no idea what you're talking about. Even if I did do any of those things you're accusing me of, which I didn't, I have diplomatic immunity." He looked at Faucher. "You'll be out of a job before noon."

"*On va voir,*" Faucher answered. *We'll see.* "But the diplomatic immunity will not help you. You might have it now, but in the role you had in 1944, your immunity did not cover murder."

Kat saw Church's haughty expression falter briefly before rallying. His voice was ugly with disdain. "You ungrateful losers. The Americans own this country; if it hadn't been for us, you'd all be speaking German. And even if you had managed to kick out the Nazis on your own, hardly likely, you'd be destitute without our dollars. You think your government wants to bite the hand that feeds it?"

Kat jumped in. "I think that once the French people hear about what you did, the French government will have no choice but to throw the book at you. And the Americans will throw you under the bus to maintain international equilibrium . . . no problem. You know how I know?"

Church didn't answer, just glared at her.

"Because Charlie Kelly is going to write the best damn story about the lengths you went to implicate him in this crime. And I'm going to be passing out that paper on every street corner in Paris."

Church stared at her, his eyes cold. Then to Faucher he said, "I insist that you contact the embassy lawyer immediately."

"Monsieur Church, you are not in the position to be making any demands at the moment. Let's go," Faucher said to the officers. Kat followed. She was going to bring her husband home.

Chapter Forty-Seven

The next evening, Kat was sitting at a table at Brasserie Lipp with Charlie, Philippe, and Jeanette. The lively room was aglow, and the champagne was flowing. Kat gingerly touched the bruise on her cheekbone and figured she'd have a headache tomorrow from it, the booze, the noise, or a combination of the three. But she'd worry about that later.

"So what do you think happened to Harold?" Jeanette asked.

Kat didn't look at either Charlie or Philippe as she answered. "According to the police, he hasn't turned up anywhere." Kat had told Charlie, of course, about La Pêcheuse and her crew's involvement in rescuing her. But she made him swear not to breathe a word of it, and she certainly wasn't going to tell Jeanette, the other journalist at the table. She didn't like keeping a secret from their friend, but *c'est la vie.*

After they ordered their meals, Charlie raised a glass. "A toast to my brave and brilliant wife, who out-policed the police, solving four murders. And her persistence prevented what might have been a fifth—mine, by guillotine."

Jeanette looked at Kat. "You know I'm going to write about your adventures for *The American*."

Kat laughed. "Of course you are!"

"So let me get this straight," Jeanette said. "Toby's death had nothing to do with the smuggling business or the murder of the doctor and his wife?"

"Correct. Claudine Roche killed him because she thought he would expose the war crimes of the chefs who were saving her business, and that her family's livelihood would be lost."

"And Marie-Hélène's death—that you were supposedly responsible for," she looked at Charlie, "was also unrelated."

"Not exactly," Kat responded. "Toby's death brought his brother Harold to Paris. Toby had told Marie-Hélène about his involvement in the killings of the Desmarcheliers, as a lookout."

"And she got the bright idea to blackmail Harold?"

Charlie laughed. "Are you interviewing her right now?"

"I may or may not have my notebook under the table." Jeanette winked at Kat.

Kat winked back. She wanted to tell her friends the (mostly) whole story, to examine every nook and cranny of it. "I'm not sure she thought of it as blackmail, exactly. More like a friendly arrangement. She finally thought she had her ticket out of Paris and France, a place that had brought her so much misery over the years."

Now Philippe asked a question. "Did we ever figure out if she called the *Tribune* that morning that Charlie found her body, or if it was someone else to set him up?"

"It was Mirielle. Harold put her up to it, with the urging of George Church. Marie-Hélène knew how to keep a secret and wasn't going to stop now." Of all the people in this sordid story, Marie-Hélène was the one who made Kat's heart hurt the most. If war hadn't come to France, she probably would have lived a perfectly pleasant, ordinary life. Instead, because of an accident of birth and history, like so many, her life had been ruined by war and violence.

"What's happening with the grocer's wife?"

"Mireille was arrested too, but she's talking to the police about everything: the drugs operation, the 1944 murders, her husband, Harold, and Marie-Hélène. Plus George Church. She knew all along that he was involved."

Jeanette shook her head. "Church. I've known him for years and never would have pegged him as a crook and a killer. How did you figure it out?"

"When we were at the party at the embassy, I chatted with Mrs. Church. She told me about their weekend home in Fontainebleau. In one of Gabrielle Desmarchelier's letters to her sister shortly before she died, she said that her American took her to Fontainebleau. As soon as I saw that, I knew."

"How did Harold and Church get mixed up together in the first place?" Jeanette asked.

"Church was a mid-level diplomat in the embassy here when Americans came back after the Liberation. Harold was in the army and stationed at the embassy. Somehow they became friends and then business partners. Killing the Desmarcheliers was a business arrangement initiated by Church."

"And Braeburn and Welch? They had nothing to do with this?"

"Nothing overtly criminal. Braeburn was trying to protect Franco-American relations by keeping American guilt under wraps. Welch was doing the same, but he was also protecting himself. He was the senior officer who received the report about the rumors of the Magnussons' involvement in the Desmarchelier murders, the report that Smithson gave me." Kat hadn't told Charlie yet that she'd gone to see Miranda Braeburn.

"What will happen to Welch?"

Kat shrugged. She didn't know. Charlie responded. "If it were up to the Army, probably nothing. But don't be surprised if you read about that letter in an upcoming edition of the *Trib*."

"It was Church who pressured Galland to detain and then arrest Charlie?"

Charlie nodded. "The charming Maurice Galland. Trust me, you haven't lived until you've been interrogated by a lion of the French police force."

"Did they hurt you?" Philippe asked.

"They didn't touch me physically. Just asked the same questions over and over, browbeat me. I think he was hoping I would get confused or desperate and confess just to get it over with." Charlie reached for Kat's hand and kissed it.

After they took Church to the prefecture the day before, Kat had waited in the lobby while Faucher disappeared for two hours. She was a disorienting mix of exhausted, exhilarated, and anxious. The exhaustion was self-explanatory, the exhilaration less so, and Kat tried to pinpoint it. She realized that, despite all the worry and danger to herself, Charlie, and Philippe over the past few days, she had loved the rush of getting to the bottom of these cases. She wasn't sure if that thrill was proper, exactly, but it was undeniable.

And she was anxious because, after all that, she still wasn't sure if Charlie would be released. She knew that Faucher was going to the prefect of the police himself to explain the situation, why Galland should be arrested, and why Charlie should be freed.

Finally, Faucher had led Charlie out. Her husband's face was pale, with dark bags under his eyes. He circled Kat in his arms, hugging her so close that he lifted her feet off the ground a couple of inches. Relief flooded her body.

Faucher cleared his throat. "You are free to go, Monsieur Kelly. Thank you for your assistance with our investigation."

"Galland said I'd be under arrest today."

"Your wife will explain. You are a lucky man."

"Thank you, Detective Faucher, for everything," Kat said.

"*Merci à vous, madame. Au revoir.*" He bowed slightly and disappeared into the prefecture.

Charlie looked at Kat quizzically. "A lot has happened in the past forty-eight hours," she said.

His fingers gently touched her cheek where Harold had hit her. "I see. Tell me everything."

And she had, only leaving out the part about visiting Miranda, for some reason she didn't take the time to interrogate. Then Charlie was at the *Tribune* by noon, writing the first of what would surely be a series of bombshell pieces. He had asked if she wanted to write with him and get a joint byline. "You're the one who cracked this case. This is your story."

But Kat had declined. She felt like she had been immersed in dirty bath water ever since she found Toby's body. It was time to get out.

This first story wouldn't name the Magnussons or Church but would include confirmation that the U.S. Army had known more about crimes their servicemen had committed than they had ever admitted. And that some of the crimes had been sanctioned or even encouraged by members of the U.S. delegation to France. And that members of the French police department had also looked the other way. No one would come out clean.

Back at Brasserie Lipp, Jeanette asked Kat, "How do you go back to cooking school after this excitement?"

"The real question is, how do I go back to being in the same class as Eugene and Vaughn. Vaughn was dishonorably discharged after taking advantage of one too many underage French girls. He and Eugene have some sort of sick bond, and I'm betting it's that they both like young women—very young women." Just thinking about it put a bad taste in Kat's mouth that the wine wouldn't wash away. She wished that one of them was behind bars for killing Toby instead of Claudine.

She felt a pang of guilt when she thought about Claudine in prison for the next decade or more. When Kat had engineered her confession and arrest, she thought it would help lead to Charlie's release. But it hadn't. Instead Mélisse had lost her mother, and Café du Vent was shuttered. How would Jules support his daughter now?

Kat wasn't a child. She understood that not everything was black and white. But she couldn't help but wonder if her actions, while right on paper, were wrong in the moral ledger.

She snapped her mind back to the table. "But I have to finish school, so I can start that column for the *Herald*. The more I know about food and cooking, the better."

"What exactly is the plan for this column?" Philippe asked.

"I still have to sort out the details with Ethan, the editor Jeanette introduced me to at the embassy party, but it will be weekly starting in January. Each one will include a recipe from

Paris, plus its background and some interesting color about who I got the recipe from. It could be a chef, a farmer, or even an ordinary person with a delicious family recipe. I'll get to taste all sorts of foods and ask all sorts of questions. Essentially, the job of my dreams."

As Kat spooned the last of her crème brulée into her mouth—no chocolate mousse tonight, *merci*—she admitted privately to herself that, after the last week, writing a cooking column sounded, well, a little tame.

Chapter Forty-Eight

The night was clear but mild. Kat wrapped her arm through Charlie's as they walked along Boulevard Saint Germain back to their apartment. Her mind drifted over the events of the past week, hopping from memory to memory, but with no purpose or direction.

Charlie spoke, drawing her back to the present. "One of Galland's favorite interrogation tactics was to say that I suspected you were having an affair with Toby, so I retaliated by having an affair with Marie-Hélène. Every time Galland insulted you like that, or in some other way, Detective Faucher glowered—literally. It was almost like a cartoon. He was sitting behind Galland, so his boss couldn't see him."

Kat didn't say anything. She remembered the moment in front of Church's house when Faucher's gaze had stayed on her cheek.

"Funny, isn't it?" Charlie asked.

"Maybe he's just a good detective who didn't like it when his boss was so obviously on the wrong track."

"Maybe."

"But it doesn't really matter, does it?" she asked. "Just like Miranda Braeburn doesn't matter . . . to us. Right?" Ever since Kat and Charlie had locked eyes in the *Tribune* newsroom in New York four years ago, they had been in sync, inseparable. But since they had walked out of the prefecture together the morning before, Kat had sensed a whisper of distance between them. For the first time since they had met, they had each undergone something profound without the other. "I went to see her, to ask her for help."

"How did that go?"

"She clued me in to Clarence Welch having a vested interest in stopping your reporting."

"That's it?"

"I think she realizes that Bob was a better match for her than you would have been. But once you've been in love with Charlie Kelly, it's hard to move on from that." She said it more lightly than she meant it. She was sure she would never move on.

Charlie stopped walking and gently pulled her so she was facing him. He put his hands on her shoulders. "Every day I wake up and know that I'm the luckiest man alive—because of you. There is no one on Earth or Mars or the moon that I would trade you for, Kat Kelly. No one." He drew her close to him and spoke into her hair above her ear.

Moments from the past week flashed through her mind: Charlie's anger after she visited Eugene, Smithson proudly sharing the photograph of his children, the familiarity between Charlie and Miranda, the agony of missing Jake, someone she had never even met. Kat leaned into his body, closed her eyes, and breathed in his smell. She had needed to hear that.

She spoke close to his ear. "And don't worry; I'm not going to trade you in either, not even for a handsome detective."

Charlie pulled back to look at her. "You think he's handsome?"

Kat pulled his face to hers and kissed him once, twice, and again on the lips, lingering there as she felt his hands around her waist and warmth flooding her body.

They began walking again, more briskly this time. But as they approached their apartment, Kat noticed a large, shiny black car idling at the curb. Charlie spotted it too and slowed down. He fished his keys out of his pocket and handed them to her. "Go inside."

At that moment, the driver's door opened, and Michel from Club du Sud stepped out. He nodded to each of them. "*Bonsoir*, Monsieur and Madame Kelly." He walked around the hood of the car and opened the door to the back seat. With his hand, he indicated that Kat should get in. "*Madame?*"

Charlie put his arm in front of her, but Kat gently pushed it away. "It's okay. I'll just be a minute." She knew who was waiting for her.

Kat slid into the car next to La Pêcheuse. Michel closed the door behind her. It was warm in the car, and in the dark, Kat couldn't see much of the woman's face except for her red lipstick.

"Madame Kelly."

"*Bonsoir*, Madame . . . Marina."

"Just Marina is fine."

"*D'accord*, and please call me Kat."

"I came to see how you are after your close call the other night, Kat."

"Thank you for your help."

Kat heard the scrape of a match and saw the flame illuminate Marina's pale face. She lit a cigarette, waved out the match, and rolled down the window. She held the cigarette outside between puffs.

"I think you know that we helped each other."

Kat nodded, and then said, "*Oui*," in case Marina couldn't see her. The woman was now rid of a formidable rival, and Kat suspected that she would take over the business that had been operating out of Marché Gaspard.

"Did you know about Gaspard? Before Philippe and I came to visit you?"

Marina took a drag and then replied. "We did. And we also knew they had protection that even we couldn't touch. But, thanks to you, we don't need to worry about Deputy Ambassador Church anymore."

"You knew it was him?"

Marina shrugged. "There isn't much we don't know."

"Why didn't you tell me that night at Club du Sud?" Kat thought of everything that could have been avoided—possibly Philippe's beating, likely the second half of Charlie's imprisonment, and certainly her close call with Harold.

"And what would you have done with that information? You didn't have any proof, and I had none that I would share." She said it almost reproachfully, like Kat should have known better than to ask such a silly question.

"What do you want?" Kat asked.

Kat's eyes had adjusted to the dim light, and she saw a small smile play on Marina's lips.

"I like you. I like your directness. It's too rare in a woman." She threw out her cigarette and rolled up the car window. "And I want you to be direct with me now and tell me whether we have an understanding."

Kat knew two things instinctively. First, that challenging this woman on their mutual understanding, or lack thereof, would likely be a death sentence for her, and probably Charlie and Philippe as well. Maybe not tonight, but soon enough. Second, she knew that neither she, Charlie, nor Philippe would ever breathe a word of it. It was cynical, but she was sure that if Marina was arrested or killed, someone else would just take her place. And in this case, the crime boss you knew was probably better than the crime boss that you didn't.

"We do."

Marina nodded. "*Bon.* You and the two good-looking men in your life are welcome at Club du Sud anytime. I should say to stay out of trouble in the meantime, but I suspect you won't listen."

Kat couldn't help but flash a quick smile. "There are just too many interesting stories here."

"You've only scratched the surface, *ma belle.* Stay in Paris longer, and you will discover that the city has more stories than a croissant has layers." Marina clearly knew her audience.

They exchanged good nights, and Kat stepped out of the car to see Charlie and Michel engaged in good-natured conversation. Of course, Charlie had already made a new friend—and likely found a new source. Although Kat was certain that Michel would only divulge the tidbits that Marina wanted shared.

The men shook hands, and Michel nodded at Kat before stepping back into the vehicle.

"Everything okay?" Charlie asked.

"*Oui.*" She took his hand and led him upstairs.

Acknowledgments

Thank you to:

My longtime agent Sharon Bowers, for the encouragement, spot-on notes, and wise counsel throughout the thrilling and sometimes harrowing roller coaster ride of publishing a debut novel.

My editor Faith BlackRoss—thank you for believing in this book!—and the rest of the terrific team at Crooked Lane, including Julia Abbott, Thaisheemarie Fantauzzi Pérez, Rebecca Nelson, Shannon O'Neill, and copyeditor Daniel Nighting.

Grace Bastidas, for saying yes when I suggested we go to Paris (and for everything else).

My brilliant early readers Danielle Wilkie, Laura Fenton, Emily Harding, Audrey Bellezza, and Elizabeth Bellezza.

My friends Allison Graham, Nicole Page, and Jessica Winchell Morsa.

My Real Simple and Engel Entertainment friends and colleagues, especially Lisa Freedman, Steve Engel, and Heidi Reavis.

The authors and artists whose work illuminated post-war Paris for me. In particular, I want to highlight two books and a film: *Paris After the Liberation 1944–1949* by Anthony Beevor and Artemis Cooper, *Les Parisiennes: Resistance, Collaboration, and the Women of Paris Under Nazi Occupation* by Anne Sebba, and Marcel Ophuls's 1969 documentary *The Sorrow and the Pity.*

My brother and his family and my parents, with so much love.

Camil, my heart—you are a light in the world.

Dave, my very first reader and an endless champion of the book and, well, me. Je t'aime.